Praise for *The Girl from*

"An unforgettable tale of friendship, lov[...]
every word of this fantastically engross[...]
author to watch!"

—*New York Times* **bestselling author Kelly Rimmer**

"A riveting story, told by a masterful storyteller who also happens to
be a fresh new voice in the genre. I absolutely loved *The Girl from the
Channel Islands* and recommend it highly, not just to fans of historical
fiction, but to lovers of good books everywhere."

—**Karen Robards,** *New York Times* **bestselling author of**
The Black Swan of Paris

"A harrowing tale of a young woman using her wits, courage, and an
unlikely relationship to stay alive on a Nazi occupied island. Lecoat
weaves a story of strength and bravery from the first exciting scene to
its satisfying conclusion."

—**Bestselling author Noelle Salazar**

"*The Girl from the Channel Islands* springs to life with cinematic clarity.
With the story's every dramatic turn, Lecoat raises profound questions
about our understanding of trust, friend, and foe."

—**Ellen Keith, author of** *The Dutch Wife*

"A captivating story of trust and betrayal, courage, survival and
forbidden love."

—**Glynis Peters, author of** *The Secret Orphan*

"Lecoat capably combines historical fact with the fictional narrative,
and offers a cast rich with multidimensional characters. Readers will be
riveted."

—*Publishers Weekly*

"An important contribution to historical fiction."

—*New York Journal of Books*

"This gripping tale of forbidden love and survival will leave you breathless."

—*Sunday Post*

"A riveting debut that reveals a rarely reported WWII story."

—*Toronto Star*

Also by Jenny Lecoat

The Girl from the Channel Islands

beyond summer land

JENNY LECOAT

GRAYDON
HOUSE

**GRAYDON
HOUSE®**

Recycling programs
for this product may
not exist in your area.

ISBN-13: 978-1-525-83154-6

Beyond Summerland

Graydon House
22 Adelaide St. West, 41st Floor
Toronto, Ontario M5H 4E3, Canada
www.GraydonHouseBooks.com

Printed in U.S.A.

For Val Lecoat, 1937–2014, whose childhood was taken by Occupation.
For all that she's missed.

BEFORE

It was the vibration, not the sound, that woke her—the violent shuddering of the front door rattling in its frame as it was hit repeatedly with powerful, angry fists. The reverberation pulsing up through the brickwork, across the joists of the house and into the legs of her bed frame. Then she heard the voices shouting outside:

"*Öffne diese Tür! Sofort!*"

Barely awake, for a second she thought it was a dream. Then she heard her mother's frantic footsteps on the staircase, half running, half falling in her urgency, followed by the uneven clanking of the metal bolt as desperate fingers struggled to pull it back. Alone in her room, she sat upright in her bed, her heart pumping fit to shatter, horror-struck to find herself so vulnerable, terrified to leave the idiotic safety of her blankets. As the front door smacked open, the sound exploded: the shouts of soldiers clattering into the hallway, their boots banging on the wooden floor that had been so lovingly mopped just the day before, her mother's anguished cry as she was pushed aside. Then they were tumbling up the stairs one after the other, a chaotic production line of orders on the move, hunting down their prey, focused only on their target.

By the time she found the courage and strength to cross the room and open her bedroom door, they had him. His pajamas rumpled from the creases of sleep, his chin and chops sprouting their morning whiskers, it was only his slight stumble along the landing that alerted her to the cuffs behind his back. She heard her own voice, high and piercing above the others:

"Dad! Dad!"

He offered no resistance as they shoved him down the stairs and asked only once why he was being arrested, while all the time her mother's low, animal wail echoed through the rooms, a bass hum in a soprano choir. Frozen, she watched through the banisters as they uncuffed him just long enough to pull on his shoes and coat, before bundling him out of the house and into the Black Maria. She saw her mother sink down onto her haunches, her nightdress hauled awkwardly around her thighs, and scream into her hands. And then there was another voice, another set of howls and wails, and she realized they were coming from deep inside her, merging with her mother's cries, and that she might never be able to stop.

1

Jersey, Channel Islands
June 1945

Excitement billowed down the street. It poured out of every doorway and crackled in the air, tickling the back of people's necks, beckoning everyone into this thrilling, historic morning. And what a morning! Yesterday's storm had vanished north over the English Channel, leaving bright sunshine and a powder blue sky. Now the whole of St Helier was waiting, rinsed and gleaming, impatient with anticipation. A stiff southwesterly gusted through the streets of the town, carrying the faint murmur of a distant, chattering crowd, and as she stood on her front path to breathe it all in, Jean felt a surge of genuine optimism. She ran her fingers through her mousy hair to revive its sagging shape, tugged at her jacket to make sure that the moth hole in her blouse was hidden, then called back into the house:

"Mum! Hurry up, or we'll get stuck at the back."

Violet Parris shuffled out, her ancient leather handbag perched carefully on her arm. Jean watched as she turned, methodically, to lock the Chubb. It was a habit that recent years had ingrained, and with pilfering still rife around the parish, it made sense to be cautious, though everyone missed the days of open front doors. "Things will settle down by Christmas," people kept saying. And perhaps they would. Jean took in the pallid face beneath the battered felt hat and considered what a frail, brittle figure her mother cut these days, the anxious, darting eyes and slight stoop of constant burden more pronounced in sunlight than in the gloom of the house. Certainly, most people would have guessed Violet to be older than forty-six. But then, Jean supposed, every living soul on this island had aged a lifetime in the last five years. She felt a sudden urge to reach out and hug her mum tightly but, knowing Violet would balk at such a display, offered her arm instead.

They set off at a pace that Jean calculated her mother could maintain for the half-mile walk. The street was filled with the sound of garden gates clanging as women shooed husbands and children onto the pavement, reknotting ties and smoothing errant strands of hair before scuttling toward the town center. One or two of them carried folded Union Jacks ready to unfurl at the crucial moment, and Jean felt a pang of envy; their own flag had been used for kindling back in the winter, and no replacements could be bought now. But then, it would be inappropriate for the family to appear in any way frivolous. Jersey was a small island. People liked to talk.

By the time they reached the end of Bath Street, the roads were already thick with people heading for the Royal Square. At the corner of the covered market on Halkett Place, two streams of moving bodies became a human river, pushing the pair of them along like paper boats, and Jean wished again that they had set off earlier. As a woman behind stumbled slightly, forcing them both forward, she felt her mother's fingers tighten on her arm; quickly, Jean tugged her away from the melee toward a quiet side street where she leaned her mother against a concrete wall, supplying a handkerchief, which Violet immediately dabbed across her forehead.

"All right?"

Violet shook her head. "So many people. Why didn't we go down the Albert Pier, see the SS *Jamaica* coming in, or find a place along the Esplanade?" Jean, who had suggested these exact choices last night, merely took the dampened handkerchief back and tucked it into her sleeve. As she did so, her eyes fell on the shop front, a small bakery set halfway down the turning. The display window had been boarded up to replace the shattered glass, but evidently the vandals had returned for a second visit, because now a huge swastika was painted on the plywood in black pitch. She glanced at her mother and saw that she, too, had become transfixed by it.

Violet jerked her chin a little. "Collaborators." Jean nodded. What had the proprietors done to earn such a reputation? Had they served German soldiers their bread? Fraternized with them? She imagined the angry faces of men rushing toward the shop in the dead of night, bricks and rocks in their hands. What had happened to this island in such a few short weeks?

Liberation Day, less than a month earlier, had been the most significant, emotional event that any islander, young or old, had ever experienced. The most longed-for day in their history had come at last, and, with the arrival of a British task force in the harbor and the official surrender of the German military, five brutal years of Nazi occupation had finally come to an end. So long and arduous had the Occupation been—Jean was a schoolgirl of just fourteen when it began—that for the first week or two of freedom she had found the transformation impossible to take in. To be able to leave the house without curfew...to speak openly on the street without fear of spies... to listen to the BBC news on a neighbor's radio! But best of all was the joy of eating a proper meal again, as the British army unloaded crate after crate of supplies, and the Red Cross ship *Vega* brought more relief parcels. Given the near starvation of the previous year, extravagances such as tinned meat, lard for cooking, sugar and tea had moved Jean and Violet to tears of relief as they unpacked their box. The sharp taste of raspberry jam, spooned straight from the jar in a moment of pure elation, would stay with her forever.

Yet those early days had also brought bewilderment. After years of inertia, with entire months punctuated by nothing but the tedious struggle for food and fuel, Liberation brought a tornado of welcome but exhausting developments. They had dutifully exchanged their reichsmarks for sterling at the local bank and watched the mines being cleared from the beaches; they had read the public announcements telling them that the non-native islanders deported by the Germans in the autumn of 1942 had been flown back to England, and that their return was imminent. They had even received, at long last, a letter from Jean's older brother, Harry, released from service and now back home with his own family in Chelmsford. Horrified at the belated news of his father's arrest, Harry spoke of his frustration at being cut off from all island information for so long but, to Jean's delight, promised that he would visit as soon as regular transport services resumed. Encouraged by a sense of returning normality, she and her mother would sit at the kitchen table of an evening, cutting out every significant article from the *Evening Post* and pasting them all into a scrapbook for posterity. And as they pasted, in a whispered voice too soft for the fickle fates to hear, Jean would dare to speak of the coming weeks and the news from the continent that even now might be on its way. Violet would nod and smile, but rarely responded. Hope, Jean calculated, was too heavy a burden for this exhausted woman in the final length of a horrendous journey; better for Jean to button her lip and direct her own dreams into the rhythmic movements of her pasting brush.

Not all the recent news was good. Among the celebratory headlines and the public announcements had been other, troubling pieces. Dreadful photographs of murderous Nazi camps where untold numbers had died. Accounts of local "jerrybags"—island women who had slept with German soldiers—being chased through the streets by marauding gangs who shaved their heads and stripped them naked. Reports of the island's insurmountable debts. And one terrifying front-page report of a local father and son, deported eighteen months earlier, who had both perished during their incarceration. After reading these, Jean would retire to her bed and lie awake for hours in the grip of a dark, low-level panic, before falling into a fitful sleep just as the sun rose. She told no one about this, especially not her mother. She could not pinpoint the exact moment when she had assumed the maternal role in their relationship, and suspected the shift had crept up on them over many months. But Jean now knew instinctively that her mother's shaking fingers indicated that Jean would need to peel the vegetables for dinner, or that Violet's single, hot tear on her book's page in the quiet of the evening required a warming drink and an early night. There would be time enough for her own feelings, Jean told herself, when this nightmare came to an end, which it surely soon would. So today, despite the sight of the boarded-up bakery and the unsettling feelings it brought, Jean squeezed out a comforting smile and placed a hand on her mother's arm.

"We can just go home now, if you want." Jean thought of their still, gray kitchen at the rear of the still, gray house and dreaded her mother's nod. But Violet just gave a little frown.

"No, we've come this far. Come on."

The Royal Square was, as expected, heaving with people. Men, women and children were squashed together like blades of grass and stewards had placed barriers across the middle of the square to contain the crowd. Jean dragged her mother through the jostling bodies and, instructing Violet to hang on to the back of her jacket and not let go, began to slither her way through the crush, making the most of any tiny gap. She smiled helplessly at any gentleman in her path until he retreated, and threw apologetic backward looks when she trod on someone's foot or dislodged their hat, until they found themselves only two heads back from the barrier just as the official cars pulled into the square. A huge cheer tore through the crowd, and by standing on her tiptoes and craning her neck Jean managed to find a sliver of a clear view.

The cars lined up outside the library. A young, uniformed Tommy opened the door of the shining black Ford. And suddenly there they were. Right there on the pavement in front of the States of Jersey government buildings, not thirty feet away, all the way from Buckingham Palace—the King and Queen! Jean gazed at King George, resplendent in his uniform, as he was greeted by low-bowing Crown officials. The Queen, magnificent in a feathered tam hat and draped decorously in a fox fur, accepted a huge bouquet of Jersey carnations. The cheers around the square were thunderous now, with snatches of patriotic songs breaking out here and there. Jean looked at her mother and saw her own excitement reflected back. But at that moment a woman next to them wiped her eyes with the back of her hand and grinned at Violet.

"Isn't it marvelous? I can't believe it!"

Jean felt her mother's body stiffen beside her as she dredged up a suitable courtesy. "Yes, wonderful."

"It's over, really over! We can start living again!"

Jean watched Violet's mouth turn to a grim line of sand-bagged wretchedness. By the time her bottom lip began to tremble, Jean knew it was over—public tears were a humiliation that could not be tolerated, and the window of fake composure was closing fast. With one last reluctant look at the graciously waving royal couple, Jean put her arm around her mother's waist and pushed out through the crowd until they were both back on the high street, breathless and unsteady. In the doorway of a shop, shielding her from passersby, Jean again offered her handkerchief, and this time Violet pressed it across her face as she sobbed into it for several moments, emanating tiny stuttering sounds like a wounded cat. Eventually the shaking eased, and she took a deep breath.

"Sorry. It was just what that woman said."

Jean rubbed her arm. "I know. But it can't be long now. For all we know Dad's already on his way home. Could be out there on a boat right this minute."

Violet nodded and managed a small wet smile. Jean, working hard to hide her disappointment at missing this once-in-a-lifetime spectacle, again offered her arm, and the two of them began the slow walk back to the house, Jean's mind whirring. Was it right to offer such optimism? No one knew if her father was actually on his way home. It was fifteen months since he'd stepped onto that German prison boat, headed God knows where. Twelve months since his last letter. And not a word from the authorities since Liberation. She told herself they had no choice but to believe, but one thing was certain—for them, the Occupation was far from over.

"Philip Arthur Parris, correct? Born March 7, 1898, living on St Mark's Road at the time of his arrest?"

Jean nudged her mother to reply.

"That's right."

"And his shop?"

"Parris's ironmongers, on New Street. It's been closed ever since."

"Well, Mrs. Parris, I'm afraid that this seems to be all the documentation available…" The Constable scratched his head, going the long way round to the far side. Jean would have put money on it that there was never an itch there. She watched him shuffle his small sheaf of papers, placing the top one on the bottom, then moving it back again. He adjusted his glasses, cleared his throat and sat back in his leather desk chair, finally looking her mother in the eye. "In fact, there appears to be no record of Mr. Parris after he was moved from Preungesheim jail in July 1944."

"That must have been soon after the last letter we received." Jean noticed her mother had deliberately raised her levels of pronunciation, tamping down the broader vowels of her Jersey accent and aping the interviewer's more educated sounds. Neither of them felt like themselves in the Constable's visitor's office with polished wood paneled walls and ancient, hand-drawn maps of Jersey in heavy glass frames, sitting in front of this elected civil leader who had cleared space in his diary to speak with them in person. No wonder her mother was sounding peculiar. Violet pressed on: "He was only supposed to serve fifteen months, you see, so he should be free now. We thought perhaps he's already been released but doesn't have the right papers to travel. Do you think maybe that's what's happened?"

But the Constable's eyes were now on the window, as the sound of far-off shouting and chanting drifted through the two-inch gap at the base of the sash. Jean followed his gaze, aware that the volume of the sound was rising. With a small sigh he got up and shut the window with a bang.

"I do apologize. Protesters, on the green."

Jean nodded. "Yes, we passed them on the way here." In fact, the sight of so many people gathered for a demonstration, after five years of strictly enforced obedience, had quite shocked her. There must have been several hundred men there, all listening intently—and in some cases, yelling their replies—to a man on a makeshift podium, behind which hung a banner hand-painted with the words Jersey Democratic Movement. The man, through a megaphone, was talking about the need for social security and something called a graduated tax system. Jean recalled her dad talking about the group a couple of years before, angrily dismissing them as a bunch of Commies who only wanted to cause trouble. Out of loyalty to him, Jean had rolled her eyes to Violet as they walked past on the opposite pavement. Hadn't the war given everyone their fill of politics for a good long time?

The Constable peered out for a moment, then returned to his seat and picked up a pen.

"Your husband was charged with illegal possession of a wireless?"

"Yes."

"Which was found on his shop's premises?"

"That's right. He thought it would be safer there than at

home. He used to let people listen to the news in the back room—customers, neighbors sometimes."

"And the trial was…eighth of February last year?"

Violet scoffed. "Call that a trial! Didn't even provide a proper translator, we didn't know what was going on. He was going to jail from the moment they arrested him. Isn't that right, Jean?" Violet's voice cracked with pain and indignant fury. Jean pressed her hand onto her mother's, while her other hand unconsciously fluttered to her neck, fingering the small gold locket her father had given her on her twelfth birthday. When she touched it, she recalled the delight in his eyes as he watched her open the box, her mother's beaming smile as he hung it around Jean's neck, struggling to fix the catch with his stubby fingers. That moment had crystallized in her mind, a perfect snapshot of their happy, loving family, and in recent months the locket had become a talisman, a connection to her father's absent self. She felt the tiny metal heart under her fingers and took a deep breath.

"What we're trying to say is, my dad's not a criminal." She looked into the Constable's eyes, willing him to see it. "He's a good man. He should never have been put in prison at all, never mind sent to some foreign jail. We just want him back…" She realized that she, too, was speaking in a strangely elevated accent and felt foolish. But her English teacher at school always said people with good vowels got to the front of the queue, and right now the Parrises badly needed official attention.

The Constable folded his hands in front of him and looked from one to the other with a solemn expression.

"Technically what Mr. Parris did was illegal, under Occupation law. Our government did warn residents not to violate such laws, no matter how unjust they felt them to be."

He glanced up, and must have taken in their startled faces, because he quickly cleared his throat again and hurried on: "But of course, you have our greatest sympathy for this distressing situation, and rest assured that the States of Jersey, as your governing body, will do all within our power to locate him. I must warn you, though, it will take time. After D-Day, German administration on the continent became extremely chaotic, and much paperwork has been mislaid." He looked back at the documents on his desk and thought for a moment. "I'm told the Red Cross can be very helpful. Would you like me to write to them?"

Violet nodded vigorously. Jean squeezed her hand even tighter.

"We'd be very grateful."

"Consider it done. I shall also see if anyone from the current Home Office contingent can be spared to look into this, while they're on the island. Quite a number of London CID officers in the Civil Affairs Unit, I believe. Smart chaps, I've no doubt." He smiled with encouragement. Jean did her best to return it.

"Thank you."

"Meanwhile do remain positive." The Constable was on his feet now, indicating that the interview was over. "We'll get Mr. Parris home soon."

Moments later, Jean and her mother were outside on the pavement, blinking in the afternoon glare. Violet fiddled with the contents of her handbag, pretending to be searching for something.

"Do you really think he can do anything?"

"Of course he can!" Jean's voice jangled with deliberate gaiety. "Look at all the things the Red Cross achieved during the war." But, in fact, Jean's attention was half on the noisy mob down the road. She couldn't see much from where they stood, but the shouting from the man on the podium seemed to be louder and angrier, as did the heckles of the crowd, and she was relieved when her mother turned resolutely in the other direction. Soon they were in the small maze of streets, filled with nineteenth-century cottages, that led them through town and toward the long, sweeping terrace of St Mark's Road, and as they reached their front door, her mother turned to her.

"Do you think he'll be the same man?"

Jean's heart skipped. "Dad? In what way?"

"We don't know what he's gone through. Look what happened to that poor father and son, how they was treated. Just wonder if he'll be the same person when he gets back."

Jean's second-favorite image of her father leaped into her head—his lanky frame draped cross-legged across a deck chair, laughing eyes squinting into the sun. She thought of his low, throbbing chuckle, the way he'd push stray hair from his forehead on a warm day. The thought of any difference was unbearable. She knew her mother must feel the same.

"Dad was sent to a regular prison over there. He'll be fine."

Violet nodded, turned the key in the lock and let them in, then pulled out her first genuine smile of the day. "Anyway, start of next week Eddie will be back. He'll know what to do."

Jean felt a numbing gloom trickle through her. Uncle Eddie, her father's younger brother. With the paunchy gut, the wiry mustache and the raucous laugh. Eddie, who shared his brother's love of an argument but lacked the grace to know when to end it, and who shouted at her when, as a child, she'd accidentally knocked over a hideous porcelain vase in his house. She hadn't seen him since the week before the Germans arrived and, until last week's telegram, had been fairly certain she'd never see him again. As she hung her mother's hat on the hallstand a clear memory surfaced of her dad, pink with fury, slamming the front door as he announced his brother's decision to evacuate. Words like *shame* and *backbone* had been spat down the hallway. But now Violet's eyes were softening with anticipation.

"Eddie knows the whole story, does he, about what happened to Dad?"

"First letter I wrote, soon as mail to England was working again. He'll know how to handle this, if anyone does."

Jean turned away before her thoughts crept onto her face and revealed themselves. "I'm sure he will, Mum. Come on, I need to make a start on dinner."

"…and where do all our Jurats and Constables hail from, these men who wield such power in our island parishes? Wealthy families who know nothing of ordinary lives! What we need is properly paid representatives, sourced from the working population of this island."

"Hear hear!" Hazel Le Tourneur heard her voice ring out across Parade Gardens toward the podium. Several male heads turned toward her, their eyes, shadowed beneath the peaks of their caps, connecting to register their shared silent mirth. But Hazel didn't care. Let them stare! Let them mutter to their friends and make their little jokes. She saw worse every day in the back row of her classroom, and such attitudes only reminded her how far Jersey had to go to take its place in the new postwar century. She tilted her chin to catch the speaker's next words as they emerged, crunched and buckled, through the mechanism of his ancient megaphone.

"And why," the young man was shouting, his finger jabbing at the air, "are our daily battles—the aging of frail parents, the illness of children, the struggle to pay rent—not at the heart of our island's policy? Why should the older worker be fearful of retirement, the laborer be afraid of sickness or injury? We need to take these burdens from the poor and create a society where everyone, not just the rich, has some protection from these realities." He lowered his device in the hope of applause, and Hazel obliged. At last. After years of being scared even to share news with a neighbor for fear of being reported by an enemy agent, this outdoor gathering in a public garden felt so much more than an airing of views. It was a restoration of hope. Small as this meeting might be— she had failed to convince any of her fellow teachers to accompany her and had slammed the door of the staff room with unnecessary force on her way out to make her feelings plain—it felt like a leap she had only dreamed of during the Occupation years. Those long, cold nights, huddled in the makeshift bed next to her father's without even a candle. Now she raised her face to the sun to relish the hot rays on her cheek, delighting in its obvious metaphor, and ignoring the instruction drummed into her throughout her childhood that girls of her snow-white complexion should never expose their skin to the June sun. But the announcement of a change of speaker pulled her back to reality and forced her to check her watch. Four thirty—time to head home.

By the time Hazel reached New Street, her bag of books was cutting into her shoulder and the rough fabric of her wooden-soled clogs was blistering her feet, making hard work of the eight stone steps up to the flats' entrance. New shoes, she decided, would be the first purchase from her next pay packet, now that supplies were starting to arrive. As she fumbled in her pocket for her key—for once, one of the other tenants had actually bothered to close the communal door

properly—she glanced down at the shuttered shop that occupied the ground floor, the painted words above it fading
and peeling for lack of attention. P. Parris, Ironmongers. She
thought of the tall, gangly owner with his badly disguised
bald patch and wondered where he might be now. Since Liberation Day a few shocking reports had appeared about the
fate of some imprisoned by the Germans overseas, but she had
heard nothing of Parris. Most likely, Hazel thought, he had
sat out the remainder of the war sewing groundsheets in some
damp French prison and, if pressed, she would say that was no
more than he deserved. In truth, she had given little thought
to her erstwhile neighbor since the day the shutters went up.

She recalled the day that soldiers had burst into the shop,
emerging minutes later with the offending wireless. Then
their second visit, just a few days later, ransacking the pitiful
stock, carrying off precious screws, tin pails and mousetraps
while residents looked on from a distance in silent, impotent
fury at this shameless robbery of vital commodities. She remembered standing at her kitchen window, which overlooked
the tiny rear yard, watching from behind the curtain as the
junior officer in command smoked a furtive roll-up and examined a small chisel he had obviously taken for his own
personal use. Even at the time Hazel had wondered what on
earth an occupying soldier could possibly want with a solitary
woodworking tool. But that was fascism, of course—take,
take, take, then work out later what you actually wanted it
for. In any case, Philip Parris himself would have no use for
it, not for the foreseeable future.

Hauling her exhausted frame up the rickety staircase, Hazel
let herself into the flat. Her father sat, as always, stooped over
in his chair by the hearth, pushing his gnarled fingers into

tortuous shapes in an effort to write in his journal, and, as always, called over his shoulder as Hazel entered.

"That you, Haze?"

"Yes, it's me." *Who else*, Hazel thought. She could barely remember the last time anyone else had crossed the threshold. Not since those odd cousins from Trinity had visited the week of Dottie's funeral. No neighbors in this building ever knocked on the door or popped in for a chat, though they were courteous enough in the communal areas. Not even that handsome, ambitious trades unionist Hazel had stepped out with for a few weeks last summer had been inside this wretched apartment, although that was largely due to Hazel's discouragement, shamed as she was by the smell from the drains.

"You go to that rally?"

"Yes, just for a bit. Not a bad turnout."

"Be careful. They'll be upsetting a few round here."

Hazel patted her father's icy, bent fingers. "Well, if they're not causing trouble, Dad, they're not doing any good, are they?" He beamed at her, amusement pushing past the pain in his eyes.

"You're right there, my love."

Hazel piled some poetry textbooks up on the tiny table and pulled back the ancient floral curtains to let in more of the golden midsummer light. Without bothering to ask, she wound up the gramophone, their most prized possession, which, by a miracle of determination, had escaped barter these last few years, and lifted the needle onto the record. The soft voices of The Ink Spots floated across the room; she waited till the melody soothed her father's weight into the back of his chair, his eyes closed in an expression of peace. Then she took the reddish-brown bottle from the shelf.

"Medicine time."

He emitted a tiny scoff. "Don't do any good."

"Doctor told me there's a new arthritis drug they've discovered in Sweden. Maybe now the war's over we can get you some of that?" Her voice was bright as glass as she proffered the spoon, but she knew from his expression and his grip on the chair that it would be a battle to get it down his throat. Just one night, she mused, if she could just have one night where everything was easy...then realized she had long forgotten what such a night would even look like. With a small sigh, she pulled the stopper from the bottle while the Ink Spots crooned out their jollity in the background.

The Albert Pier was thronged with people as the boat glided into dock, stoking a ripple of anticipation. Jean watched the thick plaited ropes being hurled across the void and listened to the shouts of seamen pierce the summer's evening, their voices pitched over the grind of the engines and the clanking metal of the cranes. The ship's towering red funnel stood bright against the pale mackerel clouds, and the gulls circled it, squawking their desire for fish. Jean pulled her jacket a little tighter and closed her eyes to smell the salt on the air, trying to push aside her black, dominant memory of this quayside: the German prison boat bobbing on the tide, the Jerries with their rifles cocked, her father being hauled from the prison truck. She had been back here since then, of course, to welcome the Red Cross ship last Christmas, and to watch the Tommies coming ashore; one bad recollection couldn't be allowed to keep her away. This dock was as central a part of Jersey life as anywhere on the island. Her father used to say it was the nature of island folk all over the world, with their innate vulnerability and dependence on larger land-

masses for survival, that instinctively drew them to piers and
harbors, filled with the hope of replenishment and the expectant thrill of the new. She looked around; everywhere,
people were hanging off railings or climbing onto the roofs
of cars for extra height, scrabbling in pockets for spectacles,
scanning the distant figures of those on deck. The excitement
was tangible, a fizzing energy from those waiting in the evening sun. For this was no ordinary boat.

Her eyes rested on a couple in their thirties huddled against
the breeze. The husband clutched at his wife's waist as if
he feared she might suddenly leap into the harbor, while the
woman herself stared at the mosaic of passenger faces on the
deck above, her own face rigid with hope and apprehension.
They were waiting, Jean was certain, to meet their child—
or, at least, the young stranger who had been their child on
a hot, frantic morning in 1940 when they had pushed them,
screaming and terrified, onto an evacuation boat. One family of hundreds who had thrown the dice in those scant, wit-
less days, reluctantly concluding that a perilous journey across
the Channel and an unknowable life alone in England was
a better bet than Nazi occupation, and that if they were not
able to go themselves, at least their children should be given
the chance. *What would such a fissure do to a family?* Jean wondered. Five years of separation, kids raised by distant relations
or foster parents with alien customs and new words, without
phone calls or letters to keep memories fresh. Would they
even recognize their parents now? And would the adults know
the windswept adolescent who walked off this ship, probably
more at home amongst the other evacuees than with their
own flesh and blood? Jean imagined a life apart from her father in those tender years and shivered.

The gangplank was put in place and passengers began to

stream off. A hub formed immediately around it, a seething throng of hugging, laughing and crying. Jean and her mother stood back, Violet's hands, as ever, gripping her handbag, Jean's folded neatly in front of her. Suddenly, amid the stream of newcomers, a bulky figure, clutching a large suitcase in one hand, clumped heavily down the gangplank, and, without even getting a good look at his face, Jean knew it was Eddie. He had lost weight and there were streaks of gray in his curly, sand-colored hair, but she knew her uncle instantly. In the previous days she had persuaded herself that seeing him would somehow be the next best thing to seeing her father, that being around his flesh and blood would somehow bring her dad closer. But as soon as she saw Eddie marching toward them, his open trench coat flapping in the wind, she realized how foolish that had been. He pulled her into a bear hug, expressing predictable surprise at how grown-up she looked, and the smell of his body—a combination of sweat, tobacco and something sickly sweet—was foreign and wrong. If anything, he felt more like the opposite of her father.

"Stone me—need to get some hot dinners in the two of you!" Eddie cackled, looking them up and down. Then he looked around. "Still—place hasn't changed too much, by the look of it."

Violet snorted. "You wait. Plenty of changes round the coast. Bloody ruined St Ouen's."

"Yeah, I heard old Adolf got a bit carried away with the fortifications. Any more news of Phil?" The question was barked, official sounding.

"Nothing yet. They say they're doing all they can."

"He'll be all right." Eddie nodded to a distant, imagined audience. "If anyone knows how to look after himself, Phil does. Right—how we getting back?" He began to make his

way up the pier, walking awkwardly to balance the weight
of the suitcase. Jean and Violet had to run to catch him up.

"Our neighbor Bill Syvret, he's going to meet us up the top
with his car. But...aren't we waiting for the others?" Violet
asked. "Where's Maureen and the children?"

"Still in Exmouth. I said in the telegram I'd be coming on
my own." He was staring straight ahead.

"No, you didn't...? Why didn't they come with you?"

"Jersey doesn't want loads of women and kids coming back,
not till they get things straightened out. Just men in certain
lines of work. Like builders." He thumped his chest with his
free hand, as if Jean and Violet were unaware of his profession. Jean thought of his wife, a slip of a woman who always
looked permanently exhausted, and the cousins she'd played
with as a child, and noticed her uncle's eyes darting around,
as if trying to avoid direct contact.

"Will they be all right over there, on their own?" Violet
pressed him.

Eddie laughed. It came out as mockery. "Don't worry about
them! Maureen, she's friends with half the town. What kind
of car does this Bill have?" Jean saw that her mother was having trouble keeping up and had placed a hand on his arm to
slow him down, but he took no notice. "Only I'd like to get
straight up to the house. Want to see what state it's in, get an
idea of what needs doing."

"Your old house? You want to go there right now?" Only
the anxiety in Violet's voice now stopped Eddie in his tracks.

"Why?" He looked from one to the other, and Jean saw
something start to disintegrate. "Why, what's happened?"

The front room at St Mark's Road was quiet and still, the
only sound the faint crack of the fire in the grate and the

chime of the grandfather clock in the hall on the quarter hour. Jean, long acclimatized to chilly evenings and steeped in Occupation thrift, had questioned the use of firewood on a June evening, even a chilly one, and argued that another jumper would suffice. But her mother insisted a small fire would make the place a little homelier, and Jean had dutifully hauled the logs from the shed just after tea.

It was just gone eight—too early to excuse herself for bed. She realized six pages in that she had read this soppy romance from the library not a year ago, and in her distraction she found herself hypnotized by Eddie's cigarette as it sat propped in the stand-up ashtray. Engrossed in his newspaper, Eddie had let it burn low in its groove, and Jean watched the tiny column of ash cling on, teetering, waiting to fall, while the coils of gray smoke rose toward the ceiling. Long ago, before the war, when tobacco was cheap and available, her father, too, would let a Rothmans burn halfway down on the same ashtray. He was home so rarely that such occasions were precious, and Jean would curl up at his feet, picking at the loose threads of his slippers, obedient to the rule that the children were not to talk until he finished the paper (chatty, impatient Harry always got into trouble for this). But silences with her dad never seemed tense. With Eddie, Jean was constantly aware of a distant, gathering squall. And since their trip to his house three nights ago, her uncle's rage had simmered like a stewing pot.

The fifteen-minute drive up to St Saviour, sliding about on the hard rear seat of Bill's car, had seemed endless. Eddie had impatiently drummed his fingers on the passenger door, while Jean and her mother exchanged silent, nervous looks. Eventually Violet sat forward in her seat and took a deep breath.

"You must understand, Eddie, what it was like here in

those early months. The Jerries went through the shops like locusts. Wasn't just food. Clothes, crockery—you name it, they took it, sent it all back to Germany." Eddie continued to stare at the road ahead. The back of his head was greasy with sweat and ancient hair oil. "Then the food ran out completely," Violet persisted. "And you needed stuff to barter with. People were desperate."

"So they decided robbing evacuees was all right?" His voice was different now, quieter and charged with anxiety and anger.

"We didn't know if you'd ever be back. You can't blame people for taking what they needed."

"It's not just that, though," Jean murmured, frightened of her uncle's coming reaction if they didn't prepare him. But her mother nudged her in the ribs across the back seat, and Jean said nothing else.

As Bill Syvret's car turned the corner of the leafy lane and pulled up in the short driveway, the look on her uncle's face told Jean everything she needed to know about his evacuation. Instantly she felt bad for all the times she had resentfully pictured him in some cozy English village, enjoying a pint in the local pub or listening to the wireless by a blazing fire. While she and her mother had spent the last five years praying for deliverance, now she saw that Eddie had spent those same years dreaming of this moment—a triumphal return to the Shangri-la he had built with his own hands fifteen years earlier. He had imagined the joyful turning of the key in the lock, finding a scuttle filled with fresh coal, bread and cheese in the larder. Now he climbed slowly out of Bill's Austin and, in the dimming twilight, strode toward the wreckage of the house, gingerly entering through the space where the front door should have been, until he was standing in the center of what had once been his living room. It wasn't the absence of his personal possessions, Jean sensed, that shocked him—the disappearance of chairs, curtains and rugs. What he was struggling to absorb was the extent of the annihilation—the smashed glass, the doors torn from frames, the holes in the floor where boards had been ripped out. The removal of the upstairs windows had allowed the rain of many months to soak and rot the upper floor, part of which had now crashed onto the floor below. Black mold sprouted everywhere, and at one point a pigeon fluttered from its nest somewhere in the upper rafters. Jean and Violet, standing well back, watched him move hesitantly toward the kitchen, where they knew he would find the sink ripped from the wall and the water heater on the floor, smashed up for spare parts. The entire place was nothing but a derelict collection of damaged walls. There was nothing for it but to gut the building and start again.

When he returned to the car, they sat in silence for several minutes. Finally Violet assured Eddie he could stay with them as long as he wanted—a sentiment Jean had anticipated but which still filled her with a mild dread—and he nodded his acceptance. Poor embarrassed Bill started the engine and began the somber journey back to town. For a long time, Eddie said nothing. Then: "How long's it been like that?"

"It happened slowly, over time," Violet murmured. "Things were really bad last winter—people burned anything just to warm themselves. Germans did the same."

"It was my home," was Eddie's only reply. For the rest of that evening, and through the days after, he had split his time between the local public house and her father's old armchair, accepting the meals and cups of tea the women brought him, and at night reading every inch of the *Evening Post*, as if the answers to this new alien world might be found within its pages. Jean watched from a distance, her sympathy mixed with undefined misgivings.

Deciding to make excuses and spend the rest of the evening in her room, Jean was just placing the marker in her book when there was a ring on the doorbell, so sudden it made both women pop in their seats. She hurried to the front window; on the doorstep stood a local uniformed policeman. Realizing no one else was going to move, she scurried into the hallway to unbolt the door. Her fingers, she noticed as she slid back the metal, had already begun to tremble.

The officer smiled benignly, but with a touch of disappointment—clearly he had hoped to speak to someone older.

"Is this the Parris residence?" he asked. Jean nodded. Her legs were losing their strength. "I have a gentleman here who has requested to speak with you." The policeman stood to one side. Behind him stood the figure of a small, hunched man of indeterminate age, who peered at Jean with sad, bush baby eyes. What little hair he'd managed to retain on his head stuck up at rakish angles, and his skin was the strangest shade of lilac gray. He looked, Jean thought, like an illustration of a goblin from a children's picture book.

"Madame Parris?" the man whispered in a strong French accent.

"Miss Parris." Jean's voice was unrecognizable to herself. "My mother—"

"I'm Mrs. Parris." Violet was behind her now, and Jean could sense the additional presence of Eddie in the parlor doorway. "Can I help you?"

The man looked hard at Jean's mother, as if assessing her. "You are…Violet?"

Jean's stomach dropped into another cavity within her

body. How did this odd little man know her mother's name? From the corner of her eye, Jean saw her mother nod.

"My name is Charles Clement." He stopped, as if this speech had been rehearsed many times, but the performance of it was not turning out as well as he had hoped. He wiped his face and began again. "My name is Charles Clement. I was a prisoner in Germany with your husband, Philip."

He pronounced her father's name the French way, with the extended second syllable. Jean reached for the door for support and saw her mother reach similarly for the frame. They waited, but nothing else came. Eventually Violet found her voice.

"You know my husband? Where is he?"

Clement hesitated, and at that moment Jean knew. In her mind she begged him not to say any more, to turn and walk away now so that she would never have to hear it. But it was already too late.

"I am so sorry, madame. I am here to tell you that Philip is dead."

2

It was his hands that she fixed upon, the delicate bony fingers of an elderly woman, white as plaster against his ragged dark trousers. Charles Clement sat rigidly still, refusing all offers of hospitality while, Jean guessed, he composed, discarded and recomposed the story to which he had now committed. Outside, incongruous laughing children played marbles in the final hour of twilight, but in the parlor the expectant silence grew in length and intensity, the popping and clicking of the dying fire the only sound. The policeman hovered awkwardly, his pleas to wait outside dismissed by Violet; Jean and her mother perched like anxious birds on the extreme edges of their chairs, waiting. Once or twice Clement glanced nervously at Eddie, who had taken a commanding position by the fireplace, scowling. From his expression alone, Jean was certain of his thoughts—that this stranger must be making all this up, perhaps to win some unknown bounty or fool them for his own ends. But when the Frenchman began to speak, finding a low, comfortable note on which to drone his faltering English, Jean knew from its simplicity that he was telling the truth.

Clement, imprisoned for sheltering a resistance fighter in his Rennes apartment, explained that he and Philip Parris had shared a cell in Preungesheim Prison in Frankfurt and had quickly discovered a connection when Parris mentioned Jersey, a place Clement had visited as a child. The two formed a friendship with a promise to support each other, such bonds being vital to survival within the German prison system. Preungesheim, he explained, was a hellhole of a place where prisoners were expected to work for ten or eleven hours a day on a starvation diet, performing grueling factory duties or clearing the rubble-strewn streets of Frankfurt. It was, however, nothing in comparison to the place they were moved to in the weeks following the Allied land invasion—Naumburg. Here, prisoners were crammed into tiny, overcrowded cells, forbidden to speak, smoke or even smile by their ex-soldier guards, and expected to survive daily on six ounces of bread and a bowl of what passed for soup. Illness was rife, and when dysentery ripped through the jail the previous winter, Parris, now severely underweight, succumbed quickly. Here Clement hesitated, glancing anxiously at the family, but Eddie egged him on, insisting despite the women's ashen looks that no detail be omitted. In a small, fading voice, Clement went on to recount how Parris had deteriorated rapidly, but that no amount of pleading from Clement or the other prisoners had elicited the medical attention he so badly needed. He died in his cell in the early hours of the morning of January 17. Clement, reaching out his skeletal hand to Violet, promised that he had whispered a prayer over Philip's body, and removed from his pocket Philip's most treasured possession—a photograph of Violet with children Harry and Jean, taken on St Brelade's beach a decade before. With that, he pulled the

same battered photograph from his own wallet and handed
it to Jean's mother.

"I am so sorry," Clement muttered. "But I have promised
Philip that if I live, I will come here to tell you in person. It
is better to know, perhaps, than to know not."

Jean and her mother stared vacantly at the photograph, a
small black-and-white picture of three carefree people who
no longer existed. Jean imagined Clement reaching into her
father's pocket for it, her father lying lifeless in the freezing
cell. She sensed the temperature of it inside her chest and felt
her world fall apart like the separating segments of an orange.
Her mother's face was drained of blood as she tried to speak.

"What happened to the body?"

"It was removed by the guards. *Je suis désolé*, that is all I
can tell you."

After that, a kind of fog descended. At some point Clement
rose and shook her mother's hand, and Eddie escorted Clement and the policeman to the door; Jean stood in the window to watch them slouch away, the policeman with his arm
around Clement's shoulders, the simple weight of it seeming
to buckle the Frenchman's knees. She stood there for a while,
trying to absorb the foreignness of this terrible new universe;
parts of the last hour were vague, a kind of nether land with
distant voices and vacant spaces, while other moments lodged
in her mind like glass splinters, each drawing blood. Eventually the deep-throated sobs of her mother, doubled up in her
chair, roused her, and while Eddie remained hunched in the
opposite corner of the parlor, lighting each cigarette from the
stub of the one before, Jean hauled her across the room and
up the stairs to her bedroom. For the next three hours Jean
sat unmoving in the tub wicker chair next to her parents' bed,
encouraging Violet to take a sip of the ancient brandy they

stored for emergencies, while sickening visions danced a hideous parade before her eyes. Her father curled up in tortured agony. His weakening body clinging to life, while he begged God for deliverance. This ghastly film played over and over, as if on a loop. Later she could not remember exactly how or when she made her way to her own room, but by dawn that was where she found herself, listening to her mother's groans and whimpers through the wall, her heart rapid in her chest as her night panic returned.

It seemed unthinkable that she would never see him again.

A little after seven she trudged downstairs to begin the only activity she could think to do, which was to make endless pots of tea. She tried not to use too much of the ration and made each pot mean and weak, but the level in the caddy still dropped alarmingly. Within the hour, Violet appeared to sit red-eyed at the kitchen table while Eddie paced from room to room with a thunderous expression. No one had the slightest idea what to say. By midday, Jean's aunt Beattie had arrived, arms filled with wildflowers and bags of potatoes from their farm, her eyes swollen and pink from weeping, and proceeded to hug her sister for so long Jean feared her mother might be crushed.

"I can't believe it. I just can't believe it," Beattie chanted over and over again, while Violet nodded, her eyes shut, throwing up her hands to indicate the implausibility of the whole scenario. Jean watched them together, thinking that barring the same blue-gray eyes, few people would have taken the two women for sisters. They were only two years apart in age but seemed more like ten, Beattie retaining the strong, handsome features of a reliable filly, while Violet looked like an exhausted cart horse in its final furlong. Beattie had married a wealthy local farmer, and everyone knew the difference money had made during the war years; farming families could always rustle up a cauliflower or a few carrots from their ploughed acres, and her aunt's family always had something put by for under-the-counter extras. Plus, Beattie had never had to watch her husband be dragged away by enemy soldiers. Watching them both bent over the table in such despair while she poured yet more cups of pale, tepid liquid from the teapot, Jean wondered how on earth her mother would ever come back from this terrible blow. How would any of them?

Toward the end of the afternoon, the slamming of the front door and her uncle's heavy footsteps down the hallway told all three women that something important was about to be announced. Eddie stood in the kitchen doorway, his chin unnecessarily high.

"Right, I've worked out what we need to do." Jean stared at him with confusion. What could Eddie have possibly figured out in these few, shell-shocked hours? Never in her life had everything seemed so unclear and insecure, a spiraling chaos that no one could fix. But Eddie nodded with confidence. "Tomorrow we're going to the Jersey States offices, straight to the top of our government. We're going to find out why this happened to my brother. And more to the point, we're going to find out who's responsible."

The sky was the palest of grays, and a tepid breeze rustled through the thick summer foliage of the chestnut trees around the square. An earlier shower had left small puddles on the granite flagstones, and a faint scent of citrusy sweetness that Jean inhaled gratefully as they walked. It was quiet in town, a complete contrast to the Royal visit last month, as if the island remained in a state of convalescence. On such a cool summer afternoon, the streets of St Helier should have been crowded with tourists, working people drawn here from all the northern cities of Britain. The high street should have been swarming with couples and families buying up cigars and checking bus timetables. Next year, perhaps, they would start to return. But today the only other people in the square were a handful of exhausted women taking books back to the public library, and one old man sat on a bench, leaning on a stick and watching the world with skeptical eyes and a downturned mouth. It was an expression Jean saw on many a face recently, especially among the elderly.

The three of them crossed toward the States administrative building, the women's clogs clattering on the granite flags of the square. They stopped only briefly for Violet to point out to Eddie the defiant V for victory that a resistance-minded stonemason had laid into the replacement paving only a few months before, right under the noses of the Germans. It made Eddie chuckle, and the wet chesty sound from deep in his lungs made Jean wince.

A young secretary ushered them through the heavy oak door leading into the government offices, then down a corridor and up a grand staircase. Moments later they were swept into an elegant office in faded duck-egg blue, with three chairs carefully arranged in a semicircle before a gleaming desk, and were requested to wait. The room was stuffy, but none of them dared to approach the tall leaded windows to see if they opened. Eddie, taking the right-hand seat, slumped with crossed arms in passive protest at the delay, while Jean and her mother rested lightly on the edge of theirs. Jean pressed her stomach to subdue its rumblings. She'd barely eaten since Clement's visit.

"Do you think I should keep my gloves on?" Violet whispered. Jean gave a small shrug to indicate it didn't matter.

Her mother looked ghastly, and Jean wished she'd been able to talk her uncle into letting her stay at home. But Eddie had insisted that it was essential Violet be present, so, tight-lipped, Jean had pulled her mother's best suit from the wardrobe to air, then hauled that spindly little body into it, helping her with the zip at the back. Now she fixed her eyes on the two chairs on the authority side of the desk, awaiting their significant posteriors.

A sudden commotion of people tumbling through the door startled all of them, and Jean sat upright with attention. There were three of them—the tallest, and clearly most senior, was a lean uniformed lieutenant in his forties with a long Roman nose and serious expression. Behind him walked a rosy-cheeked blond man in a navy suit, carrying a thick file. There was also a young clerk, around Jean's age, carrying a small stack of additional files and a clipboard, who smiled awkwardly at each of the family before finding a place in the corner to stand, as if he'd been told explicitly that sitting was beyond his remit. The lieutenant took his seat, tucking his tunic down at the back for optimum neatness, before meeting their eyes.

"Good afternoon to you. My name is Lieutenant Payne of the Civil Affairs Unit, working with Force 135, and this is Detective Constable Ashford from the Public Safety Branch of CID, based in London." The man in the navy suit nodded a greeting. Jean stared, realizing that she had not taken in a single word of their names or titles. What if she had to repeat them back? Or they questioned her and she had no idea how to address them? She felt sweat in her armpits and wriggled. "I realize that you have recently received extremely shocking news," the lieutenant continued, "and on behalf of everyone here I would like to extend our sincere condolences. However, I'm sure that your main concern today is to secure some answers to your many questions."

"That's right," Eddie replied, his voice shakier than usual. "For a start, we'd like to recover my brother's body, give him a proper burial."

The lieutenant's brows tightened. "We will do what we can, but I wouldn't raise your hopes. It's unlikely that remains can be exhumed or reinterred…" Jean whipped round as her mother's face drained of blood, enough to halt the lieutenant on that particular track. "However, regarding an explanation for these dreadful events, I'm pleased to tell you there has at least been one development."

Jean leaned forward. Could this be true? Had they discovered the mistake that had sent her dad to such a terrible, inappropriate place, perhaps identified the individual Nazis responsible? Her armpits were soaking now. She yearned to remove her jacket but was afraid to appear too casual.

"Please go on," her mother murmured.

"As you may be aware," the lieutenant continued, "much of the documentation for Mr. Parris's case has been mislaid or destroyed. But we have found a witness report that may help identify the person who informed on him."

A hollow stillness bloomed in the room, as if time had stopped. The only audible sound was the honking of a car horn out in the street. Jean repeated the words in her head, certain she must have misunderstood.

"Sorry…what?" Eddie's flushed cheeks had noticeably paled.

Violet raised her hand a little, as if in school. "No, the Germans found the radio during a random search of his shop. Just a random search."

The officer glanced at his colleague, and Jean saw the weight it contained. She heard him breathe in.

"The Germans, we now know, rarely acted on chance. In most cases, searches were instigated by a tip-off, usually someone in the local community with a score to settle." He glanced at his notes. "This didn't come up at the time of his arrest?"

"No, it didn't." Jean watched her mother's expression shift from confusion to outrage. "Now just wait a moment. I know some people informed on their neighbors—those dreadful anonymous letters that were sent to College House? But that can't be what happened here."

The CID officer looked puzzled. "If I may—why do you assume that?"

"Because no one would do that to Phil. Everyone loved him. He was more than a shopkeeper. He helped his community—welcomed people in to hear the news, despite the risks. He was a bloody hero. Pardon my French," she added, blushing.

Another silence settled on the room. The car was still honking its horn; Jean wished she could go outside and stop it. Eddie was shaking his head as if trying to dislodge water, apparently unable to take this in. Jean looked from the men to her mother, whose wide eyes were now fixed on the two men behind the desk. Once again, she found herself reaching for the gold locket at her throat. She remembered her father's clumsy fingers doing it up for her, his smile of approval. Who would want to harm a man like that? It was inconceivable.

The young clerk hovering at the side of the room stepped forward. "Would you like a glass of water?" Jean and Violet both nodded. The lieutenant announced a brief recess, and the young man soon returned with a pitcher of water and several glasses. Jean noticed the care he took to pour each glass without spilling a drop on the rug and even assisted her mother, whose hands were shaking, to take a few sips. Eddie waited until she had handed the glass back then turned to the officer.

"You said there was a witness report?"

Payne, resuming control of the interview, perused some notes in front of him. "A Mr. Le Sauteur, who lived opposite Mr. Parris's shop and had a clear view of it, reported him arguing with a woman several times in the weeks before his arrest. On one occasion, the pavement dispute became serious enough for Mr. Le Sauteur to call the police. However, by the time the bobby arrived, the shop was closed and both parties had left." Jean's mind spun in circles. She'd never known her dad to argue with any woman.

"Who was she? A customer?" Eddie demanded.

"We don't know. She was described as a tall lady, probably late twenties, with reddish hair. Mr. Le Sauteur was something of a recluse and knew few people personally. That's all he was able to say."

"Would he recognize this woman again?"

"Unfortunately Mr. Le Sauteur died toward the end of last year."

Eddie emitted a small growl of frustration. Jean could see the cogs of his mind spinning, adjusting to new possibilities. "But you think this woman might have grassed up Phil?"

"It's one possibility," Payne replied. "We can interrogate some of the German personnel now in British custody. Some are willing to provide information for a reduced sentence. But there are no guarantees." He turned to Violet. "Mrs. Parris, are you aware of anyone who may have had any kind of quarrel with your husband? Did anyone express concern about his having a wireless, for instance? Any disputes with business contacts? Anything at all?"

Jean watched her mother as she tried to answer, her mouth

twitching to move, but unable to form any words. The woman seemed to have shrunk in size in the last few minutes, and her left hand was now gripping the edge of her seat as if she expected the floor to fall away beneath her. Eventually, with enormous effort, she managed to get out the only words she could manage.

"Like I said. He was a hero."

The photograph was a flattering one, taken, most probably, by a professional photographer before the war. In it, Philip Parris, dressed in a smart tweed jacket in place of his usual brown overall, looked composed and confident, his unruly thinning hair plastered into submission. Hazel stared at it for a moment, trying to link this black-and-white image to the shopkeeper she had known. Slowly she lowered the newspaper to her lap.

"What does it say?" Her father's brows were angled into an expression of alarm.

"Just that he died in Naumburg jail in Germany last January, and the facts have only just come to light."

"Does it say how he died?"

Hazel shook her head. She was having trouble absorbing this information, and the shock of it was making her a little sick. The last time she'd seen Parris he was a reasonably healthy man in middle age. What violent events must have occurred in that prison to cause such a demise? And what did this imply for all the others? In the last three years dozens of islanders had been imprisoned abroad for wireless "offenses" or assisting Russian slave workers, but Hazel had clung to the hope that the dreadful reports of death and cruelty so far were a ghastly anomaly, and that the majority of Jersey prisoners must, surely, have been treated with basic civility. Had she, even now, miscalculated the Nazis' capacity for cruelty and barbarism? Would this turn out to be a common fate?

"There's details of a memorial service at St Mark's church next week. I should go."

Her father shifted his head back into his neck. "Seriously?"

Hazel bridled. "Dad, the man's dead, probably in terrible circumstances. You think I wanted that?"

"No, I didn't mean..."

"And you criticized him often enough yourself. Said he was a security risk to everyone in the flats."

"Well, he was. Remember that time he had the BBC on, with his back window wide-open?" He gave his head a wobble of disbelief. "But to die alone, so far from home... No one deserves that."

"Of course not. It's shameful." Hazel shook out the paper and they sat in silence for a while, the plates from their evening meal still on the table between them. The tunny fish pie she had lovingly baked now swirled evilly in her stomach. She thought of all the times she had sat in this very chair vilifying Philip Parris, condemning him. A nauseating pool of guilt welled up within her. She needed to get out of the flat, get some fresh air into her lungs. She stood up briskly.

"How about a stroll, Dad? Lovely evening." He shook his head dismissively. "Just to the end of the road? Might do you good, get your joints moving."

"I'm better off here. You go, have a proper walk."

She tucked the blanket over his legs, pulled her wrap around her shoulders and slipped out, closing the door quietly. The air was fresh and sweet, the sun still warm but no longer burning, and her feet stepped quickly along New Street toward the harbor. Within minutes, she was heading up Pier Road and the long climb up to South Hill on the edge of

Fort Regent. As she began the steepest section, feeling her blood pump and her body overheat, she wondered again why she inevitably chose this destination for her solo constitutionals. South Hill itself was certainly no beauty spot; the rugged windswept hillside was scattered with nothing but the ugly, squat buildings of the old military prison, latterly commissioned by the Germans to hold a number of American and French-Algerian POWs, now deserted but for the occasional pair of weary Tommies, sharing roll-ups or lazing against the granite walls. But the view! If she could push herself to the final hairpin bends of the road—and there had been times when malnutrition and exhaustion had got the better of her—the reward was a vista worthy of a picture in a magazine. In the distance, the glorious, mirrored stretch of St Aubin's Bay, before her, the sprawling Tudor magnificence of Elizabeth Castle. And directly below, the flat teal water of the English and French Harbours, where tiny fishing vessels, dragged from their wartime storage sheds, now bobbed once more, lobster cages stacked up in the sterns, bright buoys marking each mooring. Up here in solitude, away from the chattering of her pupils and the gentle demands of her immobile father, she could breathe deeply and stare out at the horizon with fresh hope that better days were on their way.

Tonight though, as she leaned into the breeze, her palms flat down on the ancient granite wall, there was only one thought in her mind. She had never liked Philip Parris, not even in the early days of the war when he used to top up the Le Tourneurs' jerry can with an extra free inch of paraffin, always suspecting that something would, at some point, be demanded in return. She recalled one evening years before, leaving the flats with Dottie as Parris was pulling down the shutter of his shop, and Dottie's mischievous whisper: *"Can't*

keep those kind of secrets in, no matter how many locks you turn."
Hazel snorted bitterly at the thought of it; her sister, despite
her youth, had always been an excellent judge of character.
But a death like that, in the squalor of a foreign jail, alone
and terrified... With a deepening despair she remembered
Parris's wife and daughter. She had seen them once, not long
after the shopkeeper's arrest, standing outside the store with
tight, wan faces, staring in despair at the display window as
if they could will him back to his rightful place. At the time
she had passed them without a word, embarrassed by their
grief and with no idea what to say to them. Now the memory brought a lump to her throat.

Her eyes drifted up to the ship moored out in the bay,
where, at this moment, languished hundreds of German soldiers awaiting incarceration in British POW camps. Young
men swept into a madness, their lives now ruined. She considered for the thousandth time that war was a disgusting,
hopeless practice. Even more vital, then, that from now on
ordinary people took control of their destiny, promoting
international cooperation and partnership to create a better world. With a sigh, she tightened her wrap around her
shoulders and set off for home. Tomorrow she would finalize
her membership of the Jersey Democratic Movement. She
needed to be part of something, to be useful. She needed to
feel like a decent human being.

"Fish stew."
Violet half placed, half dropped the pot in the middle of
the table and stood staring at the thick orange liquid within.
Chunks of white fish, swollen ginger mussels and small brown
limpets bobbed tantalizingly on the surface, pushing up a
delicious aroma; steam from the pot fogged the window so

thickly that rivulets trickled down the inside of the pane. The meal had been paid for by Eddie at his insistence, just like the new Marconi wireless that pumped out big band tunes from its proud position on the dresser. The music gave the kitchen a coziness that, if she squinted, Jean could almost imagine for a moment was a normal evening before the war; times when her mother would ruffle her father's hair affectionately as she served him his tea, and he would pretend to find it irritating. The good old days.

Except, of course, that it was no longer the good old days. Everything was wrong and horrible and frightening, and nothing would ever be like those days again. She did not want this meal, nor to sit at this table pretending that everything was normal. She wanted to put her head in her hands and sob. But Eddie had already had a go at her that morning for sniveling at the breakfast table, so she vowed to hold everything inside until she was in the privacy of her bedroom.

Her uncle was sitting in what had once been her father's place, looking for all the world as if he had sat there all his life. Jean cast him a sideways look as he picked up the bread knife without invitation and began to cut, his square-tipped fingers attacking the loaf ferociously, pressing too hard so that the dough crumbled and split. The slices were too thick and too numerous—there was no possibility that they would consume so much in one meal, and the pieces would harden overnight in the bread bin. Jean waited for Violet to correct him, but nothing came, so Jean gave a little cough and glanced toward the loaf.

"We're still on rations, Uncle Eddie?"

Eddie wrinkled his nose and continued to cut. "Always little extras available, if you've got the readies. Soon as that compensation comes through, you won't be going short." Jean gave her mother a sideways look, which was not returned. Three trips to his solicitor in recent days—always followed by a lengthy session in the Peirson Pub, Jean assumed, based on his breath when he returned—had yielded no concrete promises, so far as she could tell.

"Well, this is a proper treat," Violet assured him. "Couldn't get fish or shellfish for years, except a few limpets at low tide."

"Jerries didn't stop you fishing, did they?"

Jean consciously avoided rolling her eyes. Ten days home, yet her uncle still seemed to have no concept of what the Occupation had actually been like. She let her mother reply.

"Fishermen had to hand over so much of their catch it weren't worth it, even if they could get the petrol. Plus they was only allowed to fish out of St Helier and had to have a soldier with them so they didn't escape. And Jerries still called it Summerland, what a joke."

"Summerland?"

For the first time, Jean and her mother shared a small wry smile.

"What some of them called the island. These clogs we're all wearing, see…?" Violet nodded toward her feet. "All made in the Summerland clothing factory in Rouge Bouillon, 'cause you couldn't get no proper shoes. We called them Summerland clogs. Jerries got confused, thought it was our name for Jersey."

Eddie snorted. "Idiots."

"Some carried on using the name, even when we put them right. Suppose they thought they were in some kind of paradise, which they was compared to the Eastern Front. They loved the beaches, before the barbed wire went up." She snorted bitterly. "Summerland! Then they go and turn it into a living hell. Ain't that right, Jean?"

But Jean's mind was already hopping ahead. "I could get a job there?"

Her mother frowned. "What?"

"At the Summerland factory. They're still hiring. Daisy Le Coq got a job—"

"No." Violet's mouth was set on a tight line.

"Cleaning work then? We don't want to rely on Uncle Eddie for everything." In truth, the thought of being dependent on him made her uneasy.

"I said no. I need you here."

Jean had a dozen arguments lined up, but one look into those exhausted eyes told her tonight was not the time. Violet had spent all afternoon writing a long letter to Jean's brother, Harry, relating every detail of recent events, and had emerged from the parlor a little after five, ashen faced and tearful— there were even saltwater droplets on the envelope. Jean scoured her mind for another subject.

"Lovely cards, aren't they, Mum?" They took in the half dozen homemade condolence cards on the kitchen shelf. Sad little attempts made from painted newspaper and chopped-up gravy packets, which only underlined the inadequacy of the messages, and one proper, official one from the States of Jersey, handwritten by the nice young clerk from their meeting. Violet nodded.

"People have been very kind."

"Tomorrow I'll draw up a list for the memorial service," Eddie announced, his mouth full of bread. Jean saw the butter ooze between the gaps of his teeth and had to look away.

"Don't worry," Violet replied. "Beattie's taking care of all that."

Eddie nodded but Jean also spotted an indignant sniff, as if the involvement of Violet's family in the arrangements was something of a personal affront. Since their interview at the States offices earlier this week, it took very little to rile him, as if anger was a more comfortable emotion to carry around than grief. While her mother spent long hours in her bed staring blankly at the walls and ceiling, Eddie would return from his town excursions scowling and breathing heavily, padding around the house like a distressed bear until the early hours. Jean found herself wondering how long before Eddie's family returned to reclaim him, so that she and her mother could at least get their own home back. But then, she considered, swallowing hard to force down a morsel of fish, could this house ever feel like home without her father?

The last few days had been a storm of bewilderment. Everything seemed distant and violent at the same time, as the world altered before her eyes and out there, in the cobbled streets and leafy lanes she'd grown up in, nothing could be relied on anymore. Friendly neighbors now looked like smiling assassins, while the *Evening Post* was filled with reports of an island she no longer recognized. Protesters were organizing another rally, stirring up trouble with their demands for wage increases…more swastikas had been painted on the doors of those suspected of collaboration. Just weeks ago, she had felt cocooned by this island community; now old securities were shredded. Her feelings of panic at night had grown worse, happy memories of her father steamrollered by the trauma. Recollections of Christmas Days and paddling at St Brelade's were now swept aside by images of a shivering body on a stone floor, the indifferent sneers of German guards. Never again that smile, that unique scent of shop metal and shaved wood. Now even a shred of soft fish felt like a rock in her throat.

"What's the name of that rich farmer your sister married?"

Eddie's question to Violet shook Jean back into the room.

"Martin Tibot. Out near St Ouen's village."

"Bet they did all right during the war, money like that?"

Violet sniffed. "Germans took a lot of their produce. But yes, it was easier for people in the country parishes." Jean's fingers tightened around her spoon. She had learned to sense when her uncle was moving toward some kind of argument.

"I hear lots of the farmers here had a lovely bloody war."

Violet sat back a little. "Some took advantage with prices. But no one had a lovely war, Eddie." It was pointless. Eddie was already paddling hard toward what had lately become his favorite new topic.

"Don't know what's happened to people here, all looking out for themselves. You know, I'm starting to wish I'd stayed put. Still have a house if I had." Eddie put down his bread and jabbed his finger at a page of the newspaper folded open on the table. Jean's father had never read the paper over tea. "Bloody disgrace I call it."

"What is?"

"Collaboration! Locals palling up with Jerry for their own ends. Looks like everyone was at it."

The words fluttered to the floor like bomb ash. Eventually Violet stuttered: "That's not true, Eddie. A few bad apples, that's all."

"Was it? Take a look at this." He held up the page for them to see. It was filled with a petition from a local group calling themselves the Jersey Loyalists, demanding that a court of inquiry be set up in order to try every suspected collaborator on the island. This category, it suggested, included informers, black marketeers, women who had performed "horizontal collaboration" with Germans, anyone in the pay of the enemy or who had entertained them, plus any person who had assisted "in any way with the enemy." Jean thought of the boarded-up bakery on the way to the Royal Square and felt her stomach lurch. "We heard rumors in England that it was getting a bit too friendly here. Refused to believe it. Shows how wrong you can be."

Jean's voice cracked as she spoke. "You don't know if you weren't here. We had to live with the Germans, but we always knew which side we were on."

"Yeah? Fella down the pub says there's a fair few local women deserve to be tarred and feathered." The concept fixed itself in Jean's head. She replaced her spoon in her dish, her meal over with barely a bite. "I tell you this," Eddie went on, "if someone is responsible for grassing up Phil, we're going to find them." He continued chewing for a moment, then added: "Any more thoughts about this woman? The one he had the argument with?"

Violet shrugged. "I told you I don't know. Could be anybody."

Eddie was attacking his stew as if he were trying to hurt it.

"Well, whoever it is, they won't get away with it, 'cause I hold them just as responsible as the Jerries." His face reddened. "My poor Phil. What he must have gone through…"

"Don't, Eddie, please." Violet's spoon, too, was abandoned in her half-full bowl.

"Big tough fella like that would have sailed through a normal prison, no problem. When he came out of Newgate Street he looked like he'd been on flipping holiday."

It took a moment for her uncle's words to land, and to make sense. Jean slowly lifted her head.

"Newgate Street, here? Dad was in prison before?"

Eddie nodded, ignoring Violet's imploring looks, though Jean saw them clearly.

"Only for a few months, when he was a lad."

"What did he do?"

"Bit light-fingered at his first job, normal kids' stuff. Learned his lesson."

Jean looked to her mother. "You never said...?"

"Why would I? It was years ago, before we was married, and anyway, none of your business."

Eddie continued to shovel food into his mouth like a machine, and Jean could tell from the way Violet aggressively scraped out the remains of the pot into Eddie's bowl that the subject was closed. She sat completely still for several moments while Eddie demolished the remains of the meal and Violet fussed about with glasses of milk that no one had asked for, thinking of her father on the stepladder in his shop or going through the monthly accounts. A pillar of the community—a hero. They had all repeated it, many times, yet apparently he had spent months in prison for thieving. Slowly she gathered the dishes from the table and assembled them in the sink. Was there nothing fixed and permanent in her life that she could rely on? What further volcanoes might explode in the coming weeks? It was almost a surprise when she turned on the Ascot heater and found that hot water still came out of the tap.

Thirty-one people. Including the family. Jean, squashed between Eddie and her mother at the front of the church, recounted the heads behind her until Violet nudged her.

"I'm just trying to see how many people I recognize," Jean whispered over the wafting organ music. And there were several. Her father's cousin, with his wife and son. A small chap with a lazy eye from her dad's old pub, who used to drop round to the house sometimes to discuss business...two men of similar age who Jean guessed were friends from school. Aunt Beattie and her husband, Martin, had tucked themselves into the row behind, and Jean was glad to see the comforting presence of her cousin Daphne sitting between them—on seeing Jean she blew her a kiss and smiled her sensational smile. Even as a child, Daphne had always had a grace and beauty sadly absent in the rest of the family, and now, as a young woman—thinner from the war years, more angular yet more developed—she had the radiance of a Greek sculpture. Being two years older, the eldest and only girl of Beattie's three children, Daphne was the one who'd taught Jean hopscotch, how to curl her hair and how to fasten a brassiere, so occupied a special place in Jean's heart. Although the sight today of her father's arm around her, protective and comforting, felt like a punch to Jean's stomach.

The rest of the congregation, Jean assumed, were customers from her father's shop. Thinking about it, her dad had never been one for friendships… Apart from his beloved pint of Mary Ann beer on a Friday night (his greatest deprivation during the Occupation) he spent so many hours at work that even Jean and Harry had had to fight for his attention. Yet—was this it? Jean scanned the receding rows, counting and recounting. Perhaps Aunt Beattie had placed the personal advertisement in the *Evening Post* too late, or people felt too embarrassed to face the family in the midst of such tragedy. Or maybe people simply didn't want to think about the consequences of the Occupation now that life was returning to something like normality.

She spotted someone giving her a tentative wave from the other side of the aisle and craned her neck to see; it was the friendly clerk from the Jersey States offices, provider of water and writer of cards. Jean returned his thin smile and nodded her appreciation. It was nice of the authorities to send a representative, even if it was someone so junior. A mark of respect, she supposed.

The arrival of the minister brought an expectant silence. He welcomed them all before requesting the congregation to rise for "Abide With Me." Then he read the eulogy from the notes that her mother and Eddie had provided, speaking of a terrible Occupation that had taken so many lives, and everyone nodded and added amen while many of the women shed a tear. Jean kept her gaze on the stained-glass window at the end of the nave to keep herself in check. The minister spoke of Philip Parris as a valued member of the community and a fine family man, who did not deserve to die that way, and there was more nodding and amens. Another hymn was sung, then Eddie stood up to say that his big brother had always been the most important person in his life (this, in the light of his wife and children, Jean found a little odd) and ended on an ominous note that those responsible for his death would be judged by God. The minister drew the service to a close by reading a brief letter from Harry saying what a great father he had lost and how sorry he was that he could not be there in person, then instructed the island to come together in their collective grief for all those lost. Then it was over.

Jean handed her mother a handkerchief, and, taking her gently by the arm, escorted her to the main entrance to await official condolences. Beattie rushed over to give her yet another hug. Daphne extricated herself from her father's arm and embraced Jean hard, promising that they would find time to talk properly back at the farm, where a simple buffet was waiting for everyone. Jean thanked her, grateful for her cousin's warmth, suddenly realizing how alone she had felt since the news of her father's death. As the family melted back into the crowd other mourners approached to embrace

Violet, expressing their shock and repeating over and over that it was a shameful thing. But several, Jean noticed, slipped quietly past and out of the door. Jean felt a surge of anger. If they had taken the trouble to come, why not take time to speak to the widow herself? She watched them file out into the summer sunshine, glad to see the back of them.

So when the States clerk approached them with the wryest of smiles and the gentlest handshake, Jean felt a rush of gratitude. He was a fairly nondescript fellow with sandy brown hair and light freckles, the kind that in regular life you could meet several times and never remember. But his pleasant, open manner was a welcome change.

"Tom Maloret. Just wanted to pay my respects. How are you holding up?" he asked with genuine concern.

"We're fine," Jean replied, aware that this was nonsense, but that no other response was acceptable.

"Your uncle spoke to me earlier..." he went on. Jean's heart sank. "I told him that we'll do all we can to hurry inquiries along."

"I'm sure you will. Thank you."

"I realize this is a terrible time for you. And if I can ease the burden in any way? With that in mind, I was wondering..."

"Yes?" Jean noticed he was flushing pink.

"I realize this might sound a little improper. But there's a dance at West Park Pavilion this weekend. Perhaps you'd like to come along? Try to forget things for a few hours?" The flush grew deeper, and his eyes dropped to his shoes. "I'm sorry, it's clearly not the right time."

"No, it's very kind of you to ask. Can I think about it?" Jean gave him her best smile as he nodded and walked away, knowing it was all she could offer—she had no intention of going to a dance with Tom Maloret. But as she watched him walk out onto the gravel path at the front of the church and through the iron gateway, her attention was caught by a slim woman standing alone by the railings, watching the other mourners with an expression that Jean could not fathom. She wore a gray dress that had seen better days and had pale skin that would burn easily under the heat of the Jersey sun. She was also in her late twenties, unusually tall, with russet hair scraped back with a ribbon.

Jean glanced at Eddie to see if he'd noticed her, but he was standing just outside, talking intensely with the group of her dad's school chums and smoking vigorously. She gently touched her mother, who was thanking the last departing mourner.

"Mum, that woman? Do you know her?" Violet turned to Jean as if slowly swimming to the surface of a deep pool. Her eyes were red and swollen. Jean gestured to the person in question. "That one. Do you know who she is?" Violet peered at the figure, and for a moment Jean could see there was no thought in her mind whatsoever. Then Violet took in the woman's appearance and the penny dropped. Suddenly, she was intensely present and alert.

"Yes—yes, I do!" Violet gripped Jean's arm so tight that Jean flinched. "She's one of that family in the flats over the shop. The father's a cripple...youngest died of diphtheria couple of years ago."

"Did Dad know them?"

"They used to come into the shop. I think they went in the back to listen to the news a few times."

"Only the description...? The woman who argued with Dad..."

Violet was staring at the woman now, transfixed. She was way ahead of Jean.

"Le Tourneur, that's their name. I think she's the eldest." At that moment the woman must have sensed she was being discussed, because she turned toward them. Her eyes met Violet's for a moment, with an expression that was hard to comprehend. Then she turned back out of the gate and disappeared down David Place. Violet's grip on Jean's arm grew fiercer. There would be a bruise tomorrow. "That's her, isn't it?" Her eyes were still fixed on the spot where the woman had stood. "It's got to be."

Jean's heart was racing. "But why would a neighbor, someone Dad had helped, do something so terrible? And why would she come to his memorial?"

"I'm going to get Eddie."

"No!" The vehemence in Jean's voice surprised her. "Not now, Mum. We don't want a scene here. Tell him later."

But her mother was barely listening. Her voice, when it came, was the strongest it had been in days.

"It's coming back to me now, that family. Her name's Hazel." She turned back to Jean with a look of triumph. "And she hated your father."

3

The ancient oak dining table at Les Renoncules farmhouse displayed more food than Jean had seen in one place for a long time. Sandwiches filled with Spam or fish paste, bowls of cockles with fresh lettuce and a gleaming bowl of Guernsey tomatoes drew the mourners around it, filling their plates and stuffing the food into their mouths as they nodded sagely about the sadness of the occasion. Most of the church attendees had not made the long journey out to St Ouen, so the guests here were mainly Beattie and Martin's neighbors, farmers and their wives with rough, gnarled hands and accents thicker than soil. Jean had wanted the wake back at St Mark's Road, a short walk from the church, but Beattie had already offered, and Violet insisted the Tibots' farm would be a better choice. It was certainly a better buffet than anything Jean and Violet could have provided.

She nibbled on a tomato, taking care not to get juice down her only decent dress, and tried to resist the urge to fiddle with her underwear. This morning, on this most solemn occasion of the year, she had been forced to revert to an old pair of navy knickers from her school days that cut into the tops of her legs, two new pairs having been stolen from the washing line. The fact that anyone could be desperate enough to steal used underclothes spoke volumes about the state of things, for such a thing would never have happened before the war. She gazed around the dim, low-beamed room with its little casement windows, a place she once associated with family parties and board games with her cousins, and felt a door closing on her entire past. The service itself had provided no sense of resolution, the absence of a coffin or any meaningful goodbye leaving nothing but a despairing wretchedness. An overwhelming urge to cry welled inside her but she fought it hard, taking a large gulp of tea and determinedly tuning in to the conversation around her. It was, as expected, the same one that had dominated since the service.

"So Phil actually mentioned this woman to you by name?" Eddie was saying.

Violet was leaning heavily on his arm as she balanced on the edge of her chair, her eyes casting about like a frightened child.

"By name. Soon as I clapped eyes on her, it all came back. Should have thought of it when we were sat with the officers, but it was so long ago. Late '43, near Christmas. Probably a Thursday, 'cause he always worked late Thursdays doing stock take. Phil comes home, says this girl from the flats over the shop is driving him mad—always complaining about something, he said—and he tells her straight, if she carries on like that, she's not coming to any more of his wireless parties. Well, of course she'd have been livid—her family had no set of their own."

"People wrote those letters for all sorts of reasons," Beattie agreed, breaking her slow progress through the room to check that everyone had had one plate of food but no more.

"We know a chap reported Jim Rabet's piglet to the Germans, just 'cause Jim had sold him a lame horse before the war."

"And this Le Tourneur woman, she fits the description that neighbor gave?" Eddie asked.

Violet nodded. "Tall, red hair, that's her." Eddie turned to Jean for confirmation of the sighting, and Jean nodded obediently.

"Remember anything else?"

Violet gave a little start as another thought popped in. "I think her family was mixed up with those Communists, those ones been causing all the trouble."

"Bunch of idiots that lot, dangerous and all," Beattie's husband, Martin, chimed in. He was clearly uncomfortable in his one formal suit, and his tie was already pulled to one side; Jean had rarely seen him out of his farming tweeds and found this awkward attempt at conformity as touching as it was ridiculous. "Always rocking the boat during the war, causing trouble. All it did was stir Jerry up for retaliations."

Violet nodded. "Phil had no time for any of them."

"Sounds like this woman could be the one," Martin went on. "But see, do you have any proof? 'Cause if not, I don't reckon there's much you can do."

"Plenty we can do," Eddie replied, jutting out his obstreperous chin. "Pass all this on to the States, tell them to pull her in for questioning. Some Jerry POWs will name names, apparently. And I've still got a few contacts round town. Get my ear to the ground." Eddie raised his index finger to the tip of his nose, implying some kind of superior knowledge, while Martin merely looked skeptical. Jean sipped her tea, stirred by the new sense of power and agency that bloomed in the dining room. If this woman was responsible for her father's arrest, she wanted to see her herded onto a boat at gunpoint just as he had been, wanted her thrown into a freezing cell, see how she coped with it. Jean realized she was trembling just thinking about it.

"We should confront her, ask her straight out?" Violet suggested.

"No point yet, she'd just deny it. Leave it with me," Eddie replied, patting her on the shoulder. "Meantime I'm going to get myself in with these Jersey Loyalists. Seems like they're the only lot round here willing to shake things up, get some of these collaborators put away."

"The Loyalists?" Martin chuckled, pouring whiskey into Eddie's tea from a small flask, though Jean noted that he tipped a good deal more into his own. Nothing was offered to her mother or herself. "Don't think you'll have much luck there."

"Why not?" The chin was now so pushed forward Jean thought Eddie might damage his neck.

"Look, they're a decent lot—did a lot of underground stuff during the war, mapping German positions, helping escapees, stuff like that. But they're all ex-military, professional types. Not sure you'd fit in there, no offense."

"We'll see." Eddie took a hefty swig of his refashioned drink, clearly torn between annoyance toward Martin and gratitude for the whiskey. "All I want is fair play, for my brother and for Violet here. And to make sure she's looked after, of course."

Beattie gave a little cough. "Some of us have been looking after her for a while, Eddie. Those of us who stuck it out here and didn't go running off to England at the first sound of gunfire." She smiled joylessly as she proffered a plate of sandwiches before them.

"It was no walk in the park over there," Eddie snapped

back, though he took a sandwich. "Jersey didn't have to put up with the Blitz."

"I'm not saying you didn't have problems," Beattie countered. "I'm saying it was nothing to what we suffered. Lot of folk starved this last winter."

"Lot of folk helped themselves to other people's property and all." Eddie's lips pressed hard together, as he chewed, creating little white patches. Jean wondered if anyone would notice if she edged away.

"You can't blame 'em, way things were," Beattie retorted. "We managed, just about, and in case you're wondering, we always made sure Violet and the family had enough. How often did I cycle down to town with a bag of veg, or a skinned rabbit, eh, Vi? Talk about keeping me fit!"

Three times in five years, Jean thought—two Christmases and once the previous March, hardly a regular supply. But Violet merely smiled graciously.

"It's true, Eddie, family was all any of us had the last few years." Her eyes took in the room, her mind populating it with different faces. "Remember that time we all came up for Phil's birthday? You made that lovely cake?"

Beattie rubbed her sister's shoulder as if to disperse a physical pain. "That was a happy day."

"He was a fine man, your Philip, one of the best," Martin muttered. Jean restrained herself from pulling a face at the Tibots' rose-tinted version of the past. In truth, Martin had always been quite offhand with her father. Having inherited the successful parish farm at a tender age, it had always been obvious to Jean that Martin viewed his brother-in-law as a soft townie, who would never be as successful as him. Once he'd even made fun of him for not having a car.

Just then Daphne blew into the room, her mane of curly

black hair flying around her shoulders, and everyone turned
to smile at her. She moved with a light, fluid movement more
akin to a ballerina than a farm girl and had always been her
father's favorite. Until the Occupation, Daphne had received
virtually every chocolate bar, toy and pair of shoes she had
ever pointed her delicate little finger at. Jean saw the way that
she went straight to his side and how his eyes lit up when she
did so; she saw, too, the look of slight hurt on Beattie's face.

"Where have you been hiding, my girl? Plenty of dishes
to do out there."

Daphne pulled a face. "Oh, Mummy, do I have to? Won't
Gwen be coming in tomorrow?"

"Gwen left on Friday, remember?" Beattie shook her head
and turned to Violet for backup in her irritation. "Just seventeen and had to get married, silly girl. Now I've got to find
someone else from the village—can't be managing this place
with the farmwork, too."

Beattie left with a sigh to make more tea, but her words
echoed in Jean's ears. With conversation quickly returning
to the Le Tourneur woman and her probable guilt, no one
noticed Jean slip out after her aunt. She stood in the kitchen
doorway, watching Beattie rinse out the teapot, choosing her
moment, then blurted out:

"I could clean for you."

Beattie turned to stare at her. "You, Jeannie?"

"Mum says she doesn't want me working, but we can't
keep relying on Uncle Eddie. She wouldn't mind so much
if it was here."

Beattie stared at her for a moment. "Wouldn't it feel strange,
us employing you? And it's a long way to come from town."

"I'd get used to it. Buses are running again now." She
smiled to emphasize her enthusiasm.

At last Beattie nodded. "All right, I'll talk to Martin. But it's up to you to tell your mother, 'cause I'm not!" Beattie grinned, then she dropped her head to one side, taking Jean in. "You're a good girl, Jean, looking out for your mum. Your dad would be proud of you."

The compliment pierced Jean's heart. The long-fought tears pricked the back of her eyes, and she knew that she had to get away.

"Aunt Beattie, would you mind if I slipped out for a bit? On my own?"

"'Course not, my love. Take as long as you want."

Jean grabbed her jacket from the hallstand and was out the front door before anyone could see her glistening eyes or blotchy face.

A brisk walk through the field-flanked, winding lanes of St Ouen, and a half hour later Jean found herself in the wild, open expanse of the northwest cliffs, where the wind blew so hard it was like being pushed along by a giant celestial broom. Ankle deep in the purple heather, Jean gazed out at the perfect flat line of the horizon, where the vast expanse of the Gulf of St Malo blended with the wild blue of the Atlantic Ocean. It was a magical place, a regular playground for herself and Daphne as children, and even the grim cylinder of a gray German naval tower that rose out of the cliffs to the north, its seaward observation slits like a series of evil grins, could not spoil it.

She followed the path, heading south along the curve of the bay, until she reached some makeshift fencing, and peered beyond it. In the distance she could make out the concrete bunker, set deep into the earth so that only its top was visible among the gorse and heather. Battery Moltke, intended to house the largest antinaval guns of the German military until D-Day had ended that fantasy. Now it was crawling with soldiers, who were hauling out various objects and taking them to two waiting trucks. Most of the uniforms were German, with a few armed Tommies supervising activities. She imagined the network of tunnels beneath, constructed by starving, beaten slave laborers from Spain and Eastern Europe, many of whom, according to reports, had simply dropped dead from exhaustion as they worked—right here, a short walk from where the Tibots sat at their kitchen table. And she thought of the young Germans working there now, compatriots of the men who had watched her father die, who had assisted all this destruction and now lived without hope or future as they awaited their fate. But no anger materialized. Instead, she stood passively watching the shuffling figures and finally felt the tears fall, her shoulders jerking as the sobs shook her body and her wails caught on the wind and flew up among the passing gulls.

As the crying fit faded and a new calm settled, she realized what she had to do. She could not stand by any longer, smiling politely while people delivered terrible news, talked over her as if she weren't there and made decisions without consulting her. Her beloved dad was dead, and she needed to find out the truth. Tomorrow was as good a day as any. The decision brought an unexpected peace, and with a sigh of satisfaction, Jean turned to begin the walk back to Les Renoncules.

Cigarette smoke hung in the air, suspended on the sunbeams like so many chiffon veils across the length of the staff room. The teaching profession, it seemed, even its female members, contained an unusually high number of smokers; the nicotine habit had been embraced by islanders during the war years as a way to stave off hunger, before tobacco shortages forced the tragic realization that now they were plagued by two physical cravings instead of one.

Hazel inhaled the last of her roll-up and stubbed it out in the small tin ashtray next to her pile of new exercise books—another postwar luxury—freeing her left hand to turn pages more quickly. Only three more to mark and she was done. She had devised a policy of reading the bad ones first (in all honesty, she knew in advance exactly which ones they would be) while saving the most promising pupils till the end. After all, there was really only so much fourteen-year-olds had to say on Lady Macbeth's personal responsibility, and this system meant that as the repetitious nature of the essays fogged her brain, she could breeze through the last ones with relative ease. Today, though, even the efforts of her star pupils brought a degree of disappointment, with recurring themes on the "natural" concerns of women. Chewing the end of her pen, she looked around the room and spotted Elizabeth Richomme at another table, half buried in her own pile of exercise books. Elizabeth was not exactly a friend, but was around the same age as Hazel and was one of the few other staff members without formal teaching qualifications; the Occupation had necessitated some flexibility over the employment of teachers, but it was clear that the older ones who had attended training colleges before the war were far from happy about it. It gave her and Elizabeth an affinity, and Hazel called across.

"Elizabeth, do you happen to know if there are any female authors on this year's literature syllabus?"

Elizabeth stopped what she was doing and peered at her over her small round spectacles. Several other members of staff at various stages of going home also turned their heads in curiosity.

"Umm… Shakespeare, Kipling, Thomas Hardy…no, not at present."

"Thank you." Hazel wrote and circled a B plus on the last critique, stacked the books in the cupboard for distribution tomorrow and slipped into her ancient wool wrap. Somewhere on her bookshelf at home, she was certain, was a copy of Mary Shelley's *Frankenstein*. If she went through it tonight after dinner, she could pick out some pertinent passages to read in the lesson tomorrow, and perhaps engender some lively discussion. It would certainly be more inspiring, for her and her girls, than the visual imagery of *Mandalay*, as rostered by the headmistress. The idea excited her, and as she wove her way through the town streets toward New Street, her mind ran ahead with homework questions she could set on themes of morality, blame and social norms. She was still in a state of distraction when she reached the steps to the flats, and for a moment didn't notice the slight, anxious-looking young woman—a girl, really—waiting awkwardly at the bottom of the steps. Her hair was a dull brown, and she was pencil thin, but her huge, limpid eyes and delicate features reminded Hazel of a woodland creature in need of protection. Her hunched, tense gait made it clear that this person was waiting for someone.

"Can I help you?" The girl swallowed, hesitant. At that moment Hazel recognized her. Instinctively she lowered her school bag to the ground. "You're the daughter, aren't you—Mr. Parris, from the ironmongers?" She gestured pointlessly toward the boarded-up store. A nod in reply. Hazel instantly felt uneasy. "I saw the news in the paper… I came to the memorial service but didn't want to intrude. I'm very sorry."

"Is your name Hazel Le Tourneur?" Her voice was quavery, unsteady. Hazel's unease began a slow conversion to trepidation.

"It is. I'm sorry, I don't know your—"

"You live here, and you knew my father?" She was standing very still, except for the fingers that wriggled continuously.

"Yes. We're on the first floor, next to the room over the shop."

"And did you argue with him?"

"I beg your pardon?"

"Apparently he had several arguments with a woman who looked just like you?"

Hazel felt her stomach drop several feet. "Well, I...there were a few cross words..."

"I have to ask you something. I've heard... There are people who say..." She swallowed again, preparing for the climax: "Did you report my father's radio to the Germans?"

The pause that followed seemed to stretch on for minutes. Their eyes seemed locked, as if nothing but a superhuman force could break the connection. Hazel opened her mouth, which had become quite dry, and found her voice had acquired an odd tremor.

"Of course not. Why are you asking me?"

"Because he told you you weren't welcome at his radio parties anymore and he called you a troublemaker? Because you didn't like him?"

The words jangled in Hazel's ears. There was no point denying things that the girl clearly knew to be true. Another deathly hiatus. Somewhere above them a seagull squawked. A passing woman carrying shopping tutted at Hazel for standing in the middle of the pavement.

"As I said, there were cross words. That's all." She tried to sound steady and confident. The young woman took a sud-

den gulp of breath and shifted from foot to foot. Hazel suspected that she had planned out her initial questions, but that
her imagination had never taken her further than this point,
and now she wasn't sure how to proceed.

"Well, they know someone reported him. If it wasn't you,
who was it?"

"I imagine quite a number of people had cause…"

The words were out before Hazel could stop them. The
girl's eyes widened even further. She was such a tiny thing,
angry and miserable. Another ghastly pause, which neither
of them had the slightest idea how to end. Eventually the girl
spun away and began to walk off toward Val Plaisant. But a
few yards further on she turned back.

"Are you a Communist?"

To Hazel's horror, she felt a wild, uncontrolled giggle rise
up her throat. The ridiculousness of the question mixed with
the tension, and she simply could not control it. It emerged
as a kind of manic cackle, which she finally choked back,
but it was already too late—the girl had swung on her heel
and was now heading down the road at pace. Hazel thought
of chasing after her but stood rooted, watching her go, the
accusations still ricocheting round her brain. *There are people
who say…* Who were these people, and what exactly were
they saying? What did they know about Parris, about her?
She looked around—a delivery van drove down the street,
followed by a couple of kids on bicycles. People walked up
and down the road as usual, going about their business. For
a moment Hazel wondered if she had imagined the entire
episode. But the rapid beating of her heart and the shortness
of her breath were real enough. She struggled up the steps
to the front door of the flats, trying to focus. Find the book
for her class tomorrow. Prepare her father's meal and make

sure he took his medicine. And on no account mention this to him. She closed the communal door with deliberate quiet and care, checking that it was locked.

The walk from New Street back to St Mark's Road was no more than ten minutes, but this evening it felt like the longest of her life. Jean moved steadily, her Summerland clogs on the pavement pounding in time with her heart. The day had been hot, and now the baked streets of St Helier released their energy back into the air, coloring everything a golden orange and dragging every action to its slowest, stickiest form. There was no soft Atlantic breeze here, just a heat that glued itself to the tarmac roads and metal bonnets of the cars, and as shopkeepers rolled back their awnings to close for the day everyone seemed to be moving at a distorted pace, as if the thought of getting through the evening had already exhausted them. But Jean knew the sweat rolling down her back was not only due to the heat.

The encounter with Le Tourneur—older, more confident and to Jean's eyes quite imperious—had unnerved her. The coldness in the woman's tone, coupled with the vagueness of her denial only confirmed her guilt in Jean's view. But lurking below her sense of justification and righteousness, Jean could not shake off the feeling that she had made a terrible miscalculation, and if her uncle found out that she had gone against his expressed wishes, there would be terrible consequences. For one thing, if Hazel was the informant, Jean had just provided her with advance warning of the family's suspicions. And the family's lack of evidence meant that she could now go to the authorities and accuse Jean of slander. Would Jean be the one to get into trouble? Would the police be involved? And why in the name of heaven had she not thought all this through before? Her breath came short and tight, the slight upward slope of Victoria Street enough to wind her, and as she blindly crossed to the opposite side, she was almost run down by a passing cyclist.

Her idea to challenge Le Tourneur face-to-face had seemed so straightforward out on the cliffs. A direct question, delivered at a moment the woman was not expecting it, would surely provide some kind of answer. She wasn't naive enough to think the woman would confess anything on the spot, but she felt sure she would be able to glean some useful information, something she could take back to the family. And even last night, as she lay sleepless on her bed till the midsummer dawn crept around her curtains and crushed any hope of a belated doze, she had felt certain that it was the right thing, a duty to her father which no one else seemed prepared to do. But now...

Of course, if she were truthful, she knew what had upset her most about the whole encounter. That terrible, pregnant remark.

I imagine quite a number of people had cause.

What on earth did that mean? Jean had been too shocked to follow it up, too taken aback by what she assumed to be a monstrous lie. No one had ever had cause to dislike her generous, thoughtful dad, who worked all hours to put food on their table, who took care of his customers and neighbors, whose wife lived for his return home each evening and whose children adored him. Well, whose daughter adored him. Years ago, she had overheard her mother tell Beattie that Harry had married young and moved to England to get away from him. But Jean had never believed that, didn't believe it now—it was simply her mother's rancor over the premature departure of her son. Philip Parris was a hero.

A hero who was once sent to prison…

But that was when he was little more than a boy! Youthful idiocy, hadn't Eddie said so? It hadn't even discouraged her mother from marrying him. It was nothing—and should be forgotten.

So what was the Le Tourneur woman talking about?

Jean pressed on, keeping her eyes on her feet as she forced them one in front of the other, and instructed herself to dismiss the remark. The woman was just trying to smear her father's reputation to distract from her own guilt. In any case, none of this would matter in the end. The whole affair would soon be placed in the hands of the investigation team, who would no doubt have more sophisticated ways of prizing a confession out of her. On the other hand, Jean decided not to mention this when she got home. Things were tense enough there already.

She was halfway up St Mark's Road when the feeling sneaked up on her that she was being watched. Surely the woman would not have the audacity to follow her? A glance behind revealed only an old lady with a shopping bag, and Jean told herself it was just paranoia, her mind toying with her in a stressful week. The sensation continued, though, and she turned again. The old lady was now further away. Only as she reached her gate did Jean glance up and spot a scruffy schoolboy crouched on the far side of the road. He was sitting some distance apart from the usual urchins, who were kicking a football about, and as she stared at him she saw that his eyes were fixed just as intently on her. He was a fragment of a lad, nine or ten years old, with hair resistant to any maternal control, and dark eyes like glinting coal in his pale face. As she pushed the front garden gate open, he stood up and half crossed the road toward her. For a bizarre moment they stood sizing each other up on the warm concrete.

"Was there something you wanted?"

The boy looked around, awkward. He edged a little closer.

"Are you Jean Parris?" His voice was squeaky.

"How do you know?"

"'Cos this is your house, eh. I've got a note for you. But I'm not to let anyone see me give it you."

Jean's stomach began to bubble. How did this boy know where she lived? She glanced around to see whether Violet or Eddie were watching this from inside, but there was no one at the window.

"So give it to me now."

The boy hesitated. He, too, was checking for curious faces at the windowpanes.

"Said I wouldn't get my sixpence if I didn't do it right."

"Who said?"

"Not allowed to say."

"Why not?"

"I'm just to give you the note."

Jean's anxiety began to recede, turning to plain irritation. She was starting to wonder if there actually was a note and if this wasn't just a try-on for money, a wheeze dreamed up in the playground.

"Then give it to me or push off." Slowly, with obvious reluctance, the boy dug into the pocket of his tatty shorts and pulled out an envelope. His small, grubby hand held it out to her, his fingers on the very edge of the corner. Mesmerized, Jean moved close enough to take it, then watched him turn on his heel and run back up the road as fast as he could, eventually disappearing down Oxford Road. Only then did she look down at the word *Jean* on the front of the envelope. It took a moment to recognize the writing. She instantly knew who it was from, and it was all she could do to stay upright.

She glanced about her, suddenly afraid. People were returning home from work or shopping, clinking their gates as they slumped toward their front doors. The boys' football game continued further up the street. No one was paying her any attention. She looked back at the bay, and the windows of her neighbors, but could see no one at any of them. She tucked the note into the pocket of her dress and, with great care, continued her walk to the front door. She pushed it open, and to her relief heard the muffled voices of her mother and Eddie coming from back in the kitchen. With more concentration than she believed possible, she gently closed the front door with only the tiniest click, and, slipping off her clogs, tiptoed upstairs. The stairs were ancient, but she knew every creak on them from many nights trying not to disturb her mother and made it to her room without a sound. Closing the door behind her, she listened again—the voices were still coming from the kitchen; she was safe.

Only then did she take the envelope from her pocket and tear into the note inside. For a few seconds the words danced before her like an uncrackable code, as if she had never learned to read English. Finally the chaos receded and she devoured it greedily.

These days are hell. I must see you. Harbor steps, sunset Friday 20th. Please come. Tell no one. H

The note sat in her trembling fingers. It had been so long—months without a whisper of contact. Yet with these few words, every memory poured back—the glint in his eyes, the crease of his face when he smiled, his tousled hair. She had been so certain, she had convinced herself, that she would never see him again. And here was one last opportunity to be together. Of course she would be there—she would crawl across burning coals to see him. Her Horst. Her handsome, gentle *Obersoldat*.

4

The covered market was packed. Men pushing trolleys stacked with crates, young lads slinging potatoes onto scales, children clambering onto the railings around the fountain, now symbolically drained of its beauteous cascades. In twos and threes, German soldiers patrolled, their hefty boots clumping on the stone floor, the sound echoing up into the vast roof of sheet glass and sculpted struts, decorated—ironically—with the Jersey coat of arms. But mainly the central hall was crowded with women. Young, old, strong and sick, each one wearing the same threadbare coat and weary expression as they moved from stall to stall, cold stiff fingers reaching into the displays to grasp the last remaining vegetables, mouths twisting and muttering at the ludicrous cost, all the while calculating whether their meager hauls would feed their family tonight.

Jean, her wicker basket clutched tightly, pushed through the crowd to her favored stall praying for tomatoes, but found only a few stunted spuds, two manky cabbages at a price she could never afford and a small pile of swedes. His warm breath, smelling faintly of tobacco, was on her neck as she handed over a pile of change for her pitiful spoils.

"May I help you?"

The proximity of that familiar gray-green uniform was enough to cause an instant panic.

"No. Thank you."

"It is heavy, I think. Please, I carry the bag." He took it from her before she could object. The glare of disgust from the stallholder alarmed her further, but the fear of angering an enemy soldier weighed heavier than her fear of condemnation. Her plan to shake him off at the market's exit failed when he simply strode through the iron gates, her basket still firmly in his grip. Several times she opened her mouth to instruct him to leave her alone, to explain that even to be seen walking through town with a soldier was enough to bring shame. But he chattered on in his stumbling English, telling her that his name was Horst, how lovely it was to have the opportunity to talk to a local girl after months stuck in a barracks with a bunch of stinking lads, and how he relished the chance to practice this new language. Now they were walking along Beresford Street, and before she knew it, he had told her how much he missed his mother and sisters in Cologne and how glad he would be when the war ended and he could go home. By the time they turned into Bath Street, it passed through her mind that perhaps she could be smart about this. Tame soldiers were able to supply all kinds of gifts and luxuries from their stores that locals hadn't seen for years, and this might be a situation she could turn to her advantage. But at what point did that cross the line, become fraternization, get her labeled a jerrybag? She was still calculating the pros and cons when the sight of a neighbor in the distance caused her to wrench the basket from him, insisting she walk the rest of the way alone. She would never know why, when he asked her if she was always in the market on Tuesdays, she replied over her shoulder that she usually was. And when she got home, she denied to herself that the memory of his twinkling eyes and sensitive hands produced a warm, comforting sensation in her belly. But by their third "chance" meeting it seemed pointless to pretend that she did not look forward

to these snatched moments, and equally pointless to make believe that her agreement to meet him down by the harbor at dusk was due to her desperation for darning wool and French chocolate.

That first shy, hesitant meeting hidden between the boat sheds, where he had finally plucked up the courage to take her hand and she had finally let him, was the true beginning. As the days grew into weeks and the risks of being seen together increased, they became more inventive, finding deserted coves or quiet patches of woodland to huddle together, sharing stories of their prewar lives and fantasizing about a postwar world. The memories of each meeting burned themselves onto her mind. The icy day at the end of 1943 when they crouched among rocks down on La Pulente beach, finally admitting to a love they knew to be ruinous but which had flourished anyway. Her birthday, when he presented her with a posy of wild pansies beneath the cliffs. The terrible afternoon just after her father's arrest when she had wept in his arms, forcing him to swear on his mother's life that he had nothing to do with it. And his bitter denial, pointing out that he had never even known of the existence of her father's radio, ending in his heartfelt cry: "Never! Never I hurt you! If you believe this, we must part today." Afterward they cried and kissed, and he raged against the futility of this war, and she begged him to find a way to bring her dad home, while he sadly explained that as a mere private in a vast garrison, he had no power over the madness of the Nazi war machine.

Twenty months. Twenty months of secrecy, of self-reproach mixed with joy and broken pledges to end it, haunted by the terror of discovery and the certainty that this could never end well. But in all that time, never did they indulge—she blushed even to think of it—in what people would call a "full" relationship. When Jean heard her mother tutting about jerrybags, she would assure herself that she and Horst were in a different realm. Theirs was a chaste and romantic affair, the kind one might see in Hollywood movies. Nothing like the sordid physical transactions that went on in drinking clubs and billet parties around town, those brazen or desperate girls who lifted their skirts for excitement or extra rations. She could never be subject to the same censure. Yet the fact that she never told a living soul, that she swore Horst to the same secrecy and hid his gifts where they would never be found, spoke to the other side of her conscience and crushed her in the early hours. There was no way around the ugliness of this relationship in the eyes of the world, and at some point she would pay for it. But still she clung on, thrilled and ashamed, grateful for this one bright orb in a black, frightening war. She loved him.

May 4th, 1945. A chilly, sunny day, with the entire island population balanced on its tiptoes, terrified to exhale for fear that it was all a mistake, knowing that without a full surrender by the garrison, few would survive the inevitable bloodbath. They chose their favorite spot down by the harbor, behind a row of small boating sheds, gripping each other's hands and spluttering with conflicted emotions—jubilant that the war was finally coming to an end, desolate for what it meant for the two of them. They vowed to love each other eternally, Horst insisting that he was done with Germany and would gladly stay in his beloved "Summerland" forever (she had explained the misnomer many times, but he loved it and used it anyway). And she had clung to his jacket, making promises as she stroked his hair, knowing it all to be lies. Then, two weeks later, a hastily scrawled note on lined paper stuffed into an envelope bearing his last local stamp, somehow sneaked to a postbox and pushed through the Parrises' door before (by the grace of God) her mother saw it. He was seconded, he explained, to the group of three thousand or so German soldiers left on the island to help with the clear-up operation; he was glad, as it postponed his deportation for a short while, and perhaps they would have another chance to meet?

But the weeks spun by. She even stopped going up to Battery Moltke in the hope of getting a glimpse of him. The possibility shrank to such

a kernel of fantasy that she told herself he was already gone, shipped,
processed and locked away in some English prisoner of war camp. She
told herself to be sensible, to face facts. And in the weeks since, she had
come to terms with the fact that he was gone forever. She waited for
the hurt to fade, for thoughts of him to drift into the solitary confines
of her sleepless hours. They had not.

The fierce sun pierced Jean's bedroom curtains and woke
her well before her usual time. She had slept perhaps two
hours, falling in and out of a dream where Horst was running toward her along St Brelade's beach, waving to her and
shouting with urgency. Then suddenly it was no longer Horst
but her father, and as he grew near she realized he was weeping, his body skeletal and shivering, shouting something that
she could neither hear nor understand. Each time she jolted
upright in bed, only to sink back down into a pool of her
own sweat and wait for the ghastly carousel to begin again.

Rising silently, she checked that Horst's note was in its hiding place, the foolproof nook where she had kept all his notes
and gifts for the last twenty months, then she climbed back
into bed and sank into her pillow, trying to settle her fren-
zied mind. All thoughts of the Le Tourneur woman and the
encounter outside her flat had now evaporated; all she could
think of now was a week next Friday, and her first meeting
with Horst in two months. She pictured it: the first embrace, a
deep kiss beside the harbor in the fading twilight. She thought
about what she would wear and the sweet smell of his hair.
With effort, she pushed aside the fact that this would almost
certainly be their last time together.

Then, as the light bloomed in her bedroom, painting bright
golden streaks across the floor and ceiling, reality began to
creep in. She might not even get that. What if Horst's plans

to sneak off the ship came to nothing? He must have plotted with others, bribed a guard, arranged access to a small boat or dinghy—any of those could go wrong. Worse, he could be spotted by a guard and shot. Or what if her mother insisted she stay home that night for some domestic chore or family discussion? She turned over on her side, breathing hard. What she needed was a plan. If she could not affect Horst's situation, she could certainly influence her own and make sure that nothing stood in her path. She needed to prepare the ground and give no one, especially her family, the slightest reason to suspect anything. She had to think.

She must have dozed off again, for suddenly she was awakened by loud voices emanating from the kitchen. Hurriedly she pulled on her tatty old blouse and skirt and scampered downstairs, pausing to check her reflection in the hall mirror. Normally she barely paid attention to her appearance, but today she noticed what Horst would see in a few days' time—an ordinary girl with mouse-colored hair and no shape to speak of. She could only pray that he wouldn't be disappointed, for among the bubbly young girls that paraded through town on a Saturday morning, hoping to catch the eye of a young Tommy, she considered herself no catch. Why Tom Maloret had seen fit to invite her to a dance was a mystery.

Tom Maloret. She had almost forgotten him, but now an idea formed in her head. Slowly, still thinking, she walked down the hall to the kitchen and slipped in without being noticed.

Eddie was sitting at the table, red veined and highly colored from his visit to the Peirson last night, clearly in a furious mood and clutching a formally headed letter that Jean assumed to be from his solicitor. Quietly she took a cup from the dresser to help herself to tea from the pot.

"I mean, what right do they have to act as gatekeepers?" Eddie was bellowing. "We're on the same side, they should be glad of the support."

"Maybe 'cause you weren't in the services," Violet replied softly, wiping cutlery to put away. "Like Martin said, most of that lot are ex-officers."

"I'd have been an officer, if it wasn't for this dodgy ticker!" Eddie pummeled his chest in anger. "You think I wanted to spend the whole war a bloody fire officer? If those idiots had let me, I'd have joined up like that." He clicked his fingers aggressively. Jean took a deep breath as she poured her tea.

"What's happened?"

"Jersey Loyalists have said they don't want your uncle in their organization. Said their group's been working together a long time and they don't need anyone else."

"Load of jumped-up poshos," Eddie growled. "People like me frighten 'em, that's the problem. Scared I'll get too much done and show 'em up." Or perhaps, Jean thought, a professional body of military men and disciplined resistance activists had taken one look at this cantankerous ex-evacuee with a personal grudge and seen nothing but trouble. "Well, to hell with them," he went on. "Don't need 'em. Plenty of my own kind here—we know how to rattle cages. Who got the Le Tourneur woman pulled in for questioning, eh? Me, that's who!"

Jean stopped with her cup halfway to her lips.

"They've already called her in?"

"Spoke to the States investigators yesterday, told them everything. They're getting her in for an interview this week. Then we'll see some fur fly!" He slurped from his own cup, nodding to himself in congratulation on his own accomplishment. Jean stared into her warm weak tea, her heart thumping.

She pictured Hazel sitting on the same chair in the duck-egg blue office where she had sat the other week, offering the same bland defenses, but getting shorter shrift. A strange emotion filled her chest—what was that German word Horst had taught her? *Schadenfreude*—the pleasure in another's misfortune. Yes, that was what she was feeling now, the bitterness bringing comfort as the image of her father whimpering in his cell once again crashed in. For the authorities to act so fast, they must be certain of Le Tourneur's guilt, in which case that nonsense idea about Phil Parris's unpopularity could be binned forever. Jean sat back in her chair, musing that if justice didn't bring back the dead, it certainly helped the living. In the meantime, she realized she had other priorities to attend to.

"Mum, you know that old velvet curtain you saved, to turn into something smart? Would you have time to do something with it by this weekend?"

"Probably," Violet replied. "Why?"

"Tom Maloret, that clerk from the States office, he's invited me to the Pav dance. Be nice to have something new to wear. If you don't mind me going out?" As she said the words, the guilt stung her. Tom Maloret had shown her nothing but kindness, and she was about to use him mercilessly for her own ends. But the delighted look on her mother's face at the prospect of a real live suitor for her daughter told her that her plan was already working.

"Of course, I've had my sewing box out anyway to mend Phil's jacket, so I'll start on it today."

Jean followed her mother's glance to her father's favorite navy wool jacket, which was hanging on the back of a chair.

"Why are you mending Dad's jacket?"

"Because your uncle Eddie's going to have it." Before Jean could react, Violet had picked the jacket up and handed it to him. "There you go, good as new. Might be a bit tight across the back, but plenty of wear in it."

"That's champion, Violet, thank you." Her uncle slipped it on, admiring the fabric. Jean stared. It was the jacket her father had worn every Sunday when they went out as a family, the one she had clung to when she swung on his arm walking home from the park. The sight of Eddie in it made her feel sick.

"Silly for it to be hanging in the wardrobe when you need new clothes," Violet chattered on. "Very smart. You get out there and show those Loyalists what they're missing!"

"Sure you don't mind?"

Violet flicked her hand in dismissal. Jean remained very still, her teacup frozen in her hand. She wanted to scream that *she* minded, minded a lot. Wanted to shout at Eddie to take the jacket off this minute and put it back where it belonged, and demand what the hell her mother was thinking, giving away her husband's clothes so soon after his memorial service. But Jean said nothing. This week, of all weeks, she knew she had to behave perfectly and make no ripples. After all, following a catastrophic run of events, there were finally some glimmers of light. Her father's informant was heading for jail, and she was starting her new job at Les Renoncules tomorrow. Best of all, she would see Horst in ten short days. That was all that mattered now. She forced a smile.

"Right, Mum—shall I get that curtain out of the cupboard?"

The milky, bubbly water churned this way and that. Sweat from her brow plopped into the froth beneath her as she turned the posser left and right, heaving the sheets around the dolly tub, her biceps straining beneath her blouse. Outside the window, the sun beat down, but inside the scullery the steam and condensation ran like rain down every surface, made worse by the fire burning in the grate beneath the copper. Jean wiped her forehead with the crook of her arm and wondered what time it was. One thing was for sure, she would never get through her allotted chores by one, which was the hour at which her work officially finished. And all this for three and six a week.

Tipping the dirty water down the drain in the corner, she filled the tub with fresh water for rinsing, adding a Reckitt's blue bag for whiteness as per Beattie's instructions, then dragged the load over to the mangle, forcing each sheet through to squeeze out the water. It was a job Jean had done many times at home as a child, but with her older brother, Harry, doing most of the heavy turning, it had been something of a game. Now, alone in this heat, it was a titanic struggle to force the long sheets through the rollers and snake them into a clean basket on the other side. After the sheets came shirts, blouses, then underwear. Lots of underwear. Clearly out in the countryside people were not losing their personal items to laundry thieves the way they were in town (Jean had lost another pair this week and was becoming quite nervous about leaving anything on the line). Or perhaps her aunt's family simply had plenty of everything. There were certainly plenty of shoes and boots in the pile that she was instructed to polish as soon as she finished in here. The list of chores Beattie had handed her with a broad smile this morning had come as a nasty surprise. Even worse was her aunt's announcement that they had decided to pay her the same as their previous cleaner, as they knew that she wouldn't want charity. Jean had opened her mouth to object, to point out that she would have considered it no such thing, especially as she had a bus fare to cover. But then she thought of the previous evening, watching Eddie thumbing out ten-shilling notes to her mother while wearing her father's jacket and a benevolent smile, and her mouth closed again. If Jean wanted a wage, even a tiny one, it was this or nothing.

She tried to focus on the positive. The money would pay for a decent slice of next week's rations; the work would be hard, but just a longer version of what she did at home. And she would get to see Daphne twice a week. The hardest part, as Beattie had anticipated, was her new role in a place where she had always felt at home. For years a visit to Les Renoncules had meant fun and food, even if Jean suspected the abundance sometimes smacked of showing off. Many days she had romped with her cousins through the rambling hallways and rooms of the old farmhouse and the surrounding fields, before being herded into the kitchen for lemonade and Beattie's homemade biscuits. Yet this morning, no sooner had Beattie cheerfully ushered her into the scullery to show her the overflowing linen basket than she had disappeared to feed the pigs and not returned. At no point had anyone poked a friendly head around the door to see how she was getting on, and had it not been for Daphne passing by with a slice of buttered bread, asking if Jean would like one too, she'd have had no lunch. Jean smiled and got on with her jobs without complaint, but now, as she staggered into the yard to throw the huge sheets over the washing line that hung between the main farmhouse and one of the outhouses, realizing that she was barely three items down her list of allotted tasks, she found herself wondering if the real reason her uncle and aunt had so willingly agreed to this was the procurement of a pliable employee. As a child she'd often seen their French seasonal workers traipsing off to the barn where they slept, accepting Martin's argument that the accommodation was what they were used to and what they preferred; now she wondered if he and Beattie simply didn't give much thought to the needs of their employees.

The breeze and sun against her skin felt good, and when she'd hung the last sheet she sat down for a moment on an old milking stool. At that moment Martin stepped out into the yard, smoking a roll-up cigarette. On seeing her he gave a little nod.

"How you getting on?"

Jean struggled to her feet. "All right, thanks."

Martin inhaled his roll-up and nodded. "How's your mum?"

"It's hard for her. For all of us."

"Beattie'll sort you a bag of Royals to take back. I hear they've called in that informer?" Jean nodded. "Hope they hang her. Jail's too good for collaborators, hang the lot of 'em I say." Jean thought of Horst and wondered whether Martin would consign her to the same fate. She wiped her face to hide her reddening cheeks. Martin took his last drag and stubbed the fag out on the cobbles. "'Course, they won't. This lot wouldn't have the guts. And if that J.D.M. lot get in, well God help us." Jean smiled in a way that she hoped implied agreement. All she knew was that Communists were bad, but as Stalin had been an ally during the war, she found it somewhat confusing. "You steer well clear of them, bloomin' troublemakers. You know they want to stop our Jurats running the parishes?" She tried to look suitably disapproving. "And they want the farmers to form some kind of committee with the States, tell us how much to produce! Bloody Russia they want now! You steer clear."

Jean hesitated, on the threshold of a question. The subject had refused to leave her head, and she suspected this would be the only way to stop it, but she was uncertain what the reaction would be.

"Uncle Martin? Did you know my dad had been in prison, before the war?"

Martin stopped stock-still, his eyes suddenly very alert.

"Long time ago, that. Why d'you ask?"

"Uncle Eddie mentioned it. What exactly did he do?"

"It was when he was working for Pallot's. Petty thieving and handling stolen goods was the charge, I think."

Jean nodded. "I never knew. Still, it taught him a lesson, I suppose." Martin's explosive little chuckle took her completely by surprise. "What's so funny?" Her uncle rubbed his mouth with the back of his hand.

"Nothing. Like you say, learned his lesson." Jean was about to ask more, but at that moment, Daphne's arrival in the courtyard, like a bouquet of flowers being thrown onto a stage, stopped all other conversation.

"Jeannie! I hope they're not working you too hard?"

Jean forced a laugh. "I'm fine."

"Shall we go out when you're done? We can pick some flowers from the meadow and press them in my atlas? I want to make invitations for my twenty-first in September, so I need lots."

Martin rolled his eyes. "This birthday will be the death of me."

Daphne curled herself under his arm. "We're going to invite everyone we know. Make it a real celebration."

"Make me bankrupt, more like." But he was grinning. Daphne giggled and it sounded like chime bars.

"Mummy says you love to complain, but you're just a big teddy bear underneath. Isn't that right?"

Martin was laughing too now. "Yeh, well don't push your luck, young lady."

Jean suspected it was about twenty years too late for that.

"And what's this I hear about you going to the Pav with a young man on Saturday?" Daphne's eyes were full of joyful mischief, and Jean's heart sank. Nothing could be kept secret for long in this tiny island. Someone was always walking along the wrong road or glancing out of a window or bumping into someone in the market. She thought of her meeting with Horst next week and shivered.

"Just this chap from the States offices—it's nothing really."

"No, it's wonderful!" Daphne clearly saw the anxiety in Jean's expression because she added: "And you mustn't feel guilty. Your dad would want you to enjoy yourself, after the awful time we've all had. Don't you agree, Daddy? So have lots of fun and tell me all about it afterward." She glanced at her watch. "When shall I come and find you, about three?"

Jean shook her head. "I don't think I'll be finished by three. And I'll need to get the last bus."

Daphne pulled a face. "What a shame. Never mind, I'll show you the pressed flowers on Tuesday." And with that she was gone, leaving only a vague scent of lavender soap.

The rest of the day passed in a blur. Jean scrubbed the surfaces and floor of the kitchen till her arms ached, took the pile of shoes and boots and shined each one with the crumbs of remaining polish and an old rag. At three forty-five she finished chopping a pile of spring greens for the family's dinner, accepted her wages from Beattie with what she hoped looked like cheerful gratitude and ran for her bus. On the way home, she closed her eyes and let images float freely through her mind. She recalled a Christmas Eve at the farm, long before the war: her mother and father dancing to some old

jazz records, she and Daphne playing marbles on the landing for hours. Aunt Beattie's delicious chocolate mousse and
her father laughing at her chocolate-covered chin. Fun, coziness, certainty of her own world… It felt so close and real
that she reached out her fingers to touch it but felt only the
grubby glass of the bus window.

She was dreading Saturday night.

The reflection in the mirror beamed back at her, and Jean
tried her best to believe it. The shampoo and set she had had
at the hairdressers this morning, at her mother's insistence,
did give her hair a little shape. And the Coty lipstick that
Violet had fished out the back of her dressing table drawer,
somewhat dry but miraculously still usable, added a splat-
ter of color. Neither could she fault the velvet jacket that her
mother had brilliantly fashioned from the old curtain, and
which certainly lifted her tired old blouse. But no matter
how she tried to arrange her features, or how hard she tried
to project a sense of carefree jollity, all she saw was a disinter-
ested girl who would far prefer an early night with a cup of
tea. And she knew that's what Tom Maloret would see, too.

She tried to recall his face. It was friendly enough, if a little
pale from being in an office all day. He had seemed, insofar
as she had noticed anything about him, a kind and sensitive
soul. And the Pav, which she had visited only once for a children's party before the war, would certainly provide an evening of more glamour and distraction than she'd known in
many months. Perhaps it wouldn't be so bad. She practiced a
smile that would suggest friendliness without looking flirta-
tious, but could not master anything better than constipated
confusion. But a knock at the door, right on time, confirmed
that there was no way out now.

As Jean came down the stairs, trying not to trip in the heeled shoes borrowed from her mother, Eddie was playing man of the house to Tom in the hallway, and they both beamed as she appeared. Tom was in his navy work suit, Eddie was sporting one of her dad's silk handkerchiefs in his top pocket—another donation from her mother, no doubt.

"Evening, Tom. Let's get going, shall we?" She stuffed her clutch bag under her arm, almost tripping on the bottom stair in her haste, knowing that any second, Eddie might strike up an awkward conversation about the ongoing inquiries. As they slipped out of the door, her uncle gave her a wink and she heard his voice follow her down the path:

"Don't worry about getting her back early, Tom—you have fun." Jean's skin prickled with annoyance as she slammed the gate. Who was he to issue instructions about her comings and goings? But Tom courteously promised that they would.

The walk to West Park took about twenty minutes, and for most of it they managed to keep up a pleasant conversation—how they had both spent Liberation Day, and their least favorite Occupation recipes. Tom asked her questions with genuine curiosity, giving her plenty of time to reply. As they moved briskly through streets lit pink with evening sun and passed neighbors exchanging news across garden walls, she felt herself relax a little. She began to take in the scents of distant pines and petrol fumes on the early evening air and to admire the gold and gray of the sky as the sun began to dip. As the huge white wedding cake of West Park Pavilion rose up before them, resplendent with its ornate facade and elaborate windows, Tom held out his arm for her in a gesture of mock formality. Jean smiled as broadly as she could and took it, telling herself that this was simply an agreeable night out with an agreeable young man, and that nothing was expected of her.

The stairs down to the main ballroom at the Pav led into another world. The gleaming, cavernous dance hall might not have been up to its prewar best, but the shiny wooden floor, framed on each side by little square tables and wicker chairs, seemed to stretch for miles. A balcony ran the full length of the room, with French doors leading to sprawling sun terraces, and the whole place was covered by a delicately arched tiled ceiling, from which hung ornate light fixtures shedding a soft golden glow. On the bandstand, a local five-piece jazz band was playing, and couples were already swarming onto the floor, eager to feel the closeness of another body and to be swung around in someone's arms. Others gathered around the tables in twos and fours, sipping drinks and taking in the view. Many of the men were in British uniform, some of quite senior rank, and all the women surprisingly glamorous even in their tired floral dresses and old furs. Everyone looked happy and small eruptions of laughter fizzed in the air like fireworks.

"Shall we?" Tom was ushering her to a table near the back. She let him guide her to a seat and sat down primly upon it, gripping her bag like a life raft, just as her mother always did. Tom offered to buy drinks, and soon she was staring into a garish gin and orange, wondering why she'd asked for something so expensive when she would have been quite happy with squash. Tom had bought himself a bottle of French beer and clinked it against her glass before sipping at it awkwardly, at which point conversation seemed to peter out. They watched the dancers for a few minutes, occasionally smiling at each other, while Jean groped around her mind for something to say.

"How do you enjoy working at the States?" she said eventually.

Tom shrugged. "It's all right. My folks are pleased about it." Jean looked quizzical, hoping to encourage more. "I'd have preferred to work outside, be a grower like my dad. But they were keen that I make something of myself, whatever that means." He gave a small, unconvincing laugh, then pulled himself up short. "By the way, I wanted to say again how terribly sorry I am about what happened to your father."

Jean took a swig of her gin. "Thank you."

"It's just dreadful. Don't know how anyone could be so cruel."

"You mean the Germans, or the person who betrayed him?" She bit her lip and placed her drink back on the table. This was sensitive territory too early in the evening; she was doing just what she feared Eddie would do. But he just took another swig of beer, his expression unchanged.

"Both. Both behaviors are despicable."

Jean hesitated. This was an ideal opportunity to close the subject and move on. But curiosity was eating at her insides.

"I hear you interviewed Hazel Le Tourneur this week?"

Tom nodded. "The Civil Affairs Unit did, yes." Jean held her breath, but his eyes remained on the dancers.

"And do you have any idea what was said?"

Tom drained the remains of his beer, looking a little embarrassed. It occurred to Jean that such conversations outside of Tom's office might be taboo, perhaps even sackable. She wondered if the encounter on the New Street pavement had come up. "I wasn't at the interview. But I have seen the file."

"And?"

"She is known to us. She wrote a few letters to various States members during the Occupation."

Jean's heart began to race. "Letters? Saying what?"

Tom paused, considering his words. "I think she's just someone who likes to complain."

Jean took back her drink and sank half in one swallow. "Well, I know she didn't like my dad. So I wouldn't be surprised if she told lies about him."

Another hesitation. This time Tom looked down at the table, and Jean realized he was refusing to meet her eye. She felt the same unease as when her uncle Martin chuckled about her father's prison history.

"I think her complaints were quite general," Tom said eventually. "We received a lot of letters like that." He took out a packet of Capstan cigarettes and offered one to Jean, who reluctantly refused—if her mother heard she'd been seen smoking in public, she'd never hear the end of it. Tom lit one and blew a perfect smoke ring toward the distant ceiling before continuing. "In fact, we had hundreds. They poured in every week, angry about all sorts of things. Prices, rations, politicians getting special treatment...why we weren't stopping the Germans from doing this or doing that. Mostly I think those people just wanted someone to shout at. Although sometimes they had a point."

"And what was Hazel Le Tourneur angry about?"

"She took a very moral position on certain things."

"So do you think she was Dad's informant?"

Now Tom looked at her directly, and his eyes were full of pity. "I'm sorry, Jean. I really don't know. And I'm not sure this is a subject for a night out." His expression dropped further. "Is that why you agreed to come out with me tonight? To ask me about this?"

"No. No, that's not the reason." Jean was glad of the dim lighting, which hopefully hid her burning cheeks; the real reason, she knew, was so much worse. She forced out an apologetic smile. "I'm having a lovely time, really. It's just, I think about it all the time. I can't rest until I know the truth."

"I can understand that. If there's anything I can do to help you or your family, you only have to ask." He took a hefty drag then put the cigarette out, even though it was far from finished. "Now, how about a dance?"

"I'm not very good." The gin was not helping as expected, but was making her feel lightheaded and distant. She felt as if she were observing him from a faraway table. "I did country dancing at primary school, but…"

"Well, I'm no good, either. But if we push our way into the middle, we can make fools of ourselves and no one will ever know." He smiled, properly this time, with his eyes. "Come on, what do you say?"

Jean let him lead her onto the floor. He placed one hand around her waist and took her hand in the other. The five-piece struck up a somewhat sparse version of "Don't Sit Under the Apple Tree," and she let Tom lead her around the floor in an awkward, uneven shuffle. It felt phony; his were the wrong arms, his body gave off the wrong scent. She yearned for it to be Horst. But for this evening, she would simply have to pretend. She allowed the music and movement to wash into her until she felt her body blend with her surroundings and she became nothing but a jigging cog in a huge dancing machine, a speck of moving color in the dim yellow light. By the time the band had moved on to an uncertain rendition of "Jeepers Creepers," she closed her eyes and eased a little into Tom's arms, letting the rhythm, melody and gin fire her imagination. But even as her body relaxed, her mind continued to claw and grip, one thought boomeranging back again and again. Tom Maloret knew something about her father, or about Hazel Le Tourneur, that he was not telling her. And it was possible that he was not the only one.

The music from the Pavilion drifted across the park as Hazel made her way home. Inside its elegant doors, she imagined scores of colorful dancers jostled together in fun, the joy of Liberation freeing their limbs. The strands of melody she could catch were bright and jolly, and she wanted to feel happy for those people, but as she dragged her feet back toward New Street she could summon nothing but resentment. The idea that anyone could be joyful and carefree tonight, when her own world was tumbling around her shoulders, just seemed horribly unfair. She pushed on through the sultry town streets, her feet and calves aching. She must have been walking for at least four hours, extending her usual route from South Hill down to Havre des Pas then back around the harbor and along the bay to West Park. She had no idea where she was going. All she knew was that she was trying to avoid going home, where she would have to face her father and tell him what had happened.

This afternoon's interview, in the stuffy duck-egg blue office tucked deep in the States building, had begun innocently enough. She had felt nervous on her way there, but quite composed, confident in her preparation. Anticipating their questions, trying out answers. Not so different to coaching students for an examination. She had even pressed her best mauve suit, the one she kept for parent nights and special occasions, and which she hoped gave the appearance of a responsible and trustworthy citizen. The lieutenant of the Civil Affairs Unit, part of the 135 Task Force, had greeted her with great courtesy when she entered, and the pink-cheeked London DC from Public Safety had even placed a chair out for her. Buttering her up, she realized now, for what was to come.

The lieutenant started off with predictable underarm softballs. How long had she lived in the flats above Parris's ironmongery, who else lived there, what was the nature of her relationship with the late Mr. Parris? Hazel responded politely, highlighting the genial acquaintance she had enjoyed with Parris in the first year or two of Occupation. She explained that she, her father and late sister had relied on the shop in the early days of the war, when shortages came suddenly and out of the blue—who knew that nails would become as rare as hen's teeth, or that a leaking bucket would be irreplaceable?—and how happy Philip Parris had been to assist. On one occasion he even saved the family the last mousetrap in the shop, and let them have it at cost price, or so he said. After the wireless ban in 1942, he quite frequently invited Hazel to join him with other neighbors in the back room of his shop to hear the BBC news at nine o'clock. Then she explained it was toward the end of that year that things had changed.

"And what was it," the DC asked, leaning forward on his chair, "that brought about this change?"

So Hazel told them. Told them what she had witnessed from the kitchen window of their flat, the one which overlooked the shop's tiny backyard. Told them of the distaste she and her father had felt, which over the months had progressed to outrage and disgust. Told them of the curt little exchanges between herself and Parris that later became heated spats and then fully developed rows. And the officers listened, asked further questions and wrote everything down, but Hazel could see from their sidelong looks that they did not believe her answers. She felt prickles of sweat break out under her suit. The fabric was wool; this had been a bad choice on such a warm day. Presentation over practicality.

"You realize, Miss Le Tourneur, that these are very serious accusations? Do you have any evidence to support them?"

"Evidence?"

"Photographs, for instance?"

A small snort of derision escaped her nose, too late. Now they would think she was sneering at them.

"Of course not. We had to surrender our camera at the start of the Occupation like everyone else. But I know what I saw."

The two men turned away from the desk and muttered between themselves. Hazel strained to hear, but they were infuriatingly skilled at the professional whisper. After a moment they both turned back.

"So, overall you had many reasons to dislike Mr. Parris. Reasons to want him—what shall we say—removed?"

Hazel looked from one to the other. The nightmare scenario was beginning to assemble in front of her.

"But so did lots of others. That's what I've been trying to tell you."

"At this point, Miss Le Tourneur, these are simply uncorroborated allegations. Unless you can offer any other information, suggest anyone else we should speak to?"

Hazel opened her mouth but closed it again. What was the point? It was true she had no evidence, even for what she'd reported so far, and clearly it had done her no favors. Throwing more into the mix could make things worse, and the look in their eyes told her she was already half convicted. She remembered how she had laid out her suit last night, telling herself that if she were calm and rational, they would simply believe her. Now she felt like a fool.

She had left the office and, unable to face the inevitable

debrief from her father, set off on her marathon walk around St Helier. But now she was too tired and too dejected to keep going, and with a heavy heart she dragged herself up the steps of the flats. The old man was sitting in his chair, his face tight with anxiety.

"Haze, where have you been? I was worried! How did it go? Did you tell them everything?"

"Yes, Dad. I told them."

"So do they understand now? They know it wasn't us that reported him?"

"I'm sorry, Dad, I don't think they do, no." She watched the confusion and fear creep across his face like a shadow. This was what she had dreaded most. Stress of any kind always made his arthritis worse—after Dottie died, he was in bed for the best part of two months.

"But we didn't do anything! Despite everything, we never said a dicky bird! Surely they can't just let that family accuse us, take their word against ours?"

Hazel bit her lip. She would not allow herself to cry in front of him; this man had seen enough tragedy in his recent life. She removed the jacket of her mauve suit and laid it carefully over the back of a chair, then she sat down as close to him as she could get and reached out her hand.

"Dad, you remember how a few months back we talked about after the war, how angry people were likely to be? All that pent-up frustration? How there was bound to be trouble, people accusing each other of all sorts?" He nodded without any understanding, hanging on her every syllable. "Well, I think that's what's starting to happen. And I'm afraid we're both going to have to be very brave."

5

It was nearly midnight when Jean pulled on her nightdress and slithered into her single bed. The brushed cotton sheets were soft against her skin, and she let her head sink deep into the pillow. A silver slice of moonlight, just enough to define the furniture in the room, angled through the curtains and across her legs, and she relished the dimness and the quiet, which eased the throbbing in her feet and head, the result of too much dancing and two whole gins. It had been a relief to get home, and even better to return to a dark, empty downstairs, her mother already asleep and Eddie nowhere to be seen. She pushed the covers from her top half to let the fresh night air soothe her weary body. The sheer effort of talking for hours with a stranger had exhausted her, and despite her best efforts to lead the conversation back, Tom had not allowed the subject of her father to surface again. Afterward, when he had walked her right to her front door and she had thanked him, with sincerity, for a nice time, he had leaned in for what was clearly a proper good-night kiss, but instinct turned her head before he could reach her, and his dry, hesitant lips had merely grazed her cheek. She doubted she would hear from him again, or that he would give her any further information. But at least this evening would be enough to keep the family gossiping, sufficient to use Tom as an alibi next Friday. She turned onto her side. It was late, she was shattered and did not want to think any more about Uncle Martin's unexplained laughter, or Tom's awkward avoidance of her questions. She closed her eyes and tried to conjure memories of Horst. Perhaps tonight, for once, sleep would come quickly.

The sound of her bedroom door creaking open tore through her, an electric shock to her torso. In the darkness she could see the shadow of a person in the doorway. She leaped up in her bed with a small, suppressed cry.

"It's all right, it's only me." Her uncle's voice, thick with beer and induced jollity, did nothing to reassure her. "Just wondered how your night went?"

Jean's heart banged in her chest, and she pulled the covers back up her body. Eddie had never come into her bedroom before, not even during the daytime, and she had assumed that he understood the unspoken, invisible lines that separated male and female spaces in the house. But the slight swaying of his body told her that he was drunker than usual.

"You woke me up." She hoped that the words alone would convey the inappropriateness of his being here and send him scuttling away. But Eddie was too far gone for subtleties.

"Ah, sorry. Still, now you're awake…" To her despair he tottered over to her bed and half sat, half fell onto it. She felt his weight crush the springs beneath her, the chill of the night air rising from his clothes. The stink of alcohol hit her full in the face. "Tell me all about it." His body blocked the moonlight from the window so that his face became a pitch-black silhouette. Jean tried to ease her body over to the wall side of the bed without alerting him to the fact.

"Nothing to tell really. We danced a bit, chatted, he walked me home."

"Did you talk about the Le Tourneur woman?"

Jean made rapid calculations in her head. If she repeated her suspicion about Tom withholding information, he would want to know everything, and it would be impossible to get rid of him. But a lie carried too much risk of being caught out later.

"Apparently she wrote some letters to local politicians, complaining about things in general. But that's all he said." It was as bland a version as she could create.

Eddie gave a loud snort of satisfaction. "Ha! It's all starting to add up. Anything else?"

"No. He said it wasn't a suitable conversation for a night out." Surely, she prayed, that would put an end to it. But Eddie leaned forward over his knees, the way her father used to do when he was about to tell a story.

"There could be more stuff they're not telling us." Jean said nothing. She was aware of her nightdress riding up around her legs, leaving the lower half of her body exposed beneath the thin layer of covers. It felt wrong, too intimate, somehow shameful. Eddie leaned back again and now, to her horror, placed his broad hand on the blanket, on top of her leg. It was warm, but a shiver ran through her. "You seeing him again?" Her throat tightened; speech was suddenly a challenge.

"I don't know."

"Did he try and kiss you?" She could tell by the shape of the words that he was grinning as he said it.

"Not really. Uncle Eddie, I'm really tired. I want to go to sleep." The hand on her leg moved around in caressing circles.

Every hair on her body was now raised and taut. Her stomach churned. Sleep belonged to another dimension.

"He's a lucky lad, courting a nice young girl like you." He sighed. "Great times, your courting days. Don't last, though. Once you're married and kids come along…s'all different then. Lucky to get a little cuddle." Jean merely swallowed as she continued to stare at the place she guessed his eyes were. "My Maureen…said she'd rather read a good book. A bloody book!" His mood was on the move, and Jean instinctively knew that this was a point of no return. She needed to get him out of there right now.

"You should go. Don't want to wake Mum up."

Eddie's hand stopped its circular movement. For a terrible moment, Jean feared she had angered him, then felt a surge of relief as he lifted it away. Perhaps the mention of her mother had reminded him that there was someone else in the house, or perhaps he heard the fear in her voice and realized he had crossed a line. As he hauled himself to his feet, Jean pressed her lips together to contain a whimper of relief.

"We'll get her put away, don't you worry. You leave everything to your uncle Eddie. Sleep tight." He staggered toward the door and lurched through it, banging it too hard behind him.

For many minutes Jean didn't move a muscle, but remained rigidly upright in her bed while she listened to her uncle padding noisily about the landing. Eventually the footsteps thumped into the box room and the door slammed shut, followed by the distant rustling of a drunken man trying to remove his clothes and, eventually, the dull thud of his body falling onto the bed. A moment later, and she heard snoring. Only then did she sink back down beneath her blankets, clutching at them with rigid knuckles, her heart still hammering against her ribs, wishing that Uncle Eddie had never come back to Jersey, that her father was still in the next room and that the sun would rise and light up this dark, dark sky.

"Was there something else, miss?" The ratty-faced, flat-capped stallholder was peering at her over his till with thinly veiled suspicion. Jean blushed, feeling foolish. She had been lingering by the stall for a good seven or eight minutes, pretending to evaluate the cucumbers, but actually doing a perfect impression of a thief-in-waiting. With an apologetic smile, she muttered something inaudible, then moved to another stall, where she tried to look studious about carrots. Her feet ached and her shopping bag was heavy. What she really wanted was to go home. But home was also the last place she wanted to be, which was why she had spent most of the last few days, when she wasn't at Les Renoncules, hanging around the town streets or the market. Just being in the same room as her uncle brought her out in a malodorous sweat of anxiety.

It was that time. Traders were beginning to pack up their stock, and porters were pushing trolleys about. With nothing else to buy and no more money in her purse, Jean began the slow reluctant walk back to St Mark's Road. But as she reached the front door, her heart sank a little deeper. The stench of cigarettes and pipe tobacco from the parlor's open window, and the sound of raucous male voices talking over each other with impatience, told her that Eddie was hosting another of his "meetings." She opened the door and the volume shot up immediately, individual phrases jumping out into the hallway: *"too damn soft," "where's the accountability?" "those businesses should be shut down."* It was the second time this week—these gatherings seemed to be becoming a regular event.

Following his rejection from the Jersey Loyalists, Eddie had, as promised, sought out new "allies," which meant drinking in a variety of public houses around the town and buying drinks for anyone who claimed to know a collaborator. The result was a mob of embittered ex-evacuees, disaffected old bachelors and hard-drinking malingerers in search of a peg for their various resentments, though what they actually discussed at these "meetings," and what use they were, Jean could only guess. The worst of it was Violet seemed quite happy to welcome them in—Violet, who only weeks ago would have refused entry to such a rabble in her precious parlor, with their thoughtless abuse of ashtrays and wet cups on the Dutch drop leaf table.

Violet was not in the kitchen. Jean checked the backyard and the rooms upstairs. With reluctance, she turned the knob of the parlor door and poked her head around. At first all she saw was the fug of smoke and the faces of half a dozen men, one or two not long out of school, but most older than Eddie, each florid with heat and irritation, and her uncle in his habitual place in front of the fireplace, a position he seemed to feel suggested some kind of authority. But then she saw her. Violet was tucked comfortably into her easy chair and smoking a rare cigarette, which would have been surprising enough, but more shocking to Jean was the fact that she was laughing. Proper, shoulder-shaking mirth at some joke told a moment earlier, her eyes creased tight and her tiny yellow teeth finally finding the light. Not once since the news of Jean's father's death had her mother even managed a proper smile, and the sound of her laughter now hit Jean like a cold shower.

"Ah, Jean, there you are." Her daughter's arrival pulled Violet back to composure. "Help me make a pot of tea for these gentlemen, would you? They're spitting feathers here."

Jean followed her mother into the kitchen. "What were you all talking about in there?"

Violet sniffed as she filled the kettle. "Just about the collaborators—what the next step is. Authorities are dragging their feet. We've heard nothing this week."

"And how long is Uncle Eddie planning to stay?"

"Why? He's family."

"But what about Auntie Maureen and the children?"

"They'll join him when he's settled."

Jean recalled her uncle's drunken confessions about his marriage and hoped it wasn't masking a darker story. "Only he keeps bringing these people over. They're using up all our tea and sugar rations." The next sentence slipped out unguarded. "Still, you seem to be enjoying it all."

Violet whipped around. "And what's that supposed to mean?"

Jean parted her lips to speak. The things she wanted to say, the thousand questions and complaints, were lining up in her throat begging to be heard. Her confusion about her father, the hinted accusations... Violet's casualness with her husband's possessions and untimely jollity around a man Jean was starting to despise. And more than anything, Jean wanted to divulge the horror of the other night, her unease in her own room, which had no key in the lock, and her feeling of revulsion every time Eddie came near her. But each time she tried, the words evaporated. After all, what exactly was she going to report? That he had come into her room and talked to her? Her mum was likely to laugh at her overreaction. And Eddie, naturally, had said nothing, either because he had forgotten it happened or was pretending he had.

On top of all that...on top of all that, today was Thursday. Tomorrow was the day she would finally see her precious

Horst again. And no matter how much she wanted to talk to her mother, to impart all the bewilderment and disorientation of the last weeks, Jean knew she was prepared to suffer anything, swallow any pain, rather than say something which might prevent that. Instead, she let out a long, deep sigh.

"Nothing, Mum, I don't mean anything. It's good to see you smile again. Listen, Tom Maloret asked if I might take a stroll with him tomorrow evening, if you don't need me here?"

She had rehearsed this lie so often it slipped out with ease. Violet's face brightened immediately.

"Did he now? Well, you tell him you'd be delighted. And have a lovely time."

Jean busied herself by warming the teapot, an excuse to turn and hide her crimson flush.

"I will, Mum. I'm sure I will."

"Two thousand members! Who'd have thought, in those dark Occupation years, that our movement could grow so quickly? But we have an uphill battle before us and we need more."

A roll of applause went around the hall. Hazel craned her neck to get a better view of the speaker, whom she recognized from the rally in Parade Gardens. She liked this jovial man with his strong island accent and relaxed manner. Rumors abounded that in the latter days of the Occupation he had conspired with a German military official to conduct a mutiny against the local garrison, and that only Hitler's death had prevented it. She wondered what that kind of courage must feel like.

"It won't surprise you to learn," the speechmaker continued, "that our esteemed local newspaper has thrown its weight behind the new establishment party—how they have the nerve to call themselves Progressive I don't know." A ripple of dark laughter. "So in the coming weeks it will be up to you to strike the balance. In your workplaces, canteens and local pubs, ask everyone—do you feel life in Jersey before the war was fair for ordinary people? Or are you angry that rents were too high, that the old and sick were discarded, that technical and cultural advances got no investment? If so, this is our biggest, best chance to make this island work for everyone."

Applause erupted again, and Hazel joined in, her shoulders loosening a little beneath her wrap. It was a relief to sit in this hall, to lose herself in ideas and escape the darkness of recent days. Questions that nibbled at her mind like mice, thoughts of worst-case scenarios that jolted her awake in the night. Would natural sympathy for a bereaved family mean the Parrises' assumptions would be taken as truth? How did the authorities intend to treat people they considered collaborators? She kept telling herself that no court or tribunal could possibly prosecute on such a flimsy premise. But the words echoed in her head: *there are people who say…* Hazel knew only too well how rumors circulated in this island. And if the Parris family wished to blacken her name, there was precious little she could do. For days she had tried to focus on other things—her next day's lessons, her father's feeble appetite and what might tempt him to eat. And tonight, this J.D.M. meeting, a reminder that there were other things going on in the world.

A short break was announced before the next speaker, and Hazel sat back in her chair, taking in the hundred-odd crowd. She was no longer the only woman. There were seven or eight others scattered around the hall, some accompanied by husbands or brothers but a couple who had come alone or with

a friend, and it seemed that one of them was actually sched-
uled to speak. Her spirit lifted a little. Here was a hall filled
with fair-minded people who cared about justice; perhaps if
she threw herself into this group, they would turn out to be
her saviors, would take up her cause and support her. Maybe
this party was the solution to the nebulous sense of "other-
ness" that had haunted her since she could remember. In her
school days she had put it down to the early death of her
mother...later she had pinned it on the family's lowly social
status. But other kids had dead mothers and sick fathers and
lived in flats with stinking drains, and they didn't appear to
feel the same. It was something more fundamental, a radical
worldview inherited from her dad, that somehow set her at
an odd angle and stirred a prickly resentment that often left
her isolated. Now that the world really was out to get her,
perhaps this was the shelter she'd craved.

A tap on the shoulder made her jump. Jim Picot was standing behind her. She forced herself to smile.

"Jim. Nice to see you, how are you?" He was just as handsome as she remembered, hair slicked back as always. It was
almost a year since their parting, yet still her first thought was
a desperate hope that he had not seen her cry as she'd walked
away on their last evening.

"I'm well, thanks. Teaching going well?" It was a barbed
opening gambit, given that her insistence she would never
give up her job for marriage had effectively been the cause
of their split, but she felt no resentment. In fact, she realized
she felt very little toward this man anymore. Perhaps she had
never felt that strongly in the first place, or perhaps the Occupation had hardened them all.

"Very well. Enjoying the speeches? That Labour landslide
on the mainland heralds a real sea change, I think."

He nodded, but his eyes were jumping around the room, his mind clearly elsewhere. She wondered why he had bothered to come over if he wasn't interested in talking to her.

"Yes, let's hope so. Hazel, I've been asked to speak to you…"

A chill rose up from her stomach. "Asked by whom?"

"It's come to our attention…you know how fast word gets around this island…"

The chill turned to ice; it hurt her chest. "Just spit it out, Jim."

"We know that you're under investigation for informing on that Parris chap who died."

Hazel stared at him, wondering if his expression had always been so supercilious. "I am not under investigation. I was questioned, that's all. The family suspects me because they know Philip Parris and I had words, but they're wrong. I never reported him, nor would I ever do anything like that."

Picot's face softened a little.

"Hazel, *I* know that. But this collaboration issue, it's getting so divisive. Some people just want to move on, but others are out for blood."

"So?"

"So, our party is vulnerable. A lot of people saw us as troublemakers during the war. If we don't take a firm position on this, it will weaken our chances in the election."

"And by 'a firm position,' you mean condemn people who've been wrongly accused?"

"Of course not!" He placed a hand on her arm. It no longer felt good; it felt like a clamp. "No one here is accusing you of anything."

"But?"

"A few people would prefer not to see you at meetings."

Hazel swallowed involuntarily. "I'm being expelled?"

"No! But perhaps just keep your distance till all this gets sorted out."

The silence that followed might have lasted an eternity were it not for a solo clapping at the end of the room, indicating that the meeting was about to reconvene. A new, short gentleman took his place on the platform. Picot was now trapped beside her chair as the fellow began to speak.

"It's not a comfortable topic," the man bellowed out, "but we all know that not everyone supported our beloved island during the last five years. And a few who sadly went further. Profiteers, jerrybags, informants. Local politicians who doffed their caps to the Nazis for an easy life." There were angry mutterings in the hall and a good number of audible boos. Hazel sat extremely still, her eyes pointedly on Picot. "Now, despite the ongoing presence of the British task force here," the speaker went on, "the Home Office are dragging their feet when it comes to prosecutions. Chap I know at the Greffe tells me that only twenty cases have been forwarded to the London investigation team. Twenty! I think we can all agree that is pretty pathetic. And while we all want to look forward, this will only work if the bad apples are weeded out and punished. Because I say, no future without justice." A thunderous applause erupted, peppered with angry shouts for revenge.

Picot had by now assumed a "see what I mean?" expression. Slowly Hazel rose and made her way toward the exit. She pushed her way out through the door and onto the street, consciously holding herself erect while disbelief and panic shortened her breaths and brought tears of injustice to her eyes. It was less than a week since her interview with the Civil

Affairs Unit. Even she had not predicted things would move this quickly. So much for these people being her salvation.

Too upset for her evening climb up to South Hill, she headed straight back to the flat. When she got there, the first thing she saw was her father's strained pale face against the back of his chair.

"What's happened, Dad?"

"I was feeling all right earlier, so I popped down to Birds for a soft roll. Took me a while to get there, but I made it all right." He shook his head, disbelief falling from him. "Old Maisie Renouf, she won't serve me! 'Don't need your type in here,' she says. I asked what I'm supposed to have done. 'You and your girl, you know,' she says." He looked up at Hazel, and the pain in his eyes caused a stabbing sensation in her heart. "Is this how it's going to be, Haze? Is this our lives now?"

The evening was canopied by a pearly sky of faint lilacs and dove grays. At the quayside, blue metal cranes dipped toward the cargo, greedy for whatever nestled there. There were new luxuries arriving now: cooking pots, building supplies, cosmetics, fertilizers, goods to delight a population that had for years conditioned itself to expect nothing. Throughout the day, boats coursed in and out of the harbor disgorging their contents, and the dockers in their shirtsleeves and flat caps could be seen scurrying around till well into the evening, the comfort of easy chairs and hot tea postponed for the general good. A thin breeze carried their muffled shouts as they beckoned the giant hooks to their mark, while the same wind puckered the water's surface in the harbor, a reminder of squalls still in transit. In a few weeks, the days would shorten and the real storms would begin.

Along the quay, a few farm trucks revved their engines in eager anticipation of their journey to the country parishes, but there was no other traffic on the streets, or anyone else about. Jean, scampering past the main harbor front toward the quieter inlets of the east side, felt exposed, a lone gazelle on a prairie. She pulled her jacket around her and tried to look purposeful, as if she had some crucial but entirely innocent appointment to attend, glancing over her shoulder at intervals. Her new lace-up shoes, purchased that morning following rumors of a delivery and a half-hour queue at De Gruchy's store, clacked and echoed as she hurried past the commercial warehouses with their ribbed pull-down shutters. Only one thing mattered tonight—being with Horst, seeing his face, holding him again. She had spent the entire day in a state of delirious agitation, and now, only moments away from his physical presence, she felt faint with excitement.

She reached the set of stone steps leading toward the water and climbed down two of them. They were steep and slippery with sheet algae, uneven through the heavy feet of generations of fishermen, and she kept her hand on the rusting rail as she sat down to wait. In the marina, fishing boats bobbed and clanked on the darkening water, the wind in the lanyards like a child's xylophone. The sky was turning a deeper mauve, with blobs of gray clouds drifting in the rising breeze. If he didn't get here soon, it would be too late. Then she heard the slow rhythmic swoosh of a paddle some distance away, and through the half-light she saw the small dinghy making its way toward her, the familiar silhouette crouching in the stern. At that moment, her face cracked into the first true smile she could remember in weeks, and her eyes misted. By the time the dinghy was twenty yards away, his face grinning up at her as if it were the most natural thing in the world, the tears were running down her cheeks.

The little boat drew in to the bottom of the steps, the water slapping around it. There were two of them, Horst and another young man about the same age, both in their Wehrmacht uniforms for want of any other clothes, both thin, with faces that radiated exhaustion. Horst was first off, staggering up the high steps with incautious speed to reach her, and she felt a surge of warmth and joy as she reached out her arms and sank into his body. For a while, neither of them spoke but just stood wrapped around each other, kissing, then hugging again, while his friend pretended to busy himself tying the dinghy to the mooring link. Eventually prudence overcame her and she pulled back.

"How did you manage this? Won't they know you've gone?"

Horst shook his head, pushing back strands of loose hair from her face. "I pay the guards. But I must be back in one hour."

"It must be scary for you, that tiny boat?"

He laughed, delighted that she remembered. But how could she forget? A grown man afraid of the ocean, posted to a tiny island surrounded by nothing else—she had teased him about it often.

"I do anything to see you." He stepped back to look at her. "You are beautiful. But so…" He scrabbled for the word, then gave up and mimed something sticklike.

"I have so much to tell you. Come on."

Horst softly called down to his friend in German, then he and Jean hurried up the steps, following the path around the marina wall to the far side of the French Harbour. They slipped quietly between the empty hulls of fishing boats awaiting repair, hopping over the rusting chains of moorings, finally reaching the row of shacks at the far end of the wharf. Only when they were tucked behind them, squatted on the cobbles and out of sight of any passerby did Jean begin to relax. The sun had completely vanished now, leaving only a fiery gold on the underside of the clouds, the eastern sky already turning navy. She looked into his face, those warm eyes, the faint shadow of hair on his top lip, his unruly hair shaved short.

"It is terrible on the ship?"

He shrugged, clearly editing the answer in his head. "Every day we work on the beaches, in the bunkers. It is hard. But sometimes I find food in the fields. Or a boy to take a message." He grinned. "I am so happy he find you."

"Me, too." Jean smiled, then took a breath. "Listen, my father…"

He held up his hand. "I know. In the newspaper. Jean, I am so sorry. Things my country has done… I never understand." He shook his head, lost in consternation. Jean peered at him.

"Horst, I'm sorry to ask this again. But do you have any idea how the Germans got to know about my father's radio?"

He shrugged, confused. "I tell you when the arrest happens, I know nothing."

"The British investigators here, they think someone reported him, informed on him."

Horst pulled back his head in surprise. "*Spitzel?* For what reason?"

"We believe it's this woman who didn't like him…but I thought perhaps you might know more."

"I am so sorry. I wish I can help." He took her hand and leaned back against the rough wall of the shed. Tiny splinters of painted wood lodged in his hair and sparkled in the remaining light. She knew the next question would change everything but that it was her only opportunity, and that she would have to ask it no matter what.

"And what you said over a year ago—is it still true? That you never knew—about the radio?" She swallowed, tasting the poison of it. "I have to be sure. I keep going over and over it—thinking, perhaps I let something slip, or dropped a hint…"

Her meaning took only a second to jump the distance of language. "You think *I*…?"

"No, no, of course not—not on purpose!" She squeezed his fingers, trying to rake back the damage. "I know you would never hurt me. But if I said something by mistake, perhaps you mentioned it in passing… I don't know, just talking among your friends…" She had practiced this so many times, but the fact of it now was feeble and offensive. He extracted himself from her grip and cupped her face in his hands.

"My love, I know nothing of your family. For all the war, I am *Obersoldat* who sleeps in the dormitory with ten others. I do my gun practice, eat my shit rations. I know nothing of arrests, people in prison—it is *Geheimpolizei* do this. I think *spitzel* is local person. People do this in *Paris*, in *Österreich*, everywhere." He looked despondent. "But maybe you do not trust me now?" He looked so hurt that she closed her eyes, despairing. This was all so far from what she'd wanted this evening to be, and was achieving nothing except to ruin their precious time. She shook her head violently.

"No. No, I do trust you, I promise. It's just been so awful—the news of Dad, not being able to see you…sometimes I think I'm going mad. I'm sorry." She kissed him then, and felt the pent-up fear and doubt of many weeks ebbing away. He tasted of sea salt and a cigarette smoked some time before, and she wished she could stay buried in that moment forever, secure from the outside world. But after a moment he pulled back.

"Jean. They will send me to England—my boat will leave first day in September. I am straightaway prisoner of war." She bit the inside of her lip. It was only weeks away. But hadn't she always known this was coming? The least she could do for him was show some backbone. She squeezed his fingers harder and nodded, as he went on: "I will be there a long time, I think. And then?" He gazed out toward the harbor, and she saw him wrestle down his emotions. "Germany is finished. My family is gone, I have no home. I have only one thing in my future." He gripped her with a new intensity. "I know this is impossible question. But will you marry me?"

For a moment, the words bounced off her, water on metal, meaningless. Only very slowly did thoughts begin to form. How absurd that in all these months, with all the love that had poured from her and all the declarations they had made beneath dripping branches and behind rocky outcrops, marriage had never once occurred to her. Now a wild excitement exploded in her chest; her head filled quickly with images of a white satin dress, falling confetti, she and Horst lying together in a huge marital bed. But, just as quickly, she saw the two of them standing in an empty church devoid of guests, doors of properties being slammed in their faces…a solitary child with Horst's features standing alone and friendless in a playground. She realized she had been silent for too long.

"I need time to think." It was a horrible response, and she knew it. "I love you, you know that, but…"

"I know what I ask. But the world is big. If you can leave your Summerland, we can go somewhere safe. Somewhere far from the sea, perhaps, where I will not be afraid?" It was

a feeble joke, but she tried to smile. "It is possible, I believe
it. So please—you think about this?" She nodded, the tears
escaping now, though what they meant she was no longer
sure. "I can pay the guard once more, the night before we
sail. You will come here then, answer my question?"

"Of course." The hope of another meeting sent her giddy.
This might not be goodbye. She moved forward to kiss him
again, but this time he turned away and simply held her,
crushing her fragile frame, breathing hard not with passion
but with panic, a sound she knew well. And she wanted to
say so much, tell him how much he meant to her, tell him
that she couldn't imagine life without him, but that marriage
to a German made her feel sick with fear.

It was time. They slipped back through the last of the evening light to the steps where the boat was waiting, and she
watched him climb gingerly aboard and the two of them
slowly paddle out toward the harbor entrance. She stayed for
several minutes, unable to tear herself away, until his face was
a pale blur on a vague outline, then she climbed the steps and
prepared to hurry home, already preparing her made-up stories of her evening with Tom Maloret, stopping only to retie
the unfamiliar laces of her new shoes. Had she not done that,
she might never have glanced up and seen the worst sight she
could ever have imagined. A figure standing on the hillside
above on the hairpin road that led up to South Hill, a point
just high enough to view anyone coming up from the harbor steps, and to get a clear outlook onto any boats, even
small dinghies, entering or leaving the harbor; a female figure with a wrap around her shoulders, staring at her with
furious intent, with a silhouette Jean instantly recognized.
A tall, young woman with auburn hair. And as Jean picked
herself up and ran faster than she ever thought she could up

the side of the main harbor and the shuttered warehouses, running till her heart was on the point of explosion and she thought she would vomit, she already knew it was too late. She had been seen by Hazel Le Tourneur.

6

"Have one of these. My mother makes them for me every day. This one has pickle." Tom Maloret held the limp, thin-cut sandwich out to her, encouraging her with his grin. Jean forced a smile as she took it, wondering how on earth she was going to pretend to eat it right in front of him. The thought of swallowing even a mouthful made her throat close up.

"Thank you. But you must have one of mine." She handed him one of the tiny squares from her basket, the fish paste turning her stomach as its odor drifted upward. A robin, its orange breast gleaming in the golden light, hopped its way across the churchyard path, hovering in optimism; perhaps, if she feigned a generosity toward the avian world, she might be able to dispose of her lunch bit by bit. She sat very still on the bench, hoping to encourage some others to approach, but the sparrows in the trees overhead seemed content to flit from branch to branch. From the acidic smell of the cheese wafting up her nose, she couldn't blame them.

"My dad never learned to read or write very well," Tom was saying. "So he thought that if they pushed me hard at school, and got me into some kind of office, that would be a big step up from the life they've had. The day I got the States job, Mum danced a jig around the kitchen." Jean realized a response was expected and faked a little laugh. "But honestly, on days like this, when the sun's shining and the sky is this blue, walking into that enormous municipal building in the morning just feels like going back to school." He took a bite of the sandwich, then asked: "Did your dad like running his ironmonger's shop?"

Jean smiled and nodded, knowing that she was doing a terrible job of pretending to listen. She had not been able to think of a single reason to say no to Tom's picnic invitation when he'd knocked on the door first thing this morning, all smiles and hopefulness and giving her no time to think. But now, how she wished she had thought of some excuse. Her head was filled with roaring, panicky thoughts that blotted out all surrounding conversation. It had been three days and sleepless nights since Hazel had seen her down at the harbor, and Jean's anxiety had escalated with each passing hour. Last night in bed, her heart rate was so fast that she feared it would rupture. And yet... If the woman intended to confront her, surely she would already have appeared at the Parrises' door? Or, had she gone straight to the authorities, Tom would already know about it and wouldn't be sitting beside her now, yattering cheerfully about his family. All this, Jean told herself, was a good sign. But in the pit of her belly she knew this was not over. Hazel Le Tourneur was just as likely biding her time, choosing the most effective moment to bring Jean's world crashing down.

And if she did—then what? Her mother might, at one time, have tried to understand, might have listened to reason. But she and Eddie seemed to be using this hatred of all collaborators as a way to grieve, drawing strength and purpose each day from their fury. Jean might find herself chased from the family home, a packed suitcase on the doorstep. She might have to go and live with her brother in Chelmsford, assuming he would take her, and she didn't even know exactly where Chelmsford was. The thought was so alarming that even the gentlest breeze rustling the blooms on the gravestones raised the hairs all along her arms.

So anxious had Jean been about the whole business that she had hardly given a thought to the other great event of Friday night, Horst's proposal. His words echoed through her head at random moments of the day, but immediately the same contradictory images—the joyful wedding, the strained, isolated future—paraded past, tugging her emotions back and forth until she thought her skull would rupture. She yearned for a confidante, someone to ask for advice, and gave serious thought about speaking to Daphne. But Daphne's world was simple and sweet, filled with innocent divisions of sugar-and-spice girls and slug-and-snail boys, and Jean was not at all certain that she would understand. There was also the risk that Daphne would tell her own mother, which was the fastest route to Violet's ears Jean could imagine. No. Better to hold it all inside and see how the coming days transpired. Perhaps fate would take its own hand in proceedings.

"Jean? Are you all right?" Tom's voice came as a slap in the face.

"Sorry—miles away."

"My fault for asking such dull questions."

"Not at all. I was just thinking…" She hesitated, frightened to ask, frightened to hear an answer. But how much worse could it get? "Just thinking about that Le Tourneur woman, wondering if you'd had any cause to speak to her again? If you don't mind my asking," she added feebly.

Tom, too, pushed the remains of his lunch to one side, his cheeriness ebbing away.

"No, we've not spoken to her since last week. The C.A.U. are assessing what she told us. They need to speak with other people connected to that information."

Jean hid a small sigh of relief. So Hazel had, as yet, said nothing of what she'd seen at the harbor. She forced a smile, imagining the police officers interviewing a bunch of aggressive Communists.

"Some pretty unsavory characters involved, I should think."

"Oh, so you know? I didn't realize. Did your mother tell you?"

Jean stopped, her sandwich hovering near her lips, suddenly tingling with alertness. Tom, she realized, was not referring to Communists. And she knew at that moment that this was her chance to extract the truth.

"Yes, Mum told me everything. But I'd certainly be interested to hear Hazel's version."

Tom sat back on the bench, his entire body stiff and awkward. His fluttering hands began picking up the paper bags that had contained his lunch.

"I'm not really at liberty…and I really don't want to cause you any more distress."

"I doubt you'd be telling me anything I don't already know." It was shockingly brazen, but she saw him nod with resignation. She felt lightheaded and realized she was holding her breath.

"Well, your father wasn't doing anything that many others weren't. But black marketeering is not only illegal. At the scale of your father's operation, it's also viewed by people like Miss Le Tourneur as highly unethical. He clearly made a great deal of money from the back of that shop."

Jean put every ounce of energy she possessed into not moving her face a muscle. "She...she confirmed that?"

"She had a perfect view from her window. Of course, she also held a personal grudge against your father, so we're not sure everything she said is true. And her testimony itself, her strong disapproval of what he was doing, gave her a motive to report him. But Mr. Parris would have been dealing regularly with some unscrupulous people, which certainly opens up the possibilities to a wider field." He leaned forward, his face suddenly filled with concern. "Jean you've gone terribly white. Have I upset you? I shouldn't have said anything, I'm sorry."

"No, I'm fine." Her voice, even to her own ears, sounded strangulated and high-pitched. "I'm just suddenly feeling a little queasy. I think maybe the fish paste in the sandwiches is off."

Hazel stirred the stew on the tiny gas hob, pushing the cabbage, onions and potatoes around the bottom of the pan. The smell filled the apartment, and she pushed the kitchen window a little wider to let some odor escape, even though it meant the stench from the drains would soon drift inward. Of all the problems of living in these cheap flats above the shop, this was the one she struggled with most. She thought of her middle sister, Lilian, far away in south London, and wondered if she were able to open her windows. If so, what smells wafted in through her curtains? Hazel had not visited London for years but loved to look at photographs of the city and picture herself and Lilian strolling through Trafalgar Square, pigeons flying above their heads. She recalled there were hundreds of them perched on the great bronze lions around Nelson's Column, so elegantly cast from the cannons of ships defeated in the battle. It was a thrilling place. Lilian had married an Englishman and moved to the mainland in 1938, not long after their father's illness set in. Of course, as Lilian explained many times, had she any idea of how sick he would become, or known that Dottie would be taken in the diphtheria outbreak, she would never have left Hazel to cope with her father alone. But by then it was all too late, the once happy, five-strong Le Tourneur family reduced to a sad little twosome in the space of a few years. How fortunate, said the distant cousins and unhelpful neighbors, that Hazel was the tough one of the family, the one most likely to cope with the strain; acting as breadwinner while caring for her father was a task that might have cracked a less capable woman. And each time she heard it, Hazel had wanted to slap their cheeks and wail that toughness was a character trait not born to anyone, but merely assembled when required. Much as she loved her father, right now, tonight, she would have given anything to have changed places with her sister. With a sigh, she spooned the stew into bowls and took them into the main room, where her father was already sitting at the table.

"Delicious," he announced at the first mouthful, and Hazel smiled in response. It was good to see him eat after several days of pushing food around his plate like a miserable child, but she never felt able to reproach him for it, knowing his worry affected both his pain levels and his appetite. Two nights ago, he had even refused her offer to continue reading from *Wuthering Heights*, preferring to sit and stare out at the darkening sky until it was time for bed. Hazel ground her teeth as she watched him, hating the Parrises and the misery they were causing. As if this man hadn't had enough to contend with these last few years. "So," he added after a few slow bites, "have you decided what you're going to do?"

Hazel shook her head. "Every time I think I've decided, I change my mind."

"Haze!" He inclined his head, confused and disappointed.

"It's not that easy."

He shrugged to indicate the flaw in her argument. "I know that, my love, but we have to protect ourselves." He placed his spoon gently against the side of his bowl. "Look, they've done nothing but stir up trouble for us, haven't they? Based on nothing. And all that time this young woman was fraternizing herself! What do they call it? Horizontal collaboration!" He winced at using such a term in front of his daughter.

Hazel nodded reluctantly. Her memory of Friday evening was as clear as the room before her now. The light may have been fading, the moon already high and bright in the sky, but she was in no doubt. A clear view of the departing German soldier paddling out in his little dinghy, which she had guessed immediately meant a meeting with a local girl. Then, only seconds later, Jean Parris, flushed and furtive, scrambling up the harbor steps and glancing about her with obvious fear, before looking upward to see Hazel standing on the hillside. The horror in the girl's eyes told the entire story in an instant. For several minutes Hazel had stood perfectly still, watching the frightened figure run as fast as she could up the side of the black glistening harbor, as if she could escape this terrible discovery through speed alone. And ever since, Hazel had been turning over her options.

"I know, Dad. But if I report her, aren't I just becoming the informant they say I am?" She, too, leaned her spoon against her bowl, her appetite ebbing. "They might see it as proof they were right all along. Or they might think I'm inventing a nasty story to get revenge. Then my name really will be mud." She pressed her lips together hard to hold the tears back. Her father stretched out a gnarled hand and covered her own.

"They might also look into it and discover it's true. In which case that's an end to all these awful rumors about us."

Hazel sighed as she pushed her dish away. It was unlike her dad to suggest anything so mean-spirited, and a measure of how frightened he was feeling. Truthfully, Hazel herself was just as scared. A house on St Saviour's Road had recently been the victim of smashed windows and Nazi swastikas painted in pitch, punishment for a wartime crime known only to the attackers. There had been several fights reported in the local pubs. And only yesterday Hazel had been forced to go to the covered market after their usual greengrocer pretended not to have any tomatoes, which Hazel knew to be a lie. She had not mentioned any of this at home, but for the last few days her father had become edgy about getting his hands on the evening paper, evidently keen to know what might be coming his way. If these rumors persisted, the consequences for the two of them were too horrible to consider.

"Let me think about it." She gathered the bowls together and shuffled into the kitchen, filling the sink with a little tepid water to wash the dishes. She imagined herself walking back into the States offices and announcing what she'd seen. Her father was right, the facts wouldn't be hard to investigate. The Parris girl would be questioned, her lover's movements traced, and at the very least enough smoke would be created for someone to assume a fire. And that would be the end of her reputation, that skinny slip of a thing who sometimes seemed scared of her own shadow. She wouldn't be the first island girl to have fallen for a soldier, finding the invaders more handsome, worldly and courteous than the island boys, but that would not save her from society's wrath. It might cast her out of her own family, wreck her future chances of marriage. Did Hazel really need to cause this girl so much misery, simply to save her own skin?

The thoughts spun around as she rubbed the food bits from the bowls. Lilian would likely be doing the same thing about now, Hazel supposed, washing up her children's tea things before getting them ready for bed. She recalled years ago, in another lifetime, Lilian washing up at another sink in a nicer kitchen, while their mother lay upstairs in her bed, smiling through her agony, pretending that she wasn't too bad today and that she might be up for a little trip out tomorrow. That tomorrow never came. Her father had never come to terms with it. Hazel's gaze drifted across to him, hunched in his chair, wriggling his painful fingers to try and maintain just a little mobility and wincing at each tiny movement. At that moment, she realized she had no choice. She could not stand by and watch her father lose his dignity and reputation, the only meaningful things left in his life. Drying her hands on a tea towel, she walked back into the living room.

"All right, I've decided. I'm not going to report the Parris girl to the authorities." She saw his shoulders slump with disappointment. "But I am going to talk to the family. I'll reason with them, tell them they've made a mistake. I'll ask them to withdraw their accusations, put a stop to the rumors."

Her father raised his eyebrows high, then let them drop. "But they won't believe you, might not even speak to you. What then?"

"Then…then I will tell them what I saw at the harbor. And explain if they don't stop this persecution, I'll report her."

His face filled with pain. "Blackmail?"

Hazel nodded. She could feel the tension in her neck. "At least this way they'll have their chance."

"Do you know where they live?"

"I know it's St Mark's Road. I remember Parris complaining about the motor traffic before the war. One of the neighbors will direct me."

"When are you going to go?"

Hazel pulled herself up a little straighter and took a breath inward. "No time like the present."

The creak of the front door as she opened it cracked the thick silence. Jean waited for any kind of response, then, hearing nothing, stepped quietly along the hallway toward the kitchen. It was gone seven, and she expected to find her mother washing up in the kitchen or knitting in the parlor. But then she spotted a message, scribbled in pencil on the back of a brown paper bag and left on the dresser, saying that Violet had decided to attend the evening service at the Methodist church and wouldn't be back till later. Jean stood still in the center of the kitchen for a moment, running her hands over the empty table, relishing this rare moment of solitude. During the war, she had found the hours of silence oppressive, but now she preferred it to the constant background sound of this house; the padding and grumbling, the bitter muttering, the shouty meetings. She calculated she would have at least an hour before anyone was home, time to sit and digest this ever-changing situation. Taking a glass from the shelf, she poured herself a drink of water and tried to rally her thoughts.

Tom's revelation, initially, had seemed as absurd as it was shocking. Her father, the hero of his community, a black marketeer? For several moments, she had sat like a statue on that churchyard bench, fumbling nervously with the little gold locket at her throat, telling herself that this was simply Le Tourneur's desperate attempt to transfer her own guilt.

But after they parted awkwardly in the middle of the square, Tom slouching back to work with a sad look on his face, she had taken a long walk along St Aubin's beach. Somewhere toward Bel Royal, she had slumped down with her back to the gray concrete anti-tank wall, which now served as a sea defense, feeling the sand between her fingers and toes— after years of mines and barbed wire restriction it was a joyfully familiar sensation—and reached the conclusion that it had to be true. The Le Tourneurs' flat did indeed overlook the shop's backyard, and as Hazel's assertion did nothing to prove her own innocence, why would she lie? If Philip Parris had gone to jail for theft as a youngster, breaking the law was no barrier to him. It also explained her uncle Martin's amused reaction to the "learned lesson" narrative her family suggested. He knew.

And now grubby little memories began creeping out from forgotten corners of her mind. Those strangers who sometimes turned up at the house late in the evening, demanding murmured conversations with "Mister Parris" in the backyard. That unexplained tray of French tinned artichokes she once found at the bottom of her father's wardrobe. Her father's furious and baffling refusal when, on a rare visit to his shop, she had asked to use the toilet in the room above. And her mother had backed him up, insisting that she wait till she got home. Of course, Jean figured, if Uncle Martin knew, her mother probably did, too.

There were other things, as well. Those occasions when her dad had arrived home late with a skinned rabbit or a wheel of French cheese, claiming it was a gift from a customer. At the time Jean had accepted this and stuffed herself willingly, but on reflection, how would his poor, local customers have come by such things? Plenty of girls at her school never saw such luxuries in the whole of the Occupation. And those Thursday nights he claimed to be stocktaking, when there was practically no new stock to be had. Her head ached as she realized that all the time she had berated herself for her taboo relationship, her father had been doing something just as *verboten*. And the worst of it, which Jean knew very well, although Tom had never alluded to it, was that it was virtually impossible to run a sizable black-market operation during the Occupation without doing business with the Germans themselves.

She had walked home slowly, with the intention of spending the evening quietly in her room. An open window and a fresh evening breeze blowing over her was exactly what she needed right now. She drained the glass of water and was about to head upstairs when the kitchen door flew open with such force that an involuntary cry leaped from her, and the glass in her hand dropped to the floor, smashing instantly on the tiles.

In the doorway was Eddie, drunk as she'd ever seen him, purple-faced and staring at her with a terrifying grin. His voice, when he finally spoke, gurgled with beer and something unfamiliar.

"So, you're back, are you, you lying little tart?" Pieces of glass lay splintered around her feet, glinting in the rays of evening sun, but neither of them moved. Jean found herself trying to recall what time evening service ended, and when her mother might realistically be home. She struggled to find her voice.

"Uncle Eddie, calm down. You're drunk."

"Been out with one of your boyfriends, have you?"

Jean felt the flush return, her mind grappling for what could possibly be the cause of this onslaught. At the same time, she sensed she needed to stand up for herself or be crushed.

"Tom and I shared a picnic in the churchyard, what's wrong with…?"

"Not that. You know what I'm talking about. This!" He waved something in her face. It was a small, crumpled piece of paper, and for a moment Jean had no idea what it was. Then, with a slow-burning freeze that began in her solar plexus and spread through her entire body, she recognized it. It was Horst's note. "Hidden away where you thought no one would find it. But I did. And I know what you're up to."

Not since she had looked up at South Hill and seen Hazel's figure staring down had such panic gushed through her body. She instantly needed the toilet but didn't dare try to leave the room. Grasping the edge of the kitchen sink, she tried to regain some control. What she said in the next minute would define everything.

"It's from Tom. Just a little love note."

"Nice try! That's what I thought! But I looked at the writing on that condolence card, totally different. And why would he be telling you to keep it secret?" He began to move toward her, slowly and unsteadily. "So, I'm thinking…why would innocent little Jeannie be hiding notes? And I reckon you've got someone tucked away. Getting around a bit, are we? Not quite the little virgin we're making out to be?"

Jean's hand gripped the white enamel harder. Every fiber of her wanted to back away from him, but she would then be in the far corner of the kitchen, and instinct told her that was too dangerous a place. Her mind galloped forward, trying to get ahead of his. How could he have found the note? She had hidden it so securely! The same place she had hidden the little tokens from Horst over the months—the length of wool, the bar of French chocolate—right at the back of the drawer. The drawer where she… Then, instantly, she knew. A nauseous belch became trapped halfway up her throat.

"You've been in my underwear drawer!" At once she knew it was not the first time. Those missing knickers she assumed had been stolen from the washing line—suddenly it all made sense. "You've been stealing my underthings! That's disgusting!"

Instantly she realized her miscalculation. Her accusation only acted as fuel on whatever was simmering within him. The intensity of his expression told her she was now in serious physical danger, and she was trapped in the tiny kitchen with nowhere to run.

Then the doorbell rang.

The sound stopped both of them exactly where they were, as if shaken from a nightmare. No one ever rang the bell of this house. Neighbors tapped on the window; the postman simply pushed through the letters and left. The last time it had sounded was the night of Clement's visit. Who on earth would be calling on them at this time?

Sensing her opportunity to escape, Jean edged around her uncle and hurried down the hall, glad that the interruption seemed to have de-escalated the moment. But as she opened the door the panic shot back. On the doorstep, wrapped in the same green wrap she'd been wearing the other night, was Hazel Le Tourneur. So, Jean's suspicions had been right; the woman had simply been biding her time. And now, at the worst possible moment, she would confirm exactly who the note was from. She stared at Hazel's pale, sculpted face, waiting for the axe to fall. And then, the most extraordinary thing happened. An idea popped into Jean's head so insane, so audacious, she would never work out where it had come from. All she knew was that it was her last chance, her only chance, and that she had nothing to lose. In what felt like minutes, but was probably only a second or two, she figured out exactly how she would execute it. Throwing her hands to her hips as a gesture of defiance, she went on the attack.

"Well, you've got a nerve, coming here! And I bet I know what this is about."

Hazel, predictably, looked unperturbed. "Yes, I imagine you do."

Jean could hear Eddie's feet clod-hopping up the hallway and knew he was within earshot. Now was the moment to lay down her hand. *This will never work*, her conscience murmured. But it was too late: she was already in up to her neck.

"What do you think you're playing at, sending me a note, asking to meet me?" Jean watched as Hazel's expression slowly shifted from one of taut defensiveness to a sunken bafflement. The woman's eyes widened with confusion.

"Meet you?"

"Down at the harbor, last Friday. I knew immediately who *H* was." Jean turned to see Eddie behind her, trying to make sense of this new situation through his fog of alcohol. Horst's note was still in his hand, but he offered no resistance as Jean took it from him. Now it was her turn to wave it accusingly. "Thought if you got me on your own, you could talk me round? Convince me you were innocent, then I'd come back and persuade the rest of the family, get them to drop the investigations?" Hazel's eyes were growing wider, revealing their full pale blue color—not the deep sapphire of Daphne's, but a green-tinged shade reminiscent of summer rock pools. Jean locked into them and saw vulnerability and hurt amidst the uncertainty, but she ignored it. There was only one way out of this, and that was to see it through to the end. "She got this kid to deliver it," she threw over her shoulder toward her uncle. "I knew straightaway who it was from. Of course I didn't go. I was going to throw it away, but I thought it might be, you know, evidence." A cold cascade of shame chased down the panic. This was the worst thing she had ever done.

Slowly, Eddie pulled himself from the beer-soaked depths of his own befuddlement.

"You're saying…*she* wrote this?"

Jean rolled her eyes in mock frustration. Where this dramatic performance was coming from she had no idea.

"That's what I'm trying to tell you! I knew it would upset you and Mum—that's why I hid it." The words were tumbling out, the lie growing and embellished with every phrase. Eddie was frowning now, slowly piecing together this strange new fiction. She watched Eddie look from Hazel to the note and back again, connecting fictitious dots, seeing the pattern that he wanted to see. His bottom lip began to jut out as he began to nod.

"My niece is right. You've got a damn nerve coming round here."

Jean let out a little gasp. The first stage had worked: Eddie was persuaded. Now all she had to do was stem the tide of indignation and contradiction that was about to pour from Hazel herself. Jean braced herself for the onslaught as Hazel opened her mouth and began to speak. Her voice was quieter than anyone had expected.

"You're right. I'm sorry. I shouldn't have written it."

Jean felt something intangible leave her body. She was staring down at the three of them, watching from above like some curious ghost. Had she misheard? What was going on?

One of her feet involuntarily stepped back into the hallway and she almost fell. Eddie's face broke into a triumphant smile.

"So you admit it?"

Hazel sniffed and adjusted her wrap around her shoulders. Her composure was extraordinary. Jean could not drag her eyes away.

"I admit I sent this young woman the note, asking to meet her. But nothing else. Because I had nothing to do with Philip Parris's arrest."

Eddie gave a skeptical snort. Jean was long past the power of speech, and continued simply to stare at Hazel, half expecting her to disappear in a puff of smoke or turn into a cat.

"So how come you were seen fighting with him the week before?" Eddie barreled on. "Why did you write letters to the States causing trouble?"

"I never said Mr. Parris and I were friends. I didn't like him, I think we all know that. But I'm no informer." She looked at Jean directly. "I thought if I could convince one member of this family of my innocence, perhaps you'd all come to accept it. I see now I was wrong."

The cool evening breeze from the front garden was blowing through Jean's hair. She could feel her feet unsteady on the hall lino, smell the dust of the asphalt street. Yet she was still floating above the proceedings, observing. Hazel's eyes flicked back to hers constantly, as if reassuring her, and all Jean could do was to stare back. Eddie leaned forward, now back in full aggression mode.

"Think you're smart, don't you? Well, we all know you're guilty, and you're not going to get away with it. Now clear off our property."

With a final glance at Jean, Hazel turned and walked smoothly down the path, the clanking of the front gate the only sound as she disappeared into the twilight. Eddie closed the door and stood breathing heavily in the dim hallway. For several moments neither of them spoke. Jean focused only on the sensation of the note, crushed in the palm of her hand. Finally, Eddie broke the silence. "Suppose I owe you an apology."

Jean could barely meet his eye. She had zero trust as to what might happen if she did. "Forget it."

Eddie turned and shuffled down the hallway. A minute later, not knowing what else to do, Jean turned and unsteadily climbed the stairs to her room, collapsing onto her bed in a heap. The window looked out onto a clear summer sky, and she lay perfectly still until it turned black above her and the stars popped out across the firmament, wondering if what she had witnessed tonight was some kind of divine intervention, and what on earth might result from it.

With a dustpan in her hand, dragging the carpet sweeper behind her, Jean embarked on a slow ascent of the rickety farmhouse stairs. The grandfather clock in the hall below began its chimes for ten o'clock, and in her exhausted state, it sounded like a deliberate torment. Her legs were weights beneath her body, every riser a small mountain, and there were still three hours of cleaning ahead. One thing she had learned: if she was going to lie awake all night in an anxious stupor, it was worse to fall asleep an hour before getting-up time. Right this minute she could have flopped down and slept on the banister.

As she reached the top and trundled down the landing toward the boys' bedroom—it was by far the grubbiest, so wise to tick off the list early in the day—Beattie and Daphne appeared from Daphne's room, both smart as buttons in their coats and hats, ready for an outing. Daphne peered at her with concern.

"Are you all right, Jeannie? You're not sickening for something, are you?"

Jean forced a smile. "I'm fine. Just trouble sleeping."

"Cup of hot milk before bed," Beattie advised, automatically checking Jean's forehead for temperature the way that mothers did. "I'll give you a pint to take back. How's your mum doing?"

Jean knew it would be easier to sidestep everything today.

"She's all right. Coping."

"I'll sort you a bag of runner beans to take back, and all," Beattie promised. "I know she likes them. You must have lived off our runner beans during the war, I reckon. Good job we got so many plants." Jean marveled again at her aunt's naive memory. Beattie clearly believed that she had acted as some kind of personal Red Cross service to the Parris family during the war years, when several times Violet had complained how little she saw of her sister. Jean nodded and was about to push past into the bedroom when the question she dreaded came. "And what about that informant woman? Do they know yet, if it was her?"

Jean hesitated, still clutching the carpet cleaner and dustpan. How could she possibly explain anything of the last few days, when she could make no sense of it herself? And much as she longed to share the burden, there was no way to do so without revealing her own secret.

She thought of her mother and Eddie the night before, crouched like conspirators in the parlor while Eddie, smoking heavily, related the story of Hazel's visit for the tenth time. It was, he insisted, clear evidence of her guilt, for only a true collaborator would be so devious as to try and befriend a young innocent like Jean and poison her mind against her own family. Jean had listened from the shadowed privacy of the staircase, shame pumping through her veins, itching to rush in there and scream that this was all nonsense. While Hazel would no doubt demand something in return for her support—why else, after all, would she have given it?—it said nothing of her culpability. Moreover, Jean reasoned, if Violet knew about Philip's black-market dealings, she surely knew there could be other suspects? Most of all, though, Jean longed to tell her mother how her uncle had come by that note, yearned to reveal the true nature of this man her mother had chosen to trust. But that truth buckled under the weight of her own lies, and her mother's rapt attentiveness to Eddie's story told Jean that it was already too late. In the absence of her husband, Violet now seemed to cling to every word her brother-in-law uttered, in thrall to his every opinion. In the end, Jean had crept upstairs and reluctantly shredded Horst's note into a hundred pieces.

Beattie was still looking at her expectantly. Jean met her gaze, still holding the carpet sweeper in one hand.

"No. No one knows yet if it was her." Aunt Beattie nodded and turned to head downstairs. The next words shot from Jean's mouth as if bypassing her brain altogether. "Aunt Beattie, do you agree with Uncle Martin about collaborators? Do you think they should be hung?"

Her aunt stopped, taken aback. "Well… I think it depends what they did."

"What about black marketeers?" She looked Beattie straight in the eye and saw a sudden glimmer of understanding. Beattie's gaze drifted across the landing and out through the window as she considered her reply.

"Thing is, Jeannie, most businesses had little deals going

on. We used to hide piglets for our neighbor, get a couple of rabbits in return—no one thought of that as breaking the rules. It was just doing what you had to do to get by. Kept a lot of folk going, too." She gave a small meaningful smile. "It's true some people went too far, were only in it for the money. But anyone who found a way to put food on the table during the war, I say good on them."

Jean nodded. So, everyone in this family—all the adults, at least—had known what her father got up to. She was wondering how to react when Daphne, who clearly had not been following this conversation at all, piped up.

"Oh, Jeannie, I've been meaning to say! Six weeks on Saturday, are you free? It's my twenty-first birthday party."

"Oh—lovely. Yes, of course." Jean tried to inject some energy into her voice.

"It's going to be the biggest do anyone's seen in years," Daphne gushed on. "We just think everyone needs cheering up a bit. You and Auntie Vi will both come, won't you? And your uncle Eddie of course. And anyone special you want to bring." The last sentence she delivered with a knowing twinkle.

"Of course," Jean replied, the event already ruined for her.

"I'm even going to have a new dress, because Daddy had this brilliant idea of using Mummy's wedding gown. She's going to unpick it and turn it into a party dress for me, aren't you?"

"Apparently." Daphne seemed blind to Beattie's obvious irritation. Jean took a moment to marvel at the simplicity of Daphne's life. There must have been a time, as children, when they had shared that innocence. Now she doubted if Daphne could grasp the complexity of Jean's current predicament, even if she did confide in her. "Now, Jeannie, we need to get off.

Would you mind doing the silver in the dining room today, if you've got a spare ten minutes? It's looking a bit drab."

Jean stared at her aunt, wondering if her exasperation was as visible as it felt. Just this week she had found out a neighbor's daughter was getting five shillings for the same hours cleaning a far smaller house. Not once had she managed to get through Beattie's list of chores in her allotted time, often working well into the afternoon then having to wait for the six o'clock bus to get home.

"I'm not really sure I'll have time…"

"Well, just do your best. If not, there's always Thursday." Beattie was already at the top of the staircase. "Come on, Daph, I want to get into town early—apparently those Commies are having another rally. Don't want to get caught up." Daphne gave Jean an apologetic look over her shoulder as she followed her mother down the stairs, while Beattie threw back: "Help yourself to a sandwich if you get hungry. We might not be back till late."

Alone in the house, Jean dusted and polished the three bedrooms, followed by sweeping the rugs and floors, then went downstairs to begin on the kitchen. To settle her seething soul, she tried to pretend that she was a married woman cleaning her own house, with Horst coming back from work soon, and a meal to prepare for the two of them later. But her daydream turned on her, and she found herself wondering where she would shop for food and whether they would have any friends. At two, after a meager sandwich of stale bread and Spam, she went to the dining room and made a start on the silver. She rubbed the awkward nooks and curves of the handles with the soft cloth, but deliberately left a patch uncleaned on each piece, a gray swirly circle of acrimony toward her aunt. Toward Eddie. Her father's crumbling reputation and her family's lies. The blackmail the Le Tourneurs were likely cooking up at this very moment. By the time she picked up the final sugar bowl her mind swam with questions about what she might do next, what might be done to her. And she realized that in almost every case, the answers all lay with Hazel.

The corridor swarmed with giggling, shouting girls, but Hazel ignored them as she pushed through the sweaty bodies in various approximations of school uniform (new matching skirts and blazers were still not an import priority) focused only on getting to the front door and into the fresh air. In another two days, the school would break up for the summer, and it couldn't come soon enough. Never before had she had trouble with class discipline. Of course, there was always the odd note passed between chums, occasional fits of hysteria in the back row. But the last days had seen a distinct change. A sullen resentment when the girls stood to wish her good morning at the start of a lesson. Moody belligerence when they dumped a book on her desk with just a little too much force. And entering the staff room, never the friendliest of places, was now to walk into a cold storage of avoided eye contact and clipped, overcourteous sentences when communication couldn't be avoided. Wherever the information had come from, it had clearly circulated around the school like floodwater.

Shutting the main door tightly behind her and taking in a deep breath of sunshine, she turned left and headed toward the nearby cottage of a childhood pal she had not seen in ages. Company, she decided, would do her good today, and she shifted her school bag on her shoulder as she prepared to knock on the door. But at the last minute her confidence fell away, and she decided to keep walking. If her own pupils were openly discussing her alleged crimes, who knew how far this rumor had traveled? The thought of an inhospitable greeting was more than she could handle this afternoon. Only when she turned back onto the main road did the sound of footsteps too close behind her tell her that she was being followed. She spun around quickly to see the Parris girl standing a few feet behind, looking nervous. Hazel greeted her with a strong stance and an even stare.

"I was wondering when you were going to turn up." The girl stared back at her, evidently trying to return to a script she could no longer remember.

"I have to talk to you."

Hazel dumped her books on the pavement. "Are you going to scream at me again? Make up more lies?"

The girl shook her head. "Is there somewhere we can go?" Her eyes were swooping around the street, scanning the area for anyone she knew. There was a forlorn quality about her that Hazel could not reject.

"I know a place. Follow me."

The café at the top end of town was quiet and deserted. It was almost always so, since it had previously belonged to an Italian immigrant interned in 1940 and consequently was regarded with deep suspicion by most islanders. The fact that the current proprietor, Mr. Cauvain, a lifelong friend of the Milanese owner, had openly served German soldiers during the Occupation had not helped its case. While the place had so far avoided desecration, the empty tables and layers of dust on the red swag curtains told their own story. Hazel had always held the view that many local businesses had been forced into the same submission and that Cauvain probably felt as unhappy about it as anyone else. She had always found the dapper, elderly gentleman pleasant and courteous, and felt a kinship with his misfit status, especially now. She gestured to a table away from the window, where they could not be seen from outside, and watched the Parris girl take a seat opposite her. Having ordered a pot of tea for two, she folded her hands on the table in front of her and waited. Eventually it came.

"The other night. I need to know why you…did what you did."

Hazel fiddled with the teaspoon in her saucer, wondering why the answer was so difficult when she had thought about nothing else herself for the past four days.

"Let's start from the beginning. You know that I saw you at the harbor? You and your German boyfriend?" The girl made no attempt to argue the point and merely nodded. It was a look of defeat, as if this was a confirmation she had dreaded. "And maybe I wasn't the only one. If that news gets around, you'll both be in serious trouble. I hope he's worth it."

A familiar look suddenly spread across the girl's face and told Hazel everything. It was one she had occasionally seen between her parents in their younger, happier years, and on Lilian's face when she first met her husband. Hazel caught herself wondering if she would ever feel that way about any-one. Or even have the opportunity.

"His name is Horst. He's actually a wonderful man. It's not what you're thinking."

"What am I thinking?"

"That I'm some cheap jerrybag who went with soldiers for extra rations."

"Do you love him?" The girl blushed, nodding. Hazel suspected that even if they had said it to each other, this was probably the first time she had told anyone else. "But your family doesn't know?"

"They'd kill me. Especially after what happened to my father. That's why I was so scared when you turned up on the doorstep. I knew you might, I knew you'd seen us. But when you went along with my story, I was…"

"Astonished?" The girl nodded. "Well, that makes two of us."

"So, why? Why did you lie for me? And what do you want in return?"

Hazel sighed. The annoyance she felt at that last question was completely hypocritical. Until the moment the girl opened the door, Hazel had been prepared to throw the entire Parris family to the wolves to save herself. She considered her answer while Mr. Cauvain brought the pot of tea with two cups and saucers; they both waited in a tense silence until he laid everything out and retreated behind the counter.

"I don't want anything. I thought I did, at first—I mean, your family has behaved atrociously, blackening our name without any evidence. But for some reason, I…" The girl continued to stare questioningly. "Honestly? I felt sorry for you. I knew who that note was from as soon as you waved it in my face, I saw your desperation. I've seen how women like you are being treated. And in that split second…well, I just couldn't be that cruel." She poured some tea into her own cup. "I also realized that turning you in probably wouldn't help me anyway. Damage is already done."

"Thank you." The words were weighted with authenticity. Hazel poured tea into the girl's cup, as she clearly wasn't going to pick the teapot up herself. The girl stared down at it, and Hazel wondered if she was going to have to add the milk for her, too. "But won't this just make things worse for you? My mother and uncle see it as further proof of your guilt."

Hazel nodded solemnly without looking up. "Yes, no doubt."

"For some reason they're both certain it was you."

"Well, it wasn't. And I would have thought your Herr Horst would be on the list of suspects."

She shook her head. "I know it's not him. He never even knew Dad had a radio."

Hazel sniffed at the girl's credulity but knew there was no point pursuing it. "All right. But why me? Just because your father and I had a couple of arguments? I shout at girls in my class every day. I don't then go to the police and try and get them arrested."

The girl gave a short, humorless laugh. "No, I'm sure you don't." She played with her teaspoon. "You also wrote letters to the States…?"

"Yes. About our politicians taking a firmer line with the Germans. About cracking down on black marketeers, who took goods out of circulation and sold them to the fortunate few for personal profit. But I never accused any individual." Hazel shook her head. "It just makes no sense to me."

The girl sighed and lifted her eyes to meet Hazel's. "I think… I think we were all so shocked when we heard what happened to my dad. You know the Germans starved him till he became sick, then refused to get him a doctor? They let him die in front of them."

Hazel blinked at her. That detail had not been included in the newspaper article. "No, I didn't. That's terrible."

"So when we were told that someone in the island was responsible for his arrest…it just made us all so angry. I think we really needed someone to blame." She looked back down at her tea. They sat in silence for a long time. Eventually Hazel reached a hand halfway across the table.

"All right. But I swear to you, on my father's life, that despite my many problems with Philip Parris, neither I nor my dad had anything to do with his arrest. I despise the Nazis and all they stand for, and I would never have betrayed any local person to those monsters, no matter what they'd done. Now, I don't know whether or not you share your family's view. But if you do, you shouldn't be sat here drinking tea with me. I'm not going to report what I saw to the authorities, you have my word on that. But if you still think I'm your father's informant, you must leave right now."

For the longest moment, Hazel thought she was going to do just that. The only sound was the distant ticking of the café clock and the soft clinking of glasses as Cauvain continued to polish. Then the girl slowly poured milk into her cup, added sugar, stirred it thoroughly and took a long sip. Hazel fought an urge to laugh with relief. The kid sat back in her chair.

"So what happens now?"

Hazel smiled for the first time since they'd sat down. "I don't really know. I would certainly appreciate you talking to your family. Under the circumstances, I think that's the least I can ask."

She nodded. "I'll try." She pursed her lips. Hazel waited. "So what was it my dad was trading on the black market?"

Hazel swallowed a large gulp of tea. The kid was not as naive as she'd thought. "The usual things. Canned goods, brandy, tobacco. There were always people going in and out."

"Germans, too?"

Hazel nodded, blushing a little. "I saw a few in uniform, yes. I think they supplied him."

"If he was so friendly with them, how come they didn't turn a blind eye to the radio when it was reported?"

"Different sections, different people. And they couldn't afford to look lenient about radio possession—you know how obsessive they were. He was expendable, I imagine."

"But that's why you were angry with him, his collusion? That's what you argued about?"

Hazel hesitated. This kid was so fragile, she looked on the verge of tears. Any more information could be the final straw. "Yes. And the fact that he was becoming increasingly careless about his radio, inviting more people, forgetting to close the window. It put all of us in danger."

"But he wouldn't listen?"

"I don't think your father ever listened to anyone."

"My mum always told me he was a hero." A small but distinct sob suddenly burst from the girl's throat. Mr. Cauvain, concerned, glanced over but evidently decided it was not a good time to approach them. Hazel waited for her to blow her nose with a handkerchief she took from her sleeve. "I'm sorry," she spluttered finally. "I just feel as if I don't know anything anymore. Since Liberation Day we're all supposed to be happy, but everything's been turned upside down. I don't even know how I feel most of the time, except I'm always exhausted, and worried...sometimes I just wish I could run away from all of it." She bit her lip as soon as she finished speaking, as if to grab the words back, but then changed her mind. "Horst has asked me to marry him. And I just don't know what to do."

Hazel gazed at her, bemused and also filled with pity.

"Well. That's quite a quandary."

"I love him, but I could be thrown out of the island. And he'll probably be locked up for years. But then, the thought of never seeing him again..." She blew her nose again, a little harder this time. "I'm sorry. I shouldn't be saying all this to you. You've got your own problems."

"You noticed?" To Hazel's relief, she laughed a little, and Hazel laughed with her. Their eyes held each other's for a moment, and it felt comfortable. Then the girl drained her cup and put it back with a bang.

"You've been very kind. I'll talk to my mum and my uncle. Though I'm not sure it will do any good."

"Thank you," Hazel replied, and realized that she meant it.

"Thank you for the tea." She stood up to leave, and Hazel did the same. "By the way, I should have said, my name is Jean."

"Hello, Jean."

They smiled at each other again, then Jean turned and left, clanging the little bell on the door as she did so. Hazel watched her pass the window and disappear from view, the remains of her tea growing cold in her cup, and for the first time since leaving the Parrises' house, felt a warm rush that she had done the right thing. She also realized that these were the first kind words she'd had from anyone but her father in weeks, and it felt good.

7

Sawdust and wood shavings lay all over the landing floor. Her fingers were red, with a nasty blister on one thumb, and it had taken her the entire afternoon, struggling with her dad's old hand drill and some ancient screws that had seen better days. But she had done it. Now attached to the inside of her bedroom door was a slim metal bolt that slid into its casing perfectly. She pulled it back and forth several times, enjoying the clicking sound it made.

Jean stood back and examined her work with pride, thrilled by her renewed ownership of her room. Why had she not thought of it earlier? The answer had been staring her in the face. A deep rummage in the garden shed, still stuffed with bits and pieces from her father's shop, had unearthed everything she required. And when her mother had tutted and questioned the necessity, as Jean knew she would, she had delivered her well-rehearsed story that the wind was rattling her door at night and keeping her awake, adding that Eddie had too much on his plate to be troubled with such a trifling job. With a dustpan and brush, she swept the mess from the floor, a smile tweaking the corners of her mouth. She knew it would enrage her uncle, and that thought pleased her. She could no longer look at him without seeing him groping through her private drawer, his thick, stubby fingers touching the undergarments and his tongue lolling from his mouth with perverted pleasure, while the memory of him sitting on her bed kept sleep at bay on many nights. But tonight she could relax, for if her work angered him, she also knew he would not try to undo it. What possible reason could he give? She stroked the sleek black pin with her fingers. There was a dark pleasure in finding her own solution to this problem, executing it herself, and also—she had to admit it—in the notion that Hazel would probably approve.

Her mind drifted back to their meeting and that bizarre conversation in the café. She had replayed it in her brain on a continuous loop, questioning the wisdom. Blurting out her turmoil over Horst's proposal had astounded her as much as Hazel, and should it turn out she was wrong, that Hazel was the informant after all, she had volunteered dangerous ammunition. Yet she couldn't bring herself to believe that, nor could she regret her confession. Hazel's explanations had felt real and honest, and since sharing her own burden, a huge weight seemed to have lifted from Jean's body. It had been like talking to a friend, and Jean realized that, even with Daphne, it had been a long time since she had felt the security of real comradeship.

She had vowed on her journey home that she would never reveal the conversation to her family.

Downstairs, she heard the front door bang as Eddie returned, and the family convened in the kitchen for their evening meal. As always after a meeting with his solicitor, Eddie was grim-faced, muttering about the uselessness of this damn island and how disgracefully it was treating its returned evacuees. Jean watched him slop vegetable stew onto his plate with unnecessary force, while Violet encouraged him to take a bigger helping, barely leaving enough for anyone else. The gluttony, however, seemed to cheer him, and he nudged Violet as she ate.

"Fancy a game of rummy tonight, Vi?"

"Ooh, lovely. Just for matches, though."

"Afraid I'll clean you out?"

"Ha! You are a one, Eddie."

That laugh again. Jean watched her mother with a growing confusion. It seemed she had moved from intense grief to an entirely new mood in a shockingly short time. Jean picked at her food, her promise to Hazel tapping her on the shoulder, but with no idea how to broach the subject. She didn't have long to wait.

"Bumped into a chap in the Peirson earlier," Eddie spluttered through a mouthful of food.

Of course you did, Jean thought. No matter what crucial appointments Eddie had, there always seemed to be time to drink in the Peirson. "And he said that Le Tourneur woman could be in trouble with her school. Making the girls read weird books, apparently, that aren't on the syllabus."

Jean's back stiffened. Violet leaned in across the table.

"Really? Well, that's Communists for you. How'd he find out?"

"His daughter goes there. *And* he reckons that witch tried to grass *him* up to the Jerries, and all."

"No!"

"Said soldiers came round his warehouse one night looking for stolen goods—didn't find anything, luckily. But he reckons it was her who put them up to it."

"Why did he think it was her?" Jean's voice was tight.

"He'd had a row with her in the grocer's the week before—she accused him of pushing in the queue."

"That's hardly proof of her reporting him, though, is it?" Jean replied, ignoring her mother's dirty looks from across the table.

"All mounts up," Eddie shot back. "So I told this chap to make an official statement. Need to keep building up her file, see. And I bet a couple of others down there have got stories and all." He paused only to chew his way through a chunk of potato. "I reckon they'll be making an arrest any day."

"But we don't know that she was Dad's informant. Do we?" Jean pushed her bowl of stew away and felt the silence. It was the first time anyone had said the words. Both Eddie and her mother stopped eating.

"You what? Why you taking her side all of a sudden?"

"She says she didn't do it. You heard her yourself. And we've no actual evidence. I don't think it's fair to keep on persecuting her."

Violet sat back in her seat with a thud. "What's got into you? The woman rowed with your father, she wrote nasty letters...and she's mixed up with that J.D.M. lot. We know what troublemakers they are. Now we find out she's probably done it before. How much more do you need?"

"Exactly." Eddie snorted the word. "And anyway, there's no one else it could have been."

"Maybe one of his black-market contacts?" The words crashed onto the table like a dropped pot. Eddie's eyes shot immediately to Violet, who was staring at Jean as if she had just grown another head.

"I beg your pardon?"

"Come on, Mum, let's not pretend. I heard it from—"

Tom's name hovered on her lips, but she feared the repercussions "—someone in town. So I asked Aunt Beattie about it."

"Beattie said my Philip was a black marketeer?"

"No, but she didn't have to. It was obvious that she and Martin knew. And I understand that Dad was doing it for us, and that lots of people were at it. But it means he was probably working with some shifty people. He might have had German suppliers going in the back, where the radio was! Don't you think we should look into that, before we try to get an innocent woman imprisoned or deported?"

For a moment Jean thought she might have got through to them. The atmosphere was so thick she actually anticipated a discussion. Then Eddie slammed his hand down on the table, shaking the crockery.

"Do you have no respect for your elders? Why is what we say not good enough for you? And why you're listening to disgusting rumors about your father, I don't know."

"Mum?" Jean looked to her mother, pleading with her eyes. "You knew what Dad was up to, didn't you?"

Her mother straightened her body a good two inches in her seat and looked down her nose at her daughter. "I think you'd better wash your mouth out. And you'd better spend the evening in your room, young lady."

Jean sighed—it was hopeless. Her mother seemed to be disappearing further and further down a tunnel from which there was no return. Jean silently rose from the table and made her way upstairs. Just as she was about to close her bedroom door, she heard footsteps behind her and saw her uncle on the stairs. Jean took great pleasure in banging the door closed and sliding the bolt across with as much noise as she could make. He would know the score now. He would be livid but helpless. She expected to feel frightened but felt surprisingly calm.

Sitting down at her little desk, she took out a precious sheet of writing paper and tried to compose a letter to her brother, explaining what was going on in the family home and how things had changed since their father's death. But it was so, so long since she'd seen or spoken to Harry, she could no longer see his smiling face before her, or anticipate his response. She rewrote the letter three times but somehow couldn't find the right words. Eventually it dawned on her that Harry was not actually the person she wanted to talk to. And there was only one other who might be able to help her right now.

"Miss Fleury? Miss Fleury? If I could just have a minute of your time?" Hazel felt her cheeks flush pink as she was forced to canter along the corridor. She needed to overtake the headmistress's brisk march toward her private office before the woman disappeared inside like a cuckoo clock, the door slammed meaningfully shut. With an audible sigh, Fleury slowed and turned, clutching a pile of books to her chest like a shield.

"Yes, Miss Le Tourneur, what can I do for you?"

Hazel smiled awkwardly. "Would it be possible to speak in your office?"

Fleury glanced at her watch. "I have a meeting with a parent in five minutes. If it's important, we can discuss it now." So the old battle-ax was going to make this difficult for her. Hazel gathered herself and glanced about. There were several girls in twos and threes still milling through the narrow corridor who could easily listen in if they chose, a fact of which Fleury was certainly aware. Still, Hazel met the old woman's hawkish gaze, delivered over the top of tiny horn-rimmed spectacles which hardly seemed big enough for her eyes, and began her prepared speech.

"There are a number of girls in my class who have recently become quite unruly. Margaret Dupré, for one, and Barbara Ozouf have been particularly difficult."

Fleury twitched her heavily powdered nose. "Most students become fidgety toward the end of summer term. If you had been formally trained, you would know to expect that."

Hazel's teeth ground together at the back of her mouth. Her lack of formal teaching qualifications had been no barrier to her being offered this job during the Occupation, when they were desperate for anyone literate willing to fill the gaps left by evacuees. But it would be unwise to point that out just now.

"This is more than end of term high spirits. There's been some calling out, references to…well, rumors concerning my personal life, which are entirely untrue." She searched the head's eyes for a response but found none. "I was wondering if you might be able to offer some advice. When I first came here, you always said I should come directly to you with any issues." The hiatus that followed was painful. At the end of the corridor a girl shrieked in excitement at some comment from her friend, then clapped her hand over her mouth as she spotted the staff members only a few yards away, engaged in the adolescent pantomime of pretending to be diffident while at the same time vying for attention. Hazel threw them a sharp glance, then returned her attention to Fleury, who was still peering at her with a studiously vacant expression.

Finally she spoke. "I'm really not sure I can assist you. Maintaining discipline in the classroom is one of the skills teachers need to develop during their professional careers. I'm sorry that you seem to be struggling with it."

Hazel felt her head tilt back with shock. A traditional schoolmarm from the earlier part of the century, the woman had never shown her any warmth, but had never spoken as callously as this. For a moment she weighed the options, then decided she had little to lose. "Am I to take it, then, that you have also heard these same rumors?"

Fleury sniffed. "Rumors and gossip are neither perpetuated nor tolerated within this school."

"With respect, that is not what I asked you."

"Nevertheless, I think I have answered your question." Hazel saw the woman's eyes slide away to the door of her office, her intended escape at any moment. Clearly this would be her last opportunity.

"Miss Fleury, the Occupation has set terrible precedents of misinformation. There is vile suspicion between islanders now, I'm sure you're aware. I think it vital that in accordance with the principles of this school, we do not encourage blame or hostility toward innocent people." Another long interlude, filled with nothing but the sound of distant doors being slammed shut, and the even more distant voices of young girls singing outside in the street. Fleury shuffled her pile of books in a way that told Hazel the conversation was ending.

"I believe I have made my position quite clear. Good day, Miss Le Tourneur." And, as expected, she shot toward the magic door, through which no one ever passed without the obligatory "come" command, and shut it behind her.

Out on the sunny street, the hiss of summer wind in the trees, Hazel walked slowly. This time of the school year was meant to be a joyful one, with messages of gratitude from students and parents and the glow of personal achievement at another year well spent. She should be planning fun and relaxation for her own holidays, listing books to read and places to visit. Instead, a weight, heavy as silt, sat at the pit of her stomach. A web was closing around her, and the harder she fought, the more it seemed to tighten. For the thousandth time she recalled the moment she had chosen to lie for the Parris girl. She wanted to smack herself for being so soft, yet had no doubt that she would do the same thing again. There was something so vulnerable, so innocent about her, that in a strange way reminded her of Dottie. Was that what this was all about? Trying to replicate the sister that diphtheria had taken, perhaps save one soul in lieu of the one she had failed to protect? Whatever the truth of it, the girl had been in her mind often since their café conversation. Perhaps that was the reason why, as she turned into New Street and saw Jean Parris lurking sheepishly around the steps to the flats, she was not in the least surprised.

Jean perched awkwardly on the edge of the bed, clutching the cup of weak black tea to her chest and staring resolutely at her shoes. She told herself that her embarrassment sprang from being in the intimate space of a stranger's bedroom, never mind that of a woman designated her enemy. But in truth it was as much her shock at the surroundings, and the family's obvious poverty reflected in them. Hazel's makeshift bed, which Jean suspected was part of an old couch, was no more than a foot away from her father's. A few hanging garments were bunched together on a single metal rail, the rest pressed into a tiny chest of drawers at the foot of the beds. There was no other space for furniture, barely enough room for the ancient floral curtains to hang from their track, as was clear from the ugly bunching of the fabric as it met downward resistance. Jean had never thought much about her own family's class, except in comparison to Daphne's family. She had always thought of the Parrises as ordinary, and their terraced house was identical to the others on her street, but

Jean would never have been expected to share a room with her father, nor to put up with the stink of blocked drains that hung in the air throughout the whole apartment. She glanced at Hazel, embarrassed, as she sat down beside her on the bed.

"I'm sorry to force you in here," Hazel murmured. "Only my father does like his seat at the fireplace, and there's no-where else we can speak privately."

"Oh, that's all right. Thank you for the tea." Jean was grateful she had not been invited to sit in the little parlor, where the scrawny Le Tourneur father had greeted her with a frozen stare of rage as Hazel introduced her. Of course, he would know the whole story, so she could hardly expect any other reaction, but despite his obvious infirmity she did not feel safe around him. The two women sat in silence for a few moments, watching dust particles bob in the sunbeams. Jean tried to keep her eyes downward, but it was hard not to glance around at the Victorian wallpaper, peeling in the damper corners, and the mold at the base of the windows. As she held the saucerless cup, she noticed that Hazel was look-ing at her fingers.

"Your hands look sore."

"I've been charring for my aunt and uncle."

"Looks like they're getting their money's worth. What do they pay you?"

Jean almost choked on her tea. Wages was a topic that would never be allowed in her house. She had no idea how much money her father had made—legally or otherwise—and would never have thought to ask. But she could see no real reason not to reply.

"Three and six a week, for two mornings' work."

Hazel pulled a disapproving face. "Do they have money? Big house, plenty of everything?" Jean nodded. "You need to renegotiate." They sipped tea in silence for a moment. "I presume your family doesn't know you're here?"

"No. By the way, I tried to talk to them. But I'm afraid it's useless."

Hazel nodded. "I appreciate your efforts." She looked despondent, though, and Jean shrank into herself, ashamed.

"I really did try. I pointed out that there's no evidence against you, and it could easily be someone else."

"I'm afraid this isn't about evidence, or logic. After the last five years people feel lost, traumatized. They're seeking new certainties to comfort themselves. And I'm an easy target for their anger."

Jean shuffled uncomfortably on the bed. There was a metal spring of some kind poking up right under her bottom. How Hazel managed to sleep on this she had no idea.

"In what way?"

"I'm outspoken. People don't like that, especially in women. I gave your father a piece of my mind in public, not the way you're meant to behave. And I have connections to the Jersey Democratic Movement, so I'm viewed as suspicious anyway."

"You're a member?"

"Not anymore." She looked down at her hands, weighing her next remark. "But an association is enough, for some people." She looked at Jean pointedly. "You asked me yourself if I was a Communist."

Jean felt the color rise in her cheeks. Religion and politics were also forbidden subjects in her house, considered the height of bad manners. "I'm sorry."

"I don't regard it as an insult. I'd actually call myself a socialist, but some of the J.D.M. are Communists—like our Russian allies in the war. Others just want a fair deal, and securities like health care. Take my father—his illness is the main reason we live...well, that we aren't better off."

"What's wrong with him?"

"He has rheumatoid arthritis. It damages his joints and causes him terrible pain. Before the war they treated him regularly with an injection of a special gold, which helped a little, but of course nothing like that has been available in recent years."

"So he got worse because of the Occupation?"

"Yes, but I doubt it'll get much better now. Doctors and medicines cost so much, and we only have my wages."

"But you're a teacher?"

Hazel gave a wave of her hand. "Believe me, they don't pay me much."

"So why do you do it?"

"Satisfaction. It's fulfilling to see children learn and develop."

Jean considered this, remembering her favorite teacher as a child, the birdlike Miss Perchard. "When I was little, I wanted to be a primary school teacher."

"You still could be. England is desperate for teachers after the war."

She pulled a face. "I'm not clever enough to do anything like that."

"Nonsense. You don't have to be a genius, just enthusiastic and patient. I can see you being rather good with little ones."

Jean looked away to hide her pinking cheeks. Her mind was a flurry of thoughts. "So what the J.D.M. is actually asking for is fair wages and help when you're sick?"

"Those are their main concerns, yes."

"Then why does everyone hate them? Everyone in my family criticizes them all the time." She recalled her father at the kitchen table, tutting over his dinner at reports in the *Evening Post*, and recalled her uncle Martin's sneering remarks.

"People are constantly told that the poor are either lazy or stupid, or both. That's what the wealthy want you to think, so that nothing ever changes. Look at you, exploited by your own family."

Jean bridled instinctively. "I'm not exploited."

"They pay you badly. And how much do they expect you to do? Can you get your work done in the time?" Hazel pulled a wry face, and Jean stared down at her tea. It felt disloyal to her family to agree with this, to admit that the same thought had occurred to her.

"My mother got upset when I brought up Dad's black-market dealings. She seemed shocked that I knew. But I'm sure she's known for years, seems like most people did. I don't understand it."

Hazel frowned, staring at her feet. Jean saw that she was still wearing her Summerland clogs, despite the recent well-publicized arrival of women's footwear at De Gruchy's.

"If that's what you came here to talk about, I'm not comfortable saying much more about your father. I fear I may be harming your memories of him."

Jean put down her empty cup on the tiny table that separated the two beds. "I'm not really sure why I came. It's just, I've had no one to talk to for so long. I love my cousin, but I can't tell her about Horst in case…"

"In case she betrays you?" Jean nodded, aware of the irony. Hazel put her cup down, too, and sat back a little on the bed, pulling one foot up under her body to get comfortable. When the tension left her, she looked younger, and Jean realized she was really quite beautiful, her auburn hair coming loose from its bun and cascading around her porcelain white features. "Have you decided yet what you want to do?"

Jean shook her head. "No. But I have to decide before his boat sails on the first of September. Once he's in the English POW system it'll be impossible to find him. And if I don't accept now, he'll think I'm rejecting him. I'll be sending him off with nothing to hope for or look forward to."

"You said you loved him?"

"I do."

"So, what's stopping you? I accept you probably couldn't live here, there'll be strong feelings about the Germans in these islands for a long time. But it's a big world out there."

Jean gave a half shrug. "That's what Horst said. But…"

"Have you ever been out of Jersey? For a holiday?" Jean shook her head. "This is a beautiful island, but it's just a tiny dot on the map. My sister married an Englishman and lives in London now. I have a cousin who moved to France."

"My brother's family is in Chelmsford."

"Well, there you are."

"But this was a world war. We'd likely be hated wherever we lived." A deep sigh escaped her. "I can't imagine loving anyone else, though."

Hazel looked at her, her head inclined to one side. "I can't tell you what to do. But I do know one thing. If you want choices, you're going to need more than three and six a week." Jean laughed, but Hazel leaned closer. "Seriously. Women without their own money become trapped. You may have to take care of yourself, at least for a while." Jean frowned, considering this. She wasn't sure what "taking care of herself" would even mean in practice. All the girls she knew at school either still lived at home or were already married. And how did a single woman like herself acquire proper money? "I believe Summerland is still hiring," Hazel went on as if reading her mind. "I think their pay is fair." A small smile broke through. "You know, there's a J.D.M. rally at the weekend, in town. Why don't you go along, see for yourself what it's about?"

Jean wriggled. "I don't know."

"Worried you'll be spotted, labeled a rabble-rouser?"

"It's not that." But it was, and Jean knew that Hazel knew it, too.

"It's just a few speeches in the square. I promise no one will kidnap you or make you swear allegiance to the Bolsheviks." Despite herself, Jean found herself smiling back. "Tell you what, I'll come with you, if you like." Her lips pressed into a line of resolution that Jean couldn't understand. "I'm getting a little tired of being a victim myself."

The Royal Square was at its absolute best. Golden sunshine, dappling on the paving through the leafy chestnut trees, picked out the pale pink hue in the official granite buildings, while blobs of white cloud hung in a clean blue sky. A playful breeze freshened the heat of the day, and many men stood in shirtsleeves, jackets slung over shoulders, while the women—surprising in their number, Jean thought, though very much a minority—held their hats firmly on their heads, laughing. A makeshift podium had been set up on the north side, using a selection of old crates, and a few individuals stood at the back, conversing intensely. Considering what she'd imagined, it seemed quite a cheerful, normal-looking crowd, not so different from the one that had greeted the King and Queen. Jean recalled that day, squeezing through to the front with her mother, and realized with astonishment that it was barely two months ago. It felt more like two years.

Jean fingered her headscarf, stolen from her mother's wardrobe last night, to check it was still in place, and pushed the sunglasses, also her mother's, a bit further up her nose. She felt a little foolish, and Hazel's suppressed giggle when they met at the corner of Library Place had not gone unnoticed, but Jean reckoned that humiliation was worth the price of privacy. She could only imagine the row there'd be at home if one of Eddie's drinking chums recognized her at an event like this. And Hazel herself was wearing dark glasses and her hair swept up under a straw hat, which Jean calculated was meant for disguise. Jean found herself standing quite close to her, the same way one might huddle up to a tree in the rain, and returned Hazel's smile of encouragement as they waited for the speeches to begin.

As the first speaker was introduced by a young man using a megaphone, a section of the crowd broke into enthusiastic applause. An ordinary-looking chap with a long face and curly hair stepped up to take the device from him and raised his hand to encourage quiet.

"Thank you for coming today. It's good to see so many faces, familiar and new, because numbers is what we'll need in the coming months. I was told this week, on good authority, that there will be an election called toward the end of this year. And given the resistance we face from those currently in power—those for whom the current system works just fine, thank you very much—and even the local press, we are going to need the help of each and every one of you."

Jean looked toward Hazel in confusion. *The local press?* She knew that the German editions of the *Evening Post* had been full of lies and propaganda, but that was during the war. Surely now, in peacetime, newspapers simply reported straightforward facts? Behind her dark glasses, her eyebrows pulled together in a frown of concentration.

"And," the speaker continued, "should you be in any doubt how far up the system this resistance goes, I have been informed that our island Attorney General, together with the British Department for Public Prosecutions and the Home Office, no less, met recently to come up with a classification of what constitutes a collaborator." Jean and Hazel both instinctively glanced at each other, then immediately looked away. "In addition to the categories we might expect—fifth columnists, profiteers and so on—they have included, and I quote, *certain persons who sought to undermine the States administrations*." A murmur of disquiet went through the crowd. "That's right, my friends, they're talking about the likes of you and me. Anyone who had the audacity to challenge our leaders' decisions, who had the nerve to question whether those in power were doing right by their own people, at a time of national emergency. They're trying to put us in the same category as those villains who betrayed their king and country!"

The murmur became a rumble. Shouts of "shame" and "disgrace" popped up around the crowd. Once more, Jean and Hazel shared a look, but this time their eyes properly met behind their glasses, bound in recognition of each other's anxiety. The speaker took out some notes and began to talk about administrative reform of the States Assembly and a contributory scheme for old age pensions, but much of it went over Jean's head, partly because she had never heard most of these terms before, but also because she could not get his earlier remarks out of her mind. People in the British Home Office were at this moment casting her as an enemy. Even the people gathered here, these radical, freethinking rebels, considered people like her (and, without question, her father and Hazel) to be criminals. There had been no mention of any attempt to separate the guilty from the accused, or to consider degrees of fault.

"So, my friends," the speaker was saying, pushing his notes back into his pocket and preparing to make way for his successor, "I will finish with this. We must make our position crystal clear. It is no crime to complain about unfairness. There is a world of difference between responsible patriotic citizens who simply want a decent life, and the reprobates who betrayed this island. And we will not allow our good name to be smeared by anyone who tries to lump us in with them. Are you with me?" A huge cheer exploded around the square. Jean nudged Hazel, whose expression had now fallen into a sullen glare.

"I'm sorry. I think I've heard enough." Hazel nodded and without another word, they both turned and wove their way out of the crowd, gathering themselves in the furthest corner, where the square gave onto the top of Halkett Place. Jean turned to her.

"Do they know about the accusations against you?"

"Jean, you know what this island is like. Eventually, everyone knows everything about everybody." Jean felt a stab of guilt, but it was also the first time Hazel had used her name in conversation, and she liked the warmth it brought.

"Can we go now?"

They turned away to head toward the main street when a noise forced them to look back. Some kind of disturbance had broken out in the crowd, and both of them craned their necks to see the cause. For a moment it was hard to tell what was happening, then it became clear that a number of people had been struck with something and were shrieking with pain and indignation. On the opposite side of the square, by the churchyard, where just the other day she had sat with Tom Maloret, a small but robust group had rushed toward the J.D.M. crowd, hurling missiles. A victim hollered loudly, the side of his face colored scarlet, and for a terrible moment Jean thought he was bleeding. Then, as she peered more closely—they were a good two hundred yards away—she saw that it was the missile that was bright red. The man had been hit on the side of the head by a tomato. The attackers were grinning and cackling as they continued to grab handfuls of the sloppy, ancient fruits from a bag and pelt them into the crowd. Jean turned to Hazel.

"Who are they?"

Hazel stood on tiptoe, trying to get a better view. "I would say, from the way they're dressed, and the number of tomatoes they've got, they're probably farmers."

Jean turned back to look again, and that's when she saw him. Pink faced with glee, hurling tomatoes randomly into the protesters as if pitching balls at a fairground, he cut an unmistakably familiar figure. Jean emitted a soft cry of horror and disgust. Then, as some of the protesters recovered themselves and began to round on their attackers, the assailants turned and fled toward a smart, sparkling Bentley parked just off the square. When they'd hurled themselves into the vehicle in a scrambled heap of laughing, jeering chaos, the driver started the engine and the car raced away around the corner. The whole event was over as quickly as it had begun, and Jean was left staring after them, open-mouthed, Hazel watching her with some concern.

"Are you all right?"

"The one in the green jacket—that was my uncle Martin. The one I was telling you about, the one I work for."

Hazel sniffed and rubbed her nose vigorously. "The farmers hate the J.D.M. because they want better conditions for agricultural workers." Her voice softened a little. "I'm sorry. Can't be easy, seeing someone in your family behave like that."

Jean gave a little puff that was neither laughter nor despair. "He used to let me ride the pony on the farm. I've never seen him like that before."

They walked along the road toward the corner where they would part company, at which point Hazel turned to her.

"If you do decide to marry Horst, what do you see in your future? In a perfect world?"

Jean shrugged. "A nice little cottage somewhere. A garden. Maybe children."

"And if you don't marry him?" Jean shrugged again, realizing she had never given it much consideration. Getting through the Occupation had been her driving force for so long that such notions had simply never occurred to her. Hazel's head dipped to one side. "I think this war has shown the world what women are capable of. You're thoughtful, compassionate. I meant what I said. I think you'd make a good teacher."

Again, Jean found herself blushing. No one had ever suggested that she might be good at anything.

"I really have no idea what I might do. Sorry, that probably sounds foolish to you."

"It's not foolish. Much of what you held dear has been snatched away in a short time. Hard to plan your future when you have no certainty of your present." She touched Jean lightly on the arm. "I have to get back to my father. It's time for his medicine. But if you want to talk again, I'll be at the Italian café at five on Saturday." Jean nodded and watched her walk away, her tall thin frame disappearing down the street, and realized that a new idea was already forming in her mind. In fact, she wasn't sure why she hadn't thought of it before.

Her fingers shook as she placed the key in the lock and tried to turn it. As expected, it was stiff and resistant, clogged with the dirt and rust of so many months unused. She wiggled it determinedly, willing it to work, glancing about to see if anyone was watching. But the only eyes on her were those of the gulls perched on the nearby chimney pots, watching with beady disinterest as they ruffled their feathers in preparation for the first forage of the day. A few early risers passed in the distance on their way to work, and one or two figures could be seen at the windows of the apartments opposite, but they were busy with their own dawn activities and unlikely to notice a girl on the street opening up a shop. Even one that had sat empty and unused for eighteen months. And if they did—well, it was still her father's premises until the legal formalities disposed of it, and Jean could inform any challenger that she had a right of access. Although the furtiveness with which she had crept out of the house before sunrise told a different story.

Click. The key gave suddenly, and she was in. The bell over the door was no longer functional—perhaps the clapper had been stolen—so she was able to slip inside in virtual silence. The darkness was intense, all light blocked by the boards that had been nailed over the window just days after her dad's deportation. Using the shaft of daylight from the open door, she reached for the electric switch on the wall and pressed it downward. To her astonishment, a light bulb suspended at the back of the shop burst into life, and instantly the room appeared around her. The ancient, high wood counter, the cubbyholes behind it where her father spent his days searching for screws and bolts and washers, the display shelves on the opposite wall—almost entirely empty now, with only the occasional tool or upturned storage jar to indicate they had ever been used at all. A thick layer of dust lay on everything, cobwebs hung in most corners and Jean jumped as a scrabbling sound indicated a startled mouse. But as she closed the door, letting the dim yellow light color the entire space, the silence was stifling. Memories flooded in: occasional visits here as a child on Saturday mornings, watching her dad in his brown shop coat, chatting and joking with customers as he bagged their purchases and took their change. Her brother, Harry, up a ladder refilling jars of square-headed nuts, rolling his eyes at her father's constant corrections. The smell of wood and polish and turpentine. Her eyes filled as her father returned vividly to her, the first tangible memory she had had in weeks. But she wiped the tears away quickly. The place now smelled only of must and mold, and she was not here to reminisce. Tiptoeing in fear of disturbing the ghosts, she made her way through to the back room her father had used as storage.

The idea had taken firmer shape as she had walked home from the rally. Hazel was right—her confusion about a past she no longer understood or trusted was fogging her mind. Perhaps if she could find out more about her father's life within these walls, she would be able to make sense of things, perhaps even find a clue to his real betrayer. It might, at least, satisfy her raging curiosity. At a little after midnight, she had climbed onto the little stool in the pantry and taken the keys from their special place in the top-shelf jar. Then it was simply a matter of slipping out this morning before anyone else in the house was awake.

The back room of the shop was just as she remembered

it—a small space containing a filthy sink with cold running water, and a workbench for repairs. But if Jean had half hoped to find crates of illicit goods stacked in corners or lurking under drop cloths, she was to be disappointed. Of course, if such items had ever been here, they were long gone, looted along with the shop's stock. But her eyes fell on the small wooden door. The room upstairs, containing the tiny toilet cubicle! She had seen it once when she was very little. Tentatively she pulled the handle and wrenched the door open. A few wooden stairs went steeply around a corner and led into total darkness. At the bottom of the stairs was another light switch. She flipped it, but this time was not so lucky, and there was no way she was going to risk her neck by going up there in the pitch black. For a few moments Jean scrambled around the downstairs area, feeling about on the shelves behind the counter, reaching into the cubbyholes for anything that might help her, and was on the point of giving up when she opened the cupboard beneath the little sink. Right at the back of its shelf, clearly overlooked by the soldiers who routed the place, was a sliver of dirty soap next to an old cloth, a box of matches and—hallelujah—the stub of an ancient candle. She took the matches and the stub in her fingers, struck a light and lit the wick. As the golden flame flared, she smiled to herself; if ever she needed a sign that she was meant to do this, surely this was it?

As she started up the stairs, her heart raced. It was warm in the sealed-up building but she felt goose bumps creep up her arms as she took each tread slowly, afraid it might give way. At the top she looked to the left where, just as she recalled, was the toilet cubicle. The rest of the attic room was in complete blackness, and only as she held the tiny flame out did her eyes begin to adjust. Afterward, she wondered

what it was she had expected to find and could think of no
answer. But what she did see there had certainly never entered her head. For in the small space with sharply sloping
eaves there was only one piece of furniture. A single metal
bedstead with a slightly grubby single mattress.

8

"You must wear something nice. What about your blue dress?"

"It has moth holes."

"So put a cardie over the top. Blue is your color."

Horst likes me in yellow, Jean thought, and recalled a time the two of them had hidden among the rocks at Bouley Bay, her favorite yellow cardigan wrapped tightly around her. Oh, the promises they had made that day, the secrets they shared! Last night at midnight, Hazel's words skimming through her mind, she had decided she should marry him and hang everything else. Fifteen minutes later, she had decided it was a terrible idea. Right now she could hardly make a decision about what cup to pick from the dresser.

"I'm sure he won't even notice what I'm wearing."

Violet ignored her as she dropped a precious egg into the mixture and began to beat it. Jean stared at the stodgy brew—this flour was better than the almost-cement powder of Occupation but not by much—and thought of the entire week's ration of sugar Violet had just poured into it, despite Jean pointing out that it would mean a week of unsweetened tea for the whole household. But her mother was in no mood for listening today, no more than she was yesterday when Jean had fiercely opposed inviting Tom Maloret to tea.

The idea, of course, had come from Eddie, and the announcement, pitifully disguised as a casual notion, had been made over their evening meal last night. Eddie, it seemed, had bumped into Tom in town and had thought it "only polite, in the circumstances" to issue an invitation. Violet had immediately declared it a brilliant idea. Jean had fought it until she was exhausted, throwing up every excuse she could. It was an imposition on Tom's time, it was too soon in their "courtship" (Jean had spluttered the word), rationing was still too severe, she had no polish for her shoes. What she longed to say was that it was cruel and deceptive to imply a growing commitment that she did not feel, and even more monstrous for the Parris family to hold out a lantern toward a marriage proposal she had no intention of accepting, a family tea being a well-known light on this road. And, of course, there was the second, even worse agenda. Eddie clearly intended to pin Tom Maloret to a parlor chair and interrogate him about the current state of the Le Tourneur prosecution, demand to know why no arrests had been made. The poor man would find himself skewered by her family and trapped until they had satisfactory answers—although the irony of them also using Tom for their own ends did not escape her.

But neither Eddie nor Violet would take no for an answer, muttering tired, thought-free phrases about it being the done thing to meet one's daughter's beau and not letting the side down. In the end, Jean's only victory was a promise that no reference would be made to weddings, engagement rings or prospective grandchildren while Tom was in the house. Now Jean faced the prospect of an excruciating afternoon squashed in the parlor, not only with Tom but Eddie, too, a bunch of fools in a parody of a happy family. She told herself it would just be a couple of hours and that she had endured worse. If things went well, she might even be able to slip away by five to meet Hazel, a rendezvous she was keen to keep. But neither Hazel nor Horst was at the forefront of her mind today. Right now there was just one question that had lingered since her trip to New Street. She hovered awkwardly around the table, pretending to be tidying while her mother worked. Violet had always been happiest when she was baking, and now with a few basic ingredients available she was clearly starting to enjoy it again. Eddie was outside, dispatched by Violet to clean the front windows in honor of their guest's visit, and if his usual work speed was anything to go by, would probably be a while yet. Now was her opportunity.

"Mum, I went round to Dad's old shop the other day." Her mother was facing away from her, but she saw her shoulders tighten. "I didn't mention it before so as not to worry you. I just wanted to check the tap wasn't leaking or that pigeons hadn't got in."

"Really? You weren't snooping around looking for black-market goods, then? Because you shouldn't listen to rumors. Some people have nothing good to say about anyone."

Jean considered several answers before deciding to ignore this. "Everything looks fine in there, just a bit grubby. But I was a bit surprised by something I saw."

"What's that?" Violet's focus remained firmly on her mixture.

"I went up to that little room at the top, you know where I mean? I thought it would be empty."

"And?"

"And there was a bed. A single bed with a mattress. Suppose the Germans couldn't be bothered to drag it down that tiny staircase. But why would Dad keep a bed above the shop?" The words drifted like dust in the air. Violet continued to stand with her back to her, banging the mixture on the side of the bowl with her spoon to test its texture. Even with the egg and sugar and the few raisins she had found in the market, it was looking less than appetizing. Jean waited, but still nothing came back. "Mum, did you hear what I said?"

"Of course I heard. How do I know why there's a bed there? Maybe he was storing it for someone, selling it on."

"I thought that," Jean replied, "but no one stored anything for long during the Occupation, did they? If you didn't need it yourself, you bartered it straightaway."

"I told you I don't know." Violet's voice was full of tension.

"And anyway, we could have used it here. I asked for a new bed loads of times and was told they were impossible to get. If he had one sitting up there—"

The spoon went down with a bang, and her mother turned, anger spilling from her. "For heaven's sake, Jean, why do you have to go sneaking around up there? You should learn to keep your big nose out. It's none of your business."

Jean's insides chilled. "Why? What isn't my business?" Her mother pushed the mixing bowl away and it scraped across the table.

"Think you're so clever, don't you? Think you're the only one that knows anything. Well let me tell you, you know nothing, my girl. Nothing." Jean continued to stare at her, praying that Eddie wouldn't come back into the house. They were hovering on the precipice of something, and any interruption now would destroy it.

"I don't understand."

"You think I didn't know? You think I'm a fool? I was

married twenty-five years. Believe me, after that long, you know what's what."

"Mum…what are you saying?"

Her mother's eyes were brimming as if a dam were about to burst. "Do I have to spell it out?"

Jean's heart was banging in her chest. If the next sentence escaped her lips, it would be out in the world forever, and neither of them would ever be able to forget it. But the half-formed idea had been clanking around the inside of her head since she reached the top of that wooden staircase, and she had no power to stop it now.

"You mean, another woman?" The despair on her mother's face pushed her onward. "More than one?" The silence answered eloquently. "Oh, Mum, no! That can't be true?"

"That's what I thought, the first time. Till I got to recognize the signs."

"Signs?"

"After half a dozen, you know."

Jean lowered herself onto a chair. "I had no idea."

"'Course not, no one did. Think I'd let on something like that?"

"But you and Dad seemed so happy?"

"And that's what everyone will continue to think!" The snap in Violet's voice chilled her. "A happy devoted couple, that's how I want them to remember us. I mean, it was true, once."

"Are you saying you…you stopped loving him?"

Violet's squawk of laughter contained no mirth. "Love! You believe that's anything to do with marriage, you're a damn fool." She picked up the spoon again, the cake mixture the new victim of her anger. Jean stared at her, her parents' entire marriage now disintegrating in her head.

"Did you know who these women were?"

"No, didn't want to know. But I'll tell you this—I'd bet any money that one of them was that Hazel Le Tourneur."

All the oxygen seemed to leave the room. Jean reached out and grabbed a chair to sit on before her legs gave way. She remembered the warm touch of Hazel's hand on her arm. This was too alarming, too horrible to take in.

"Why? Why do you think it was her?"

Violet continued to attack the mixture in the bowl, though there was no pretense that she was any longer thinking about her cakes.

"Woman's intuition. He was always asking her to those radio parties. She was round there all the time."

"But so were lots of other people…and we know that he and Hazel fell out?"

"Well, can't you figure it out? He obviously broke it off, she threw a paddy. That's why she informed on him, get her own back." She wiped her eyes with the back of her hand and turned to face Jean. Composure was slowly returning, stiffening her body and tightening the line of her mouth. "And that's what your dad got for playing around. But no use crying about it. Take my advice, don't expect anything from a marriage, and you won't be disappointed. Like me. Like Eddie."

Jean, still trying to absorb the impact of all this new information, just managed to latch on to this vital coda.

"Why, what's happened to Eddie and Maureen?"

"That woman's been no proper wife to him. Serve her right if she never saw him again." Jean felt her stomach sink. Maureen's return was a hope she still clung to, despite the glum indications.

"So is she coming back or not?"

"It's none of our business what they do." Her eyes flickered away from Jean, giving Jean the distinct impression her mother was keeping something from her. "Anyway, that's already far more than you need to know. And not a word of any of this to Eddie if you know what's good for you." The drawbridge was being tightly wound up, and Jean knew right then that she would never get her mother to speak of this again. "Now, I need to get these in the oven, and you need to get changed—we've got a guest arriving in under an hour. Chop-chop."

But for several moments Jean didn't move. She just sat, watching her mother drop blobs of mixture onto a baking tray while determinedly humming the melody of an ancient hymn, as if such desperate theater could wipe out the horror of the last five minutes. Then, for want of anything else to do, Jean slowly rose, made her way upstairs and put on her moth-holed blue dress, a cardie over the top. At the same time, she touched the gold locket her father had given her all those years ago. For the first time since her twelfth birthday, she considered removing it, but there were still too many questions to answer. The only thing she felt certain of now was that she could be sure of nothing anymore.

"So what exactly is the official position now, Mr. Maloret?"

"Please, call me Tom."

"Tom. And do help yourself to a rock cake."

The four of them were perched like crows in the front room, the furniture around them gleaming with freshly applied polish. The old wooden clock, a wedding present her mother had always treasured, ticked too loudly on the mantelpiece. Tom balanced nervously on the edge of the easy chair, while Violet poured milk into her best cups from her favorite Worcester jug, which she always saved for occasions.

The poor man had been in the house less than four minutes and already the questioning had begun. Jean watched Violet calmly wipe a rogue drip from the lip of the jug, smiling at her guest and smoothing down napkins as if all was right with the world, and marveled at her composure. Yet perhaps it wasn't so surprising, Jean considered, given how much practice she must have had.

Jean herself was having difficulty keeping still in her seat. Anger and confusion fogged her brain; left to her own devices she would run through the room pushing over chairs and smashing ornaments. In her head she found herself flipping back through a hundred memories, ordinary domestic days in this very house, recoloring each one with this new poison crayon. How often had her father returned from work, slinging his hat casually onto the hallstand, with the perfume of another woman still clinging to his collar? How often had her mother served the family their tea, smiling and chatting about the prices in the market, while underneath rage and suspicion barreled through her stomach as she imagined another woman's arms around her husband and sordid fumblings on that filthy little bed? Jean thought of her parents strolling together through the park, discussing the news of the day over the paper—yes, and that Christmas, dancing together to an old jazz tune—and realigned every picture as a lie. So, their entire marriage had been a pantomime, a fake! A facade of cups of tea and washing up and chats about children's shoes, while beyond closed doors another life churned and heaved, stinging and scarring but never talked about. Perhaps her mother was right, and a marriage to Horst would end up just the same.

Worst of all...Jean's bowels complained as she thought of it...was her mother right about Hazel? Had it been Hazel's soft red hair tossed back over that stained striped mattress, her pale fingers beneath his shirt? Had Jean inadvertently initiated a friendship with her father's mistress? For a friendship was what she would have to call it now. She glanced at the clock—she had nearly two hours to decide if she wanted to meet with her later. But did she still want to go, and what would she say? She took a deep breath and tried to force herself back into the room.

"Well," Tom was saying, taking tiny bites of his cake so as not to speak with his mouth full, "it's difficult for the authorities. We have a number of similar cases, where a family is sure that a certain party is responsible for a crime of betrayal. But if that party denies the charge, and we have no evidence, it's very difficult to prove."

"But listen here." Eddie rose to his usual position in front of the fireplace, legs apart and cup placed on the mantelpiece even though Violet had asked him many times not to, rubbing the end of his nose with his palm. "We know there's a number of cases already been passed up to London for prosecution. And that chap who just came over, the Director of Public Prosecutions, he said he's looking into some cases personally. So, seems to me things can be moved along, if there's the will."

Tom took a quick swig of tea to wash down his mouthful before replying. From her own cake, Jean knew it was partly the dryness—they had come out of the oven the texture of a sweet, stale loaf—but she could also tell that he was trying to buy himself thinking time. She wondered whether he had anticipated this interrogation when he accepted the invitation, and whether he could tell that she was hardly listening. Why did the poor fool keep coming back for more? She cursed herself for ever involving him in this mesh of deceit.

"But it's not yet decided what will happen to those people either," Tom went on. "There's no law on the statute book with which to charge them. Other than treason, of course."

"What's wrong with treason? Sounds right to me," Violet chipped in. Jean dropped her head, shocked by her mother's hypocrisy. Had her father returned from prison alive, he would very likely be one of the accused. Or did her mother hate her father so much she would have willingly seen him charged? She wondered what Tom was making of this.

"It carries the death penalty." Tom's voice was soft, walking the line between stating facts and impertinence toward his hosts. "The last thing the British government wants to do at the end of a long and painful war is start hanging its own citizens."

Jean pictured Hazel strung up on a gallows, a thick rope around her neck. She pictured herself hanging next to her. A spike of vomit rose up her throat.

"Why not?" Eddie demanded. "Collaborators got people killed. Plenty of us think hanging's an excellent punishment."

"Eddie!" Jean's mother's voice was sharp enough, for once, to pull Eddie back. Perhaps she was thinking of her late husband after all, or simply viewed capital punishment as an unsuitable topic for teatime. Tom placed the little plate with his half-eaten cake back on the occasional table.

"I fully appreciate your strength of feeling, Mr. Parris. But the fact is that if you're going to execute people, you need to be absolutely sure you've got the right ones, which in most cases is impossible. Plus, the British would then have to apply the same punishment to their own quislings and profiteers. Include them, and you could be talking thousands of cases." He played awkwardly with his cuffs beneath the sleeves of his suit. It was the same one he had worn in the office the first day they'd met, the one he'd worn to the Pav dance, and was frayed around the seams. "The other factor," Tom continued, "is that, from what I understand, there are certain... hesitancies in London around the whole issue of Channel Island collaborators."

Jean's eyes drifted to the window. The parlor was dim and stuffy and forced her to take huge in-breaths to get enough oxygen. Outside was freshness and sunshine, and she longed to be out in it, out among the strolling couples and playing children. She wanted to take great gulps of air and think about what she had learned today, not suffocate in this hideous chatter about collaborators and executions.

"What do you mean, hesitancies?" Eddie's voice droned on.

"The British government never wanted the Channel Islands to be abandoned to the Germans. Now the war's over, there's a lot of pressure to—well, put the whole episode behind them, so to speak."

"You mean, the British are ashamed for letting Jerry just walk in here?" Violet's eyes widened with indignation. "Well, so they should be. And now they're not even compensating us. Not a penny for people like Eddie, who's lost his home."

"Actually," Tom retorted, "there was a meeting at the Home Office this week, and they accepted that the islands cannot meet their war debts without British help. There's talk of repairs compensation, too."

"Paid to individuals?" Eddie charged in.

Tom wriggled. "Probably not."

"So, let me get this straight." Eddie's lips were pursing and squeezing in a way that Jean had learned to dread. "People like me who lost everything won't actually get a penny? Any cash the Brits do cough up will go straight to you lot in the States, so we all know that's the last we'll see of it. Meanwhile the animal who got my brother sent to Germany to die, they're probably going to walk free so as we don't embarrass the Brits? That about the size of it?"

The hiatus that followed hummed with tension. Jean knew Tom was throwing her desperate appeals for help but kept her eyes firmly on her cake crumbs. She wished now that she'd fought harder against this invitation—it was unforgivable to torture this harmless young man this way. She felt the heat build in her body.

"Look, Mr….Tom… We want to put this episode behind us, too." Violet was leaning forward in her seat as if physically to create a bridge across the table. "No one wants to move on more than us. But how can we, when those responsible for the death of my husband are still unpunished?"

"Exactly." Eddie's face was coloring its habitual red. "And you know what's going to happen if nothing gets done? People will take things into their own hands. What do you call it? Vigilantes. And I for one wouldn't blame them."

Tom put down his cup and sat back in his seat. Jean sensed that he was growing weary of this but was clinging to his naturally courteous nature.

"Mr. Parris, I assure you, we in government are well aware of that risk. But behavior like that would be a disaster for this island." Jean's eyes darted to Eddie then back to Tom. Was he giving her uncle a warning? "We're talking about the breakdown of law and order, maybe hundreds of arrests. Believe me, no one would benefit from a situation like that, particularly the perpetrators. Anyway!" He pushed out a tired smile that convinced no one. "Perhaps we should talk about more cheerful matters. How are you finding supplies in the shops, Mrs. Parris? Are you managing to restock all right?"

To Jean's relief, Eddie stepped back and let Violet take the lead in some meaningless chatter. For the next hour they spoke of reliable greengrocers and favorite bathing spots around the island, Jean trying to rise to the occasion whenever Tom turned to her in a forlorn attempt to draw her in. At least her mother kept to her side of the bargain and did not at any point mention engagement rings or babies. But Jean's eyes kept drifting toward the street outside, and her troubled mind continued to jump around. Was her uncle thinking of taking personal revenge against the Le Tourneurs? Just yesterday Jean had listened at the parlor door while he and his cronies muttered about petitions and citizens' courts and "giving them what for." Eddie had already proved himself to be a pervert and a sneak. Given what she now knew, perhaps it ran in the family. Did that explain her own lying and manipulation? Was it in her genes? And still she kept coming back to Hazel, the woman she had entrusted with her most vital secret. If she had misjudged this…if her mother was right… if she had ruined her life for the sake of a confidante…

"What do you think?" Tom was asking with a beaming smile.

"I beg your pardon?"

"A little stroll up Vallée des Vaux? It's a lovely day, and it's really peaceful up there…"

"I'm sorry." Without any thought at all, Jean found herself on her feet. She had to get out of this room, immediately. It was almost five, and she was suddenly overcome with an insuppressible need to go to Hazel and challenge her. She could not get through the night not knowing the answer, and the thought of more empty hours of chitchat with Tom Maloret was more than she could bear. "I'm really sorry, Tom, but I've just remembered I have to return a library book."

"What are you talking about? They'll be shutting anytime

now?" Violet's eyes burned with accusation—she knew her daughter was lying. Jean's only option was to pretend she hadn't spoken and continue toward the door.

Tom shrugged a little. "All right, let me accompany you…?"

"No, really. Not necessary." Her voice was shrill and unnatural, and she could see both Eddie and her mother glaring at her. But the force within her was too strong to resist. "It's been lovely seeing you, Tom. Perhaps we could have lunch again in a week or two. Have a safe trip home." And she was out of the parlor and through the front door before anyone could stop her.

It was cold for December, and the dank gloom matched the mood of everyone in the town. All day long, locals had queued at any shop that purported to sell firewood, no matter how damp or green, in the hope of a little heat and comfort over the approaching season. Skinny, hungry children gazed despondently in shop windows devoid of toys, dreaming of racing cars and dolls their elder siblings had received from Santa in happier Christmases—proper Christmases, before Occupation. In the late morning an Allied plane flew high above the island to write a giant V in smoke before disappearing back into the blue, untouched by frantic antiaircraft fire; it had caused a stir of excitement in the streets and was widely regarded as a festive gift from Mr. Churchill. But Hazel merely watched it with dispassionate eyes, thinking that an airdrop of food or even information leaflets would have been more warmly received. It had been eighteen months without any reliable news of the war's progress, other than the gossip one could pick up at the market or the occasional invitation to Mr. Parris's wireless parties. And clearly she would not be attending any more of those.

Dinner was a meager affair. She had managed to find a scabby

Savoy cabbage at one stall, and they still had two decent-sized po-
tatoes left, but without butter or salt Hazel struggled to create any-
thing close to an appetizing meal. She watched her father ease the
food into his mouth a little at a time, noting that his fingers looked
more bent and useless around his spoon each day, knowing that the
cold was only making it worse but nervous about using their last burn-
able log. "Damn this war," she muttered to herself as she washed the
dishes in cold water. How much longer was anyone supposed to put
up with this misery?

The muffled sound from through the wall, a regular event every
Thursday evening, started a little earlier than usual. The first time
she had heard it, about a year before, she had not been entirely sure
what it was; having no personal experience and no recollection of simi-
lar sounds from her parents' bedroom, she found the rhythmic bang-
ing and moaning quite confusing. But her father's mortified reaction
soon made it clear what was going on. To cover their embarrassment,
they had quickly established a way to cope with these weekly inter-
ruptions: Hazel rapidly placing a record on the wind-up gramophone
and playing it over and over at full volume until the sound ended.
Tonight, though, as she raised the needle to place it at the start again,
she became aware of a new and different noise. It was the sound of
a man and woman having a furious argument. The words were too
muffled to make out, but there was no denying the emotion and vit-
riol, particularly on the woman's side.

"What's all that?" Her father was upright in his fireside chair,
his face a picture of concentration.

"Trouble in paradise?" Hazel quipped, sitting in the other chair
to listen. The moral outrage they had felt when Parris had first begun
his weekly antics had faded over the months into dark little jokes and
ironic remarks. "Maybe his wife's found out."

"Maybe he wants too much money for his black-market tunny
fish." They both giggled at that, but both were still listening intently.

"I could put a glass against the wall?" Hazel suggested.

"No, behave. Just because he's got the morals of an alley cat doesn't mean we have to join him."

"But I need to hear her voice. I want to know if she's German."

"Why are you so convinced she is?"

"That coat she always wears, the dark green one with the velvet collar. It looks European, nineteen twenties. I used to see them in magazines. You can't buy coats like that in Jersey. You couldn't even before the war."

"Well, wouldn't be the first Jerry to spend time round there, now, would it?" her father sallied.

The shouting ended as abruptly as it had begun, and they listened as feet clattered down the stairs. Quick as a cat, Hazel rushed to the rear window. As usual, she got a good look at the back of the woman in her green coat and tightly tied headscarf as she slammed the rear door and marched out, letting the yard door bang behind her. It was infuriating to be so close, but never at the right angle to see the woman's face. But this time a single, spat word floated up, loud enough to penetrate: "Schwein!"

Hazel dropped the curtain back into place and turned back to her father.

"Well, I think that answers my question. But I don't think we're going to see her again."

"Won't take him long to find a replacement." Her father pulled a face he usually saved for Hitler and Lord Haw-Haw. "Men like that, honestly, they want a beating. No respect."

The days ground on, slow and dark. The old year gave way to the new, chilly and treatless, and Hazel and her father plodded on with their dull vegetable stews and daily searches for firewood. But they congratulated themselves on their accurate prediction, for the mysterious woman in the green coat never appeared at the shop again, and apart from an obvious bad temper often taken out on his customers,

Parris continued as before, opening the shutters at nine each morning and closing each day at five. It was in the early days of January, just after the start of the new school term, that Hazel was forced to the shop to make an essential purchase. On that afternoon she found Parris on the pavement brushing down the awning.

"Don't suppose you have any putty for a loose windowpane?"

The smile with which he turned to her made her feel a little queasy. "I can mix you something up that will do the job. Pop over tonight and pick it up."

"Tonight?"

"We can listen to the news at the same time."

Hazel took a step back and threw him her darkest look. "I don't think so. Not after the last time."

His look of mock innocence enraged her. "You're not still upset about that? I told you it was just a misunderstanding."

"There's little to misunderstand about a hand on my leg, Mr. Parris. Nor the suggestions you made to my late sister, who by the way was only sixteen years old at the time."

His face clouded and he took a step toward her. Hazel was grateful they were outside and not in the darkened privacy of the shop.

"Now listen here. You go spreading lies about me…"

"Lies? My father and I heard you every week through the wall of our flat. Never mind the black-market goods that German corporal delivers to your yard. Your other customers may consider you a pillar of the community, Mr. Parris, but I'm afraid we know rather better."

The rest of the conversation, when Hazel tried to recall it, was something of a blur, with Parris shouting and waving his arms threateningly, telling her that she and her idiot father could whistle for paraffin in future and that if she ever repeated her slanders she would know all about it. Hazel had held her own for several minutes before running back to the flat, hiding her anxious breathing and reddened cheeks from her father for fear of upsetting him. Two weeks later, she

had heard of Parris's arrest from a neighbor and, in all honesty, felt
nothing but a wave of relief. The windowpane had eventually fallen
from its frame and smashed in the yard below, the space stuffed with
the torn-out sleeve of a disintegrating jacket for what Hazel assumed
would be the rest of the war. And each time she looked at it, she heard
Parris's voice in her head, and entertained the uncharitable thought
that he had got exactly what he deserved.

Jean sat perfectly still, her fingers around the pretty Italian glass of water provided for her by Mr. Cauvain. Hazel's face was taut and strained.

"You can see why I didn't want to tell you any of this. But if your mother believes I was one of Philip Parris's conquests… well, you at least should know the truth."

Jean stared into the glass, trying to absorb the shock waves. Her father. The hero. Daddy with the ice creams and the Christmas presents, having relations with a German woman on that filthy bed above the shop. Every week for a year, on the Thursday nights he told them he was stocktaking. Most likely one of the young secretaries or translators the Jerries had shipped over at the height of the garrison. While all that time she had tortured herself with guilt for her chaste, loving meetings with Horst on the beaches and in the woodlands. She could not name the emotions running through her at this moment.

"Have you told anyone else about this? The officers who interviewed you, the Civil Affairs Unit?"

Hazel shook her head. "I told them about the illicit trading, not about this."

"Why not? That woman must have known about the radio—she was probably the one who reported it. That's one thing my mother did get right. Tell them about her, and you're off the hook?"

Hazel offered a humorless smile. "I intended to tell them. But they were so skeptical about the first part of my account, it seemed pointless to make *more* accusations I couldn't prove. Now it's too late. It would just look as if I'm throwing dirt in self-defense."

"If we could find that woman…?"

"She's most likely been back in Germany for months."

"Could you get your father to back up your story?"

"He'd be seen as a sick old man saying anything to protect his daughter. Once people have marked you as the enemy, it's hard to change their minds." She sat in silence while Cauvain topped up their water glasses. Jean threw him a smile of gratitude, then he returned to his counter. For a while neither of them spoke. Jean ran a hand through her hair.

"I do have some news for you. This chap who works in the States offices…" She considered explaining her relationship with Tom but realized how humiliating it would be to say it aloud. "He says there's no law to prosecute collaborators. So at least they can't put you in jail."

Hazel's sarcastic cackle shocked her.

"Oh, Jean. They don't need to prosecute. They'll just ostracize us. Work, shopping, social events. In classical times they called it banishment. But it turns out you don't need to send people away—you can banish them perfectly well in their own homes." She nodded to their host, who was studiously wiping unused wineglasses, and gestured around the room. "You see anyone in here since Liberation? Mr. Cauvain told me he initially refused to serve Germans but was threatened with imprisonment. His friend Mario, the original owner, only left Italy to get away from Mussolini, thought he could make a decent life for himself here. But no one's interested in the truth. They just want someone to punch."

"It won't be that bad for you, surely? I mean, in time...?"

"Jean, I was sacked from my teaching position this week."

Jean stared. She felt the blood drain from her face. "No!"

"Services no longer required. They're saying they want staff with formal qualifications now the war is over. But we both know the real reason."

Jean reached across the table and touched her arm. "I'm so sorry. How will you manage?"

"I'll figure something out." But the hopelessness leaked out of her.

"This is terrible. And my family is responsible."

Hazel shrugged. "My employers chose to believe the rumors."

"What if I talked to the school? Tell them they've made a mistake?"

"I appreciate the offer, but it's too late for that."

"Can I at least help out with money?"

Hazel gave an ironic laugh. "On your three and six a week?"

"But you need food, and medicine for your dad." With a sudden flash of inspiration, Jean lifted her hands behind her neck and undid her father's gold locket. "Here. This has to be worth something, it's eighteen-karat gold."

Hazel bristled as the locket was thrust at her over the table. "No, I couldn't."

"Take it. It was a gift from him—I don't want it anymore."

Reluctantly Hazel took it, examining it in the palm of her hand. Jean wasn't sure but suspected she could see a wetness in her eyes. "Thank you. That's...very kind." She peered at the engraved heart. "It's beautiful, so tiny. I'm scared I'll lose it."

"The safest thing is probably to wear it."

Hazel hesitated, then raised her arms to clip it around her own neck. Again, they shared a small but meaningful smile.

And then it happened.

Facing the rear of the café, Jean didn't see the pane of glass shatter and fall. All she knew of it was the almighty crack as the brick came through the window. By the time she turned her head, the floor in the front half of the café was a glittering pool of jagged shapes and shards, heaped like a chaotic treasure chest beneath the wooden frame, spilling across toward their table. For several seconds no one moved; Jean, Hazel and the owner stayed rooted, staring at the shimmering rubble and listening to the sound of feet sprinting down the street. By the time Cauvain had recovered himself and rushed outside, his directionless panic and frantic glances told Jean that the perpetrators had long disappeared. Hazel leaned across to touch her arm.

"Are you all right?"

Jean glanced down and was astonished to see the lower half of her legs ribboned with blood.

"Oh, dear Lord, what happened?" Violet's hand flew to her mouth as the young constable escorted Jean into the hallway. Jean gave her mother the broadest, most relaxed smile she could manage, accompanied by a dismissive wave of her hand.

"I'm fine, Mum, don't make a fuss. It's just a few cuts and grazes." She touched her mother's arm to enforce the point, even though a few of the lacerations were still smarting badly, and the blood was stubbornly pushing through a couple of the bandages donated from the café's first aid box. "Someone threw a brick through a window and I caught some of the glass. But I'm all patched up, and there's no harm done."

"What window? You said you was going to the library!" Violet flapped and fussed around her, peering at the one small cut on her chin before bending down to examine her legs. "Poor Tom, he waited half an hour for you to come back. Mind, I'm glad he's not here to see you in this state." Jean reflected on the irony that her mother's concern for her health was largely to do with the potential damage to her marital prospects.

"I'll apologize to him tomorrow. Right now I need a sit-down and a cup of tea."

"But where were you? Where did this happen?"

Jean opened her mouth to give the answer she had hastily prepared on the way home, but she had not reckoned with the exhilarated policeman, who had insisted on accompanying her back despite her protestations. Now it seemed he was determined to grab his slice of the excitement.

"It was an Italian café, ma'am. Much maligned for its Jerry clientele during the Occupation, hence the attack." He straightened a little as he delivered the words, delighted to be part of a real criminal event. "But we'll find whoever did it. Luckily the place was empty apart from your daughter and her friend, and like she says, nothing worse than cuts and grazes."

"See, Mum, this is what Tom was talking about," Jean jumped in, a rapid attempt at deflection. "When people start taking things into their own hands, people get hurt." But it was already too late. Her mother had latched on to the key words and was already peering at her with suspicion.

"An Italian café? What were you doing in a place like that? Who were you with?"

Jean felt her stomach sink. "No one you know. Now how about that tea?"

"Someone from school?"

"Just a friend, it doesn't matter."

"What was her name?"

"Mum, can I just go and sit down?"

"You'd better not be two-timing young Tom!?"

"Hazel Le Tourneur was the name, ma'am. Also received only minor injuries." The constable, out of Jean's eyeline, had whipped out a small notebook and leafed through his notes to find the correct information. He beamed at his own professionalism and perceived helpfulness, oblivious to the acrimonious look Jean was throwing his way. "And both ladies have provided as much information as they can. We'll let you know soon as we make an arrest. Well, now that the young lady's safely home, I'll leave you to it." He gave a little nod and backed out of the open doorway, utterly unaware of the grenade he had tossed into the house. Violet slammed the door behind him with unnecessary force. At that moment Jean saw Eddie coming down the stairs into the hallway.

"What was that about an attack? Was that a policeman?" He looked flushed, and Jean suspected he'd already sneaked a bottle of beer since Tom's departure. He took in Jean's bandaged legs. "What's happened?"

"I'll tell you what's happened." Violet's hands were now firmly on her hips. "This one's only been sitting in Italian cafés with that Hazel Le Tourneur, almost getting herself killed."

Eddie slowly moved toward her. Jean began a mental calculation as to whether or not she could rely on her mother's protection in the next few minutes, and decided it was unlikely.

"She's been what?"

The controlled anger was worse than any tantrum. Unprepared for a battle, Jean leaned heavily against the banister, trying to dredge up the strength to fight. Her legs were now throbbing at the sites of the deepest cuts, and feelings of lightheadedness came in waves. The lovely nurse at the café, so fortunately passing on her way home from her hospital shift, had told her it was probably shock. As she knelt before Jean and Hazel, dabbing at their wounds with iodine spotted onto Mr. Cauvain's cleanest napkins, she had insisted they should go home and rest for the remainder of the evening. Right now, that was exactly what Jean wanted to do, but Eddie was already warming the argument like clay in his thick fingers. She struggled to pull herself upright, sensing that to yield now would be a mistake. But she had no energy for further lies.

"Yes, I met Hazel. She told me she's been fired from her job because of our accusations." And so much more, Jean wanted to add, but what was the point? Neither Eddie nor her mother would accept anything that came from Hazel's lips, even if Violet suspected in her heart that it was true. And beneath lurked the fear that her mother might drop dead on the spot if she discovered that her husband's lover had been a Jerry tart.

"I knew it!" Eddie growled. "That evil little bitch has got to you, hasn't she? Ever since she wrote you that note, you've constantly taken her side."

Jean cursed the tangle she had pulled tighter around herself. But she could feel strength rise with her indignation.

"Just listen, please. I've got to know her, and I don't believe she's guilty. I know you're upset and angry about Dad. I am, too. But all we're doing is ruining a good person's life, while the real informant…" The words whirled up like a typhoon, but she beat them back down. "The real informant will never face justice." She looked to her mother in the vain hope of a shadow of understanding. But her mother was staring at her throat.

"What happened to your locket?"

Jean felt the last air leave her sails. "I gave it to her. Her father needs medicine."

Violet gave a little cry and clutched at her own neck with both hands. What emotions she must juggle, Jean thought, to find such indignation on behalf of a man she resented so deeply. But Eddie was right in front of her now, his hot breath on her face.

"So not only have you sided against us with this woman, but you're now giving her stuff?" Jean said nothing. Even a simple *yes*, she calculated, would be seen as belligerent. "And," Eddie bulldozed on, "you go with her to a place run by *other* collaborators?"

"Mr. Cauvain hated the Germans! And the owner only came here to escape Mussolini!" She regretted it as soon as it was out. All it achieved was to lift the lid on her uncle's simmering rage.

"My God, no wonder this island's in the state it is! Locals running businesses for bloody foreigners, a government that lets every bastard collaborator go free! But the cops…the cops won't arrest them, will they? They'll go after the locals who want them out! Regular blokes standing up for what's right, they'll be happy to chuck them in jail!"

His arms were flailing loose in the dimming light of the hall, as if to batter the many people who'd assaulted him— the Nazis, the looters, the solicitors and officials, his wife and now his brother's daughter. For a moment it looked as if the fury might tip over into agony and he might fall weeping to his knees. But, instead, he pushed past the two of them and stormed out into the street. Within five minutes, Jean reckoned, he would be back in the Peirson pub, demanding comfort and confirmation from his rabble of pals, gulping down the booze that both fueled and calmed his wounded heart.

As the door slammed, Violet looked at her daughter with distaste, shook her head, then turned and walked purposefully up the stairs, slamming her bedroom door behind her. Jean put out a hand toward the banister to steady herself, realizing that she felt quite faint, and slumped down on the bottom stair with her head between her knees. As her equilibrium slowly returned, she looked down at the bright red spots permeating the bandages, wondering if her wounds would scar. She wiped the sweat from her forehead and sat back, squinting against the final shafts of sunlight from the glass panel above the door. She was exhausted, shaken and utterly disillusioned. But through the wretchedness she realized that she had come to a decision.

Her life until now had been run on presumption and a fear of doing wrong. But around her, the world had been operating on different rules. Now it was clear that she had nothing to live up to, and nothing to lose. Whatever challenges it might bring, her future was now entirely clear. She, Jean Parris, was going to marry Horst.

9

"So," Beattie announced in a businesslike tone, "we'll set the buffet in the dining room, keep the kitchen clear for preparing food. I'm going to speak to Batterick's tomorrow, see about fresh crabs for sandwiches. The rest will have to be tinned sardines or corned beef."

Jean, who sometimes felt invisible to her aunt, and even to Daphne, while she was performing her cleaning duties, continued to mop the kitchen floor. Beattie and Daphne were sitting at the table with a notepad, making a long list of "to-dos" for Daphne's party; the big twenty-first event was now fast approaching, and its planning seemed to have taken over the entire household. Jean let the mop knock into the legs of the chairs a couple of times to let them know that they were in her way, but neither of them seemed to notice.

"How many crabs do you think we can get?" Daphne asked her mother.

"Well, they're not rationed, but he has a lot of regulars, so we'll have to put an order in. I reckon we might get away with six. Have you worked out a final guest list?"

"If the Rabets come from St Mary, I make that forty."

Jean's mop stopped momentarily on its journey across the flagstones. Forty people at a private party? And six crabs for a single day? In her house, one was a treat. She thought of Hazel and the locket she would need to sell in order to get money for food, and realized she was gripping the mop a little too tightly.

"We'll need to see that chap your dad knows about some extra sugar for the cake," Beattie went on. "And drinks. Old Jean-Paul has offered a barrel of cider."

"Daddy says we should try and get some champagne."

Beattie drew herself up. "Champagne?! Your dad and I didn't even have that for our wedding anniversary!"

"He says you're only twenty-one once."

Sullen-faced, Beattie wrote it down. "I'll see what I can get in town. Need to go in next week anyway."

"What for? Is it my present?" Daphne's eyes sparkled mischievously. Jean's gaze drifted toward the two of them. All this, and Daphne was getting a present on top? When it came to his daughter, it seemed Martin was incapable of saying no.

"I've told you, that's a secret. Now run upstairs and see if I need more thread for your dress."

Jean watched her cousin scamper upstairs excitedly, her glossy black mane flying behind her, while Beattie licked her pencil and wrote down random thoughts as they occurred. Both women had expressed concern about the state of Jean's legs when she arrived this morning, but they had readily accepted her story about falling in a patch of brambles. Beattie had asked if she felt well enough to work but had not removed any items from her list of chores. Jean herself had been unsure this morning, still in some pain and her fingers trembling as she relived the moment of the cascading glass. But the atmosphere at home was still tangibly poisonous, her mother having risen with the sun, breakfasted and returned to her bedroom before Jean was awake, and as she did not want to lose a day's pay, she decided on balance she was better off going to Les Renoncules. She dragged herself to the Weighbridge to get the bus, staggered through the lanes to the farm and knuckled down to blacking the kitchen range before starting on the floors. But as she worked, barbed, caustic notions grew through her mind like knotweed. It seemed that Hazel's revelations last night, and her consequent epiphany, had cracked open a vault to new and rebellious thoughts.

Plunging the mop into the old tin bucket, she found herself wondering what Daphne would consider to be the worst day of her life. Other than the day that German bombs fell in the harbor, Jean's reckoning was that her cousin's life had been completely devoid of trauma. Ever since Martin had taken a picture of her perched on her rocking horse with his old box Brownie camera and placed the photograph in a silver frame on the dresser for everyone to admire, Daphne had existed in a kind of enchanted bubble. In her life, no soldiers would ever smash their way into the house to drag her father away, nor would a stranger ever knock on the door to inform her that he had died a horrible death in a foreign prison. And never in a thousand years would she ever have to sit and listen to someone tell her that the dad she loved and trusted had spent hours each week in the company of a German slut while her mother was at home cleaning and sewing and stretching their meager rations, pretending to be the happiest wife in the world. The waspishness broiled in her gut and was directed not just at Daphne for her charmed life. It was now turning on her father for his shocking betrayal of his family, her mother for not taking a stronger stand, at Hazel for knowing about it so long ago and at this faceless woman, who had most likely consigned her father to an early death. She imagined a blonde, bosomy femme fatale, no doubt far younger than Violet, draped in an exotic green coat, the velvet collar pulled high around her neck like a movie star, and wished she could slap her.

As she finished the final corner and squeezed the mop out for the last time, she decided it was time to seize her moment. It was the only way she could continue to help her friend, and if that meant a difficult conversation, then that would have to be the cost. And anyway, she reminded herself, if she were going to marry a German boy, then she was going to have to get used to confrontation.

"Excuse me, Aunt Beattie?" Her aunt turned with some surprise, seemingly startled to find Jean in the same room. "I was wondering..." Her confidence stuttered but she pushed on. "I was wondering if I could ask for a raise?"

She was met with an expression of complete bafflement.

"A raise? You want more money?"

Jean forced herself to straighten her back and look her aunt in the eye. She reminded herself of Hazel's assertion that the family were exploiting her, and thought of all the additional unpaid hours she had put in. And Beattie could hardly plead poverty after the conversation Jean had just witnessed. "If it's not too much trouble. And if you're happy with my work."

Beattie's eyebrows shot upward. The mop and tin bucket stood between them like some silent referee. "Of course we're happy with you, Jeannie. But you've only been working here a few weeks. Three and six is what we paid young Gwen from the village. Why do you suddenly need more?"

Jean opened and closed her mouth. Explaining the real reason was impossible; Beattie's reaction would be the same as her mother's, and Beattie would make it her business to tell Violet about it at the first opportunity, which would only make things worse at home.

"Just for groceries and bills. We don't want to have to rely on my dad's brother all the time." Beattie sat back in her chair and frowned. Jean tried to judge the look and hoped it might be capitulation.

"Well, how much are we talking about? I mean, we've got this party to pay for. And we're going to have to hire pickers for next spring."

Jean was about to make her bid when the door to the courtyard opened and Martin appeared in the doorway. He was wearing his usual work clothes of patched trousers, Wellingtons and an ancient plaid shirt, and his hair was uncombed and full of soil dust as he marched to the tap to pour himself a drink. As soon as she saw him, Jean felt her luck evaporate. After all, her uncle's recent antics in town could hardly have made his attitude clearer. To her dismay, Beattie jerked her head toward Jean as soon as he stepped into the kitchen.

"This one's asking if we can pay her a bit more."

"Is she now?" His voice was gruff, though she sensed a trace of humor in it. Jean rallied herself; if she crumbled now, she had no chance at all.

"I was wondering if you could pay me five shillings a week. Only I usually do a lot more than half a day, and I have to pay my bus fare to get here. I am family." The last remark was a desperate appeal, but immediately she knew it had backfired.

"Exactly!" Martin's joviality vanished. "Family, that means looking out for each other, not taking advantage." Jean winced. Was Martin claiming that *she* was exploiting *him*? "I think you're forgetting all the help we gave you and your mother during the Occupation. All those extras Beattie used to take down for you." Here it was again. Two bags of vegetables and a single rabbit for the entire war, and Martin considered this to be regular support? Her uncle shook his head in a display of world-weariness. "I don't know what's going on with people since Liberation. All this about higher wages and less working hours. Must be those Commies in town." Jean remembered his gleeful face and childish enjoyment, reveling in his mischief as the rotten tomatoes hit the protesters. The bubbling became a boil.

"I'm just asking for what I think is fair."

"Fair? Was it fair when the Jerries stole our piglets? Is it fair we still can't export spuds to England, with this Colorado beetle business? What you don't understand, Jeannie, is that it takes money to run a farm, and we're not made of the stuff. If you don't like working here, no one's forcing you." Slamming his glass on the draining board to be washed, he turned and disappeared out into the courtyard again, leaving a chill in the warm kitchen. Beattie stood with obvious embarrassment.

"Sorry, Jeannie."

"Could you not talk to him?" But the purse of her aunt's lips showed that she had already drawn a line.

"You heard what he said."

Jean carefully leaned the mop against the range, taking care not to make any unnecessary noise. She did not want Beattie to report, after the event, that her words were issued in temper.

"It's fine. And thinking about it, he's right, isn't he?"

Beattie smiled with relief, anticipating an awkward scene avoided. "Well, I'm glad you can see that, my love. So many expenses at the moment."

"No." Jean smiled back. She wondered if her aunt could sense the acrimony beneath. "I mean, he's right that no one's forcing me." She glanced at the kitchen clock. "And actually, that's my four hours for today. If I stop now, I can get the lunchtime bus. So if you can pay me for this morning, and I give you three days' notice for Thursday, we should be all square, shouldn't we?"

Beattie stared. "You're not coming back? But I thought you needed money?"

"Exactly." She kept her tone bright and sunny. "I'm going to get myself a full-time job, with proper wages. I hope you manage to find someone else in the village to replace me. It's such a big house to keep clean, isn't it, and Daphne's party coming up, too." She removed her pinafore and hung it neatly on the hook on the door.

The bus, for once, was right on time. And as she sat back and watched the emerald lanes spin by, Jean smiled to herself. If this week had seen the collapse of her beliefs and certainties, she was now soaring from the ruins, a gull ascending into the sky. She was no longer allowing herself to be buffeted by events but taking control of her destiny. For the first time in weeks, she could picture a future, and it felt like Liberation Day all over again.

When the crash came, she was in a deep sleep. At first it might have been a part of her dream, then perhaps it was the neighbor's cat, knocking over a flowerpot from a windowsill. But within seconds, some sixth sense tore a white streak of panic through her body, and she was violently awake.

She sat up in bed, listening. Something was wrong. Within the house. Hazel glanced over to where her father was beginning to stir in the next bed and glanced about. The shapes of the room, outlined in the slate gray of the night, looked as they always did. The danger was elsewhere. Her heart pounding, she threw off the blankets and grabbed her old dressing gown, the pink candlewick that had belonged to her mother, fighting to find the sleeve openings. Tiptoeing toward the door—no point alarming her father until she knew what she was dealing with—she opened it as quietly as she could. The night was hot—hotter than it had been when she went to bed three hours ago. Then the smell hit her, and she knew.

As she opened the door to the little parlor the heat smacked her in the face. The fire was already raging in a rough circle in the middle of the floor, her father's chair already caught in the flames. Hazel stared at it for several seconds. How could this be happening? Could she still be dreaming? Then the billowing smoke set her coughing and snapped her from her stupor.

"Dad! Dad! Wake up! There's a fire!" To her relief she heard a sleepy, questioning grunt from the bedroom. "Wake up, Dad! We have to get out of here!"

Hazel sprinted toward the tiny kitchen at the rear, thankful for the moonlight through the window that lit the silhouettes of the shelves. She grabbed the largest pan she could find and thrust it into the sink, turning the single metal tap. After the usual sputtering the tap began to run, but dear God, how slow it was! She stood watching the glinting surface of the water rise, muttering futile incantations to speed it, glancing in dread over her shoulder at the swelling blaze. When the pan was two-thirds full, she lifted it from the sink with difficulty and staggered into the parlor, hurling the contents over the flames. But, to her horror, the fizz and smoke she expected was replaced with a whooshing sound, as the fire seemed to leap upward and outward at the same time, tiny fireballs exploding around the room, setting light to items previously safe. Hazel let out a small scream before the smoke started her coughing again. Why, why had the water made this so much worse? The answer dropped into her mind, a flash of memory from a science book she had owned as a child: petrol. Water will ignite a petrol fire further. Only then did she register the smashed glass of the parlor window and realize that this was not a result of the fire, but its cause. A petrol bomb.

There was no time to consider the implications. No time even to try to grab precious possessions from around the room—the framed photograph of her parents' wedding, her leather school bag on the table, now lost behind a rising wall of flame. She rushed into the bedroom, where to her huge relief her father had managed to raise himself to a standing position.

"We have to put it out," he cried.

"It's too late, Dad. We have to go. Now."

"My things…"

"There's no time."

But it was almost impossible to shift him. His stiff, painful leg joints that took so long to get moving every morning would not function at such short notice and at an unexpected hour. As she tried to half push, half drag him toward the bedroom door, ignoring his shouts of pain, she could feel the burning heat growing closer, see and smell the smoke billowing into the hallway in blooming, evil clouds. The tiny hallway was filling with it, and she could no longer see the flat door—even if they were able to reach it, it would be impossible by then to find the latch to open it. Her coughing was getting worse, and she felt her lungs ache for oxygen; if she were to pass out, they would both be burned alive before there was any hope of help reaching them.

"Window." She turned her father around and shoved him back into the bedroom, pushing shut the bedroom door against the black curling smoke. She glanced up and registered the panic on his face.

"No! We're too high!"

"Only one floor." She could hear voices and rapid footsteps above—thank goodness those in the flats upstairs were aware of what was happening. But there was no guarantee that her neighbors would be able to break into the flat, or even that they would try if the fire continued to progress at this rate. This was the only way. "Come on, Dad, please." She hauled him across to the window. She thanked her stars that here in the tiny bedroom the furniture was rammed closely together, giving her father plenty to grab and lean on as he dragged himself across the room. Another couple of steps and they were there. She looked around and saw smoke drifting in under the door and felt the heat of the fire bleeding through the wall. They were both coughing now.

As they reached the window, she used both her hands to heave the sash up. It was a window they rarely opened more than a few inches, given the proximity of the street, and the ancient rotting wood of the frame protested as she forced the lower half upward, but with a strength that surprised her, she managed to open it most of the way. Her father's stricken face stared in terror at the concrete below. It was a worrying drop for anyone, and Hazel could only guess what fears it must hold for a man who had so little control of his body. But she knew they had only moments, and that waiting for help was simply not a choice. She gripped his arm.

"Dad, you must lower yourself down. I'll help you. It's not that far." She helped him ease one leg out of the window, and then the next, so that he was balanced on the frame on his stomach, facing her. His weak, useless fingers gripped the inside sill as hard as he was able.

"I can't, Haze. Please."

"You can. Easy does it." She placed her arms under his armpits to hold him as he slowly wriggled his body nearer and nearer to the tipping point. For years he had seemed so tiny and frail; now, supporting his entire body weight, he felt like a sack of lead in her arms, and every sinew of her body screamed for release. "Grab the sill. Hang on." He did so and she felt a gigantic tug as his body slid away from her, slamming against the exterior wall. She heard a cry of pain he barely had the strength to emit as he hung there for several seconds, mustering every ounce of strength to support his own body weight in a way he had not done for years. But even before she could issue instructions to drop gently, to try to maintain his balance and be sure to bend his knees as he landed, the arthritis ripped his hands from the sill, and he fell backward. Not daring to look, Hazel clambered out, easing herself across the window's threshold, hanging on to the frame until her legs were dangling as close to the ground as she could get them, then forced herself to let go. The drop was probably no more than six or eight feet but seemed eternal. As she landed, the force shot up through her feet, legs and hips, jarring every bone in her body with its power. A searing pain shot through her right ankle—only then did she remember her feet were bare. But as she toppled back onto her bottom, banging her wrists and elbows on the concrete, she had only one thought.

"Dad? Dad, are you all right?" Her father was laid out on the ground, positioned at such an unnatural angle, his legs in different directions. She scrambled toward him and took hold of his head. "Dad, Dad, speak to me, please." He looked up at her face. Despite the growing cacophony around them, the shouts of neighbors and the trundle of numerous feet running down the front steps, the hollering of people from windows across the street and the distant sound of a fire engine bell, all Hazel saw and heard was the small loving smile her father gave her as she cradled his head in her hands.

"And a pound of apples, please."

The stallholder weighed them out and poured them into her wicker basket, asking if there was anything else. Jean told him no; in truth she hadn't even needed the apples, but she felt like celebrating. She handed over the coins and set off through the market, taking in the sights and smells. Beresford Street market was very slowly returning to its prewar glory. New stalls were popping up, some run by familiar faces, some entirely new. Produce that hadn't been seen for months—green beans, cucumber, even rhubarb—had begun to appear in the displays, and housewives with scarves knotted under their chins filled their shopping baskets and gave grateful smiles, thanking the stall owners for their treasure haul. With her basket swinging at her side, Jean headed to the central Victorian fountain, leaning against the iron railing that encircled it and letting her fingers drift for a moment in the cool water. Sunbeams poked through the arched windows high above her and lit the plaster cherubs on their water pots. It seemed absurd under the circumstances, but for the first time in weeks, she felt happy.

She had arrived at the Summerland factory at eight sharp and spoken to a very nice woman, who explained that there were indeed vacancies. With Liberation taking a number of girls back to domestic duties, all Jean had to do was fill in the form and return it by Friday, and she could start next week. Jean promised she would, albeit with apprehension. The hours would be longer than she was used to, and (though naturally she did not mention this) she knew there would be a fight at home about her taking the job at all. But, given other events this week, she figured this was likely to pass almost unnoticed. Her mother was still sending her to Coventry, and last night Eddie had disappeared for such a long drinking session that she had not even heard him return. On that basis, it seemed the ideal week to announce her new plans. How much worse could things possibly get?

Her main focus, though, was that the end of the month was almost upon them, and her final meeting with Horst was now a mere week away. Tinted with the rosiness of her new resolve, the evening now took on a dreamlike quality in her imagination. She saw herself on the twilit quayside, Horst's arms around her, his face breaking into a joyful smile as she accepted his proposal. Then he would gawp in wonder as she explained her brilliant plan—how she would spend the next year, or however long Horst's sentence turned out to be, working at the factory and squirreling away money for their future. By the time he was released, they would have enough to get married and travel anywhere in the world. She pictured them at the door of some pretty cottage on a foreign hillside, wrapped in each other's arms to defy all prejudices, and the future seemed to stretch out before her, sunlit and carefree. She pushed back thoughts that this would be their last encounter for what might be ages, and that this fantasy life was likely years in the future. It was enough that she would see him soon. She took a rubber band from her pocket and wrapped it around the third finger of her left hand. She liked the look of it. Mrs. Horst Klein. It even sounded good.

She was initially unaware of the two women standing a little further round the fountain, both holding baskets of shopping and chatting in low voices. Then some of the words floated toward her.

"I heard the fire engine about three."

"Did them in the flats get out alive? Flipping death trap, they are."

"I think it were only one of the flats went up, but my neighbor works at the hospital, she heard one of them's dead."

"Dreadful. Be in the *Post* tonight, I suppose."

Slowly the meaning of their words began to penetrate her consciousness, and through some instinct, Jean felt a tremor of anxiety. She turned to the woman nearest to her.

"Excuse me, are you talking about a fire?"

The woman nodded solemnly. "New Street last night, the flats over that old ironmongers. Terrible business." Then, presumably seeing Jean's changing expression, she added: "No one you know, is it?"

But Jean was already gone, the apples spilling from her bag in her haste and rolling across the concrete floor of the market, spinning under the feet of shoppers or against the edge of nearby stalls. By the time she reached New Street, she was gasping for breath. On reaching the site, she stood on the pavement, staring up at the boarded windows and the slicks of smoke damage and silt on the render, trying to absorb it. At first her mind attempted to block the information, as if buying her more time to prepare. But reality slowly hacked its way in, evident through her drying mouth and thumping heart. She pictured the flames, the heat and the panic, imagined Hazel and her father struggling to escape the confines of the flat. The women in the market said that someone had died…surely, surely that had to be a mistake? She had to know more. Another sprint back to the General Hospital, her legs and lungs now strained to breaking point, left her standing at the main reception desk for half an hour, finally told by a uniformed staff nurse that no information could be given to anyone until blood relations had been traced and informed. Jean wandered the grounds of the hospital for a while, as if her presence there would somehow connect her to the people inside, then gave up and dragged her shaking body home.

As she entered the kitchen the first thing she saw was Eddie sitting at the table. The *Evening Post* was already in front of him, and he appeared engrossed in it. Without pausing to consider the consequences Jean marched over and snatched the paper from him. Eddie did nothing to resist though she could feel his eyes on her, watching her reaction. A photograph of the flats was on the front page, showing smoke pouring from the window and fire engines gathered outside in the dawn light. But it was the headline that leaped off the page. Tragic End to Flats Fire. Her eyes skimmed across the words below—a description of the "fatal blaze" and a report beneath that a family man in his early fifties, described by the journalist as a cripple, had died trying to jump from the first-floor window, his daughter escaping with less serious injuries. She scanned the text again, then raised her eyes to meet Eddie's, where she was horrified to see a small but discernible smile.

"Terrible, eh? Still, these things happen."

The next sentence tipped out before she'd had time to weigh its implications. "And where were you last night?"

"Me? Out with my pals."

"All night?"

"Went back to Jimmy's place. What's it to you?"

"I think you know." Images tore across her mind: the swastika painted on the bakery, the brick through the café window. Eddie and his pals sprawling in the parlor, raging at those they blamed for their ruined lives. His rant at Tom Maloret about vigilantes. He was going to force her to say it. She no longer cared.

"Did you have something to do with this?"

His laughter was explosive and humorless. "Don't talk daft. Fires start for all kinds of reasons. Cigarette ends, faulty electrics."

Jean continued to stare at him. She knew that if any building was likely to have faulty electrics, it would be those run-down flats over the shop. But the universe felt out of kilter.

"I don't believe you."

The laughter turned to a repulsive smile. "Can't help that."

"You did this to hurt Hazel and get back at me for helping her."

He stood, slowly, raising himself to his full height and looking down at her. "You better be careful, making accusations you can't prove. You heard what Tom Maloret said— nothing but trouble down that road." To her horror his arm lifted toward her head, where he proceeded to ruffle her hair with his thick-fingered hand, as if she were a child. "Now, I think you'd better get the tea started for your mum, don't you? I'm going out." And he left Jean alone in the kitchen, holding the newspaper in her hand and shaking in every muscle of her body.

The corridor was long and bright, its fluorescent tube lights bouncing off the green linoleum and forming a sickly brilliance. The pale pink of the walls and the strong smell of disinfectant, mixed with other less obvious chemicals, added to an ambience that seemed designed to nauseate, rather than heal. But Jean pressed forward, her bag clutched tightly at her side. She had never been in this part of the hospital before, and her eyes darted around the signage, where arrows instructed her toward the correct ward. A notice reminded her that visitors were restricted to close family, and she felt like an intruder, almost expecting someone to stop her. But she could always quote the permission of the kindly woman on the reception desk, who had nodded her through with a wink when she saw Jean's desperation. Nurses in starched white uniforms marched purposefully past her without a second glance, and a porter pushing a wheelchair containing an elderly woman with no teeth and a wild-eyed expression barely acknowledged her existence. Jean checked her watch—visiting time didn't end for another half an hour. She just had to find her way through the maze.

At the end of the next corridor, just as long and bright as the first, she found the ward she was looking for and cautiously pushed open the swinging double doors. Rows of beds lined each side of the room, most containing women of middle age or older, some of whom were sleeping, while others conversed in hushed tones with their visitors. There was a nurses' station in the center of the room, but Jean had no intention of drawing attention by asking for information. Instead, she pretended to examine the contents of her bag while she glanced around. The door to one of the side rooms was ajar, and Jean decided to take her chances. Moving quietly across the room, she reached the door and peered in.

Hazel lay on the solitary bed, propped up on several pillows, her eyes closed. Her hair was brushed back from her face, her left hand was encased in a thick white bandage, and an oxygen mask attached to a metal cylinder beside the bed was clamped over her nose and mouth. Jean, uncertain what to do next, stood helplessly in the doorway. She had stupidly assumed that all patients were awake during visiting time, and disturbing a sleeping patient seemed cruel. She was about to tiptoe from the room when Hazel half opened her eyes and raised her head. Jean suddenly regretted coming at all. She stood quite still, wondering if she moved very slowly, as one did with an aggressive cow defending a calf, she would remain practically invisible...

"Jean?" Hazel removed the mask to speak. Her voice sounded different, hoarse and crackly.

"I didn't know if you'd want to see me." Jean's voice didn't sound too solid, either. She realized she was holding on to the doorframe.

"Of course I want to see you. You're one of the few still speaking to me." Hazel replaced the oxygen mask with her uninjured hand, slumping back on her pillow. Jean took a deep breath and moved a little further into the room.

"I'm so sorry about your dad. Do you want to tell me what happened?"

Hazel swallowed, preparing for the anticipated pain of speaking. "The only way out was the front window. He broke his back as he fell. He lived a few hours, then..." Tears welled in her eyes. "Never even had a chance to say a proper goodbye."

"Oh, Hazel..."

Hazel blinked furiously to stop the flow, with little success. "I tell myself it's a release. He would never have coped with an injury like that. But the truth..." She stopped and coughed dramatically for several seconds. "The truth is, he should have had many good years left. We never even finished *Wuthering Heights*." Her tears flowed. Jean's own clouded her vision. She scolded herself for being so selfish when she had vowed to be strong.

"What about you?"

"A sprained ankle, smoke inhalation. I'll be all right."

"And the flat? Can it be repaired? Can you go back?"

Hazel shook her head. "Has to be gutted. The landlord may have a room in another house where I can stay for a bit."

"And after that?"

She gazed at Jean, and the hopelessness was hard to watch. "You tell me. No job, no home, no family. Persona non grata everywhere I go." She gestured toward her neck, and Jean saw the glint of the gold locket beneath her hospital gown. "At least I still have this. I'd planned to take it to the jewelers next week. Now it will have to go toward a funeral."

She sank back, exhausted by the effort, and sucked at the mask again. Jean took her deepest breath to ask the final and worst question.

"Do they know how the fire started?"

"The police are investigating. But I already know." She hesitated as if she wasn't sure what Jean's reaction would be. "It was a petrol bomb, thrown through the window."

Jean felt her head swim a little and steadied herself. "I feared as much."

"I knew from the start something like this could happen. Just hoped my name would be cleared before it got this far."

Jean's cheeks were burning hot. She wished Hazel would say it, but it was becoming evident that it would have to come from her. "And do you think this might have something to do with my family?"

Hazel slow-blinked her acknowledgment. "Do you?"

The word climbed reluctantly through her mouth. "Maybe." Another breath for a few short sentences that would lead her to a different country. "I know my uncle is…not a good man." She prayed Hazel wouldn't ask for details. "And he's spoken about taking things into his own hands. He knows we were together when the café was attacked, and that I'd given you the locket—he was furious about that. I can't prove anything, but if it wasn't him, I think he knows who it was." Hazel's eyes blinked, two blue pools against the whiteness of the pillow. Eventually she pushed herself up a little and took several gulps of oxygen in preparation for what she was about to say. Jean watched intently, waiting, and eventually Hazel removed the mask.

"Jean, you have to decide now whose side you're on. Tell the police what you've told me." Jean nodded. "I still don't truly know what you think of me. But if your uncle was involved in this, he's an accessory to murder. If you don't speak up now, it will be too late." Gasping, she lay back with the mask once more, her eyes closed with the exertion. Jean watched her, the figure that seemed so powerful and assertive now so diminished and frail in that hospital bed.

"I understand that."

Hazel struggled again for a moment, but her determination to get this out was obvious. Jean waited patiently.

"Do you, really? You realize what it would mean for you and your family?" Jean nodded again but Hazel saw straight through it. "They might never forgive you, even if no action is taken. And it could destroy your family's reputation. I know what that's like."

"But do I have a choice?"

Hazel gave a tiny shrug to indicate her powerlessness. "I have to trust you. Because just now, you're all I have." Then Hazel smiled at her, a small, provisional smile that nevertheless went deep. It seemed to convey weeks of blossoming trust, even affection, and it sent a shot of heat through Jean's body. Jean returned it with the same intensity, and for a moment they remained suspended in the moment, content in its communicative silence. Then Hazel closed her eyes, and Jean turned and walked out of the ward.

As she left the hospital, pushing past medical staff and visitors in the corridors, at one point almost crashing into a porter pushing a gurney, Jean realized that this time, perhaps due to the sheet-whiteness of her face, or her panting little breaths, she was attracting a good deal more attention in the way of worried looks and muttered remarks. But she didn't stop until she was down the main staircase, through the entrance doors and out to the hospital's exterior, where she made use of the nearest flower bed to retch up bile and water, which was all she had in her stomach.

It was dark when Jean returned to St Mark's Road. Several lights burned in the windows of the long terrace and the street was silent and empty of children. Back in the town, the clock of the Catholic church at the bottom of Victoria Street began its chime for ten o'clock. Her feet dragged and she longed for a drink; hours of walking the streets had exhausted her, and her fingers were pink and puffy with the humidity. But it had calmed her to weave through the quiet streets of St Helier, past the darkened windows of the shops, hearing only the seagulls and the occasional laughter of inebriated men stumbling from the public houses. At one point, she had passed West's Cinema and watched the chattering crowd spill out onto the pavement, their faces filled with the wonder of the silver screen, listening to broken refrains from "The Trolley Song" and the compliments about Judy Garland as they drifted away down the side roads. She had been careful to avoid the New Street flats and the Italian café, any of the places that marked this summer's terrible path, sticking instead to peaceful spaces where she could breathe and think. She had ended up in the hushed greenery of the How-ard Davis Park, slumped gratefully on a bench to watch the flamingo skies form over the graves of the Allied soldiers, and remained there until the park-keeper had politely chased her out to lock the gates. At that point, there was nowhere to go but home.

As she neared the house, bracing herself for whatever might follow, she was surprised to see that there were no lights on. Assuming her mother to be in bed early—a continuation of her cold-shoulder policy, no doubt—Jean tried the front door but found it locked. She scratched her head, wondering what had happened. Eddie would of course be in the pub, but her mother had been nowhere in the evening since New Year's Eve 1941. Finding her key at the bottom of her bag she let herself in and padded through the silent house, every sense pricked to maximum alertness. She could not recall the last time she had found herself alone here in the hours of dark-ness, and every shape and shadow, even the creak of her own footsteps, seemed strange and alarming. As she entered the kitchen, only a little moonlight through the window and the flame of the Ascot bathed the room in a silvery-blue light. Her hands ran over the smooth tabletop, the sides of the dresser, the handles of the drawers.

Something was amiss, askew, but she could not identify it. Then, as she glanced outside, where a shaft of moonlight was falling across the cobbled yard, she spotted it. The padlock on the door of the shed was hanging open, as if someone had hastily tried to close it and had failed to check it before turn-ing away. Cautiously she opened the back door and tiptoed across the yard toward it. The padlock gleamed where the moon caught its metal side. Gingerly she pulled open the door, holding her breath in fear of—what? That someone would be hiding in there? That some wild animal had broken in? She chastised herself for being such a child and peered inside. The interior was just as it always was, dank and musty, packed with shovels, half-empty paint tins and lengths of hosepipe, things her father had brought home from the shop for house-hold repairs that were rarely completed. Perhaps her mother had put something away earlier in the day and simply failed to close the padlock properly. She was about to close the door again when her foot caught on something. She looked down to find a bulky hessian sack she could not remember seeing before. Curious, she bent down and untied the top. Inside, crouched in the darkness, sat a pair of men's boots. Worn and a little scruffy, the kind of footwear any workingman might own. But the most striking thing was the smell that ema-nated strongly from their surface. It was, without question, the stench of petrol.

Jean's heart beat so fast she thought she might faint. Why would anyone—or to be realistic, why would Eddie—hide petrol-soaked boots in the shed, the day after an arson at-tack? And if that didn't constitute grounds for investigation, what would? She continued to stare at them, the options tumbling through her head. Should she take them now, hide them away as evidence? What if Eddie returned and found them missing? What if she left them here, but later discov-ered Eddie had disposed of them to cover his tracks? She was on the verge of taking the sack and hiding it in her room when she heard the sound of a key in the front door. Fast as lightning, she pulled the sack shut and pushed the shed door close but unlocked, just as she had found it. Then she scur-ried back into the kitchen, reaching the light switch just in time. For at that moment Eddie and her mother burst through the kitchen door.

Such was the shock of their demeanor, it took Jean several seconds to register what was going on. Both of them were squawking with laughter and somewhat unsteady on their feet. Eddie's arm was draped around Violet's shoulders, and the smell from their collective breath told her that they were both drunk. Jean found herself stepping back in abhorrence—outside of a medicinal brandy, her mother never touched the stuff, and in her entire life Jean had never seen her mother inebriated.

"What's going on?" Her voice sounded schoolmarmish, hardly recognizable as her own. "Where have you been?"

Their rheumy eyes slid toward her, and Eddie pulled Violet closer toward him, his arm now around her waist in a manner that made Jean a little sick. Violet herself gave a girlish giggle, which ended in a belch. This only made her laugh more as she covered her mouth with the flat of her hand.

"We've been celebrating."

Jean felt a wave of disgust. Celebrating? Surely not the fire, the death of an innocent man? Even if Eddie could be that callous, her mother would never sink so low.

"What do you mean?"

Eddie looked from Violet to Jean and back again, clearly relishing this moment as something of a triumph. A broad grin spread across his face.

"Got a bit of news for you, Jeannie. See, your mum and me—we went down the register office this afternoon. We're married."

10

The first thing that hit her about the room was the dinginess and the smell of damp. *Home from home*, she thought, savoring the irony. The place was small, containing only a single bed, a table and chair; in the corner was a grubby sink with one cold tap. Being a basement, the window was set high on the wall, bringing to mind a prison cell. Well, Hazel considered, if that was so, at least she would not allow herself to be a prisoner here for long. A week, two at the most.

She placed her bag on the table. It was an ugly, ex-army thing made of canvas, kindly provided by a staff nurse to carry the items donated by a hospital charity: a hairbrush, toothbrush, some undergarments, a small tablet of soap, and a spiral notebook with a pencil. A handful of essentials that now constituted her entire worldly possessions. A meager trousseau, she considered bitterly, for a woman of her age. She thought of all the items she had treasured at home—the collection of Brontë novels inherited from her mother, her father's journal. Even her sister Dottie's red woolen jumper with the animal border that their mother had knitted years ago; it had never fitted Hazel, but it still smelled of her sister and sometimes she would take it to bed.

She wondered if any of them had survived the fire. Perhaps, at some point, she might be allowed into the flat to see for herself. On the other hand, she had no desire to smell the smoke now embedded in the bones of the building or relive the horrors of that night. In the end, what did books or even mementos matter anymore? She wished she had some photographs, but the important pictures were already imprinted in her mind. It was almost cleansing to be free of everything physical, to rise like a phoenix—again irony overwhelmed her, almost raising a bitter smile—from the ashes of her former life.

The pain in her ankle drove her quickly to the table to sit down. The burn on her hand throbbed, too. She had been given some pills to get her through the first couple of nights on her own, but already knew they would be nowhere near enough. Strangely, though, the pain didn't bother her, even if it drained her energy. In an odd way, it was useful to have something physical to focus on, a force to pull together her scampering mind. It was also a bizarre relief, in these days of numbness and shock, to know that she could still feel anything at all.

Yesterday she had sat on the side of her hospital bed, her legs dangling over the edge of its high metal frame, looking up at the two St Helier police officers who had come to question her. Having described everything she could remember about that night, including details of the smashed window and what she assumed to be a homemade petrol bomb, she told them about Eddie Parris and his band of vigilantes, courteously suggesting that it might be prudent to question them. The elder of the two policemen nodded, his face solemn but devoid of emotion. The fire damage, he explained, might prove too severe for investigations to be conclusive. Naturally all lines of inquiry would be followed up and witness statements would be taken, should any witnesses come forward. But, given the time and nature of the attack and the "unusual circumstances" of these events, she was not to raise her hopes that any charges would necessarily be brought. Hazel peered at them, not initially understanding, until she noticed the sly little looks that passed between them, the glances at their watches and reluctance to write anything down. In that moment, everything became clear. She was unworthy of judicial priority. A suspected collaborator with no one to vouch for her, she was also a woman with questionable political connections, who had recently been dismissed from a reputable job. Not to mention the neglected nature of the property, where accidents were likely to occur. In their view, nothing she said could be relied on. There would be a half-hearted investigation for the sake of appearances, perhaps a few formal interviews to create a respectable file and satisfy their seniors, but without material evidence nothing would ever move forward. As they left, she thanked them for their time and wondered if they caught the sarcasm in her voice.

Taking the hairbrush from her bag she pulled it through her dry, damaged hair, her once crowning glory reduced to a haystack of auburn straw, and heard the crackle. Dust floated in the light from the window. So often in the hospital, with the constant drone of nurses and cleaners and visitors in the perplexing blur of night and day, she had longed for solitude. Now that she was here, she realized that loneliness would soon devour her. So what, she mused. What were emotions anyway, but a temporary chemical state, soon to be replaced by another? Biting her lip against the pain, she dragged herself to the sink and washed her hands and face. Somewhere outside the chimes of a distant church bell struck. It was time.

It was only a short walk to the small church on the outskirts of St Helier, but in her weakened state it took her almost half an hour. The minister greeted her with kindness, but there was no real connection. This was the only church in the parish willing to accept the burial of a barely practicing Quaker; neither she nor her father had any link to this man or this place, and with Hazel herself in no fit state to issue instructions, it was clearly going to be the simplest of services. Inside the quiet, dim little chapel, she embraced the cousins that she had not seen since Dottie died, and an elderly friend of her father's from his days as a cabinetmaker, who had to remind Hazel of his name. But by three o'clock it was clear that no one else would be attending. Tucked into the end of the front pew, Hazel held herself as upright as she could as she rose for "Nearer My God to Thee," too numb and too angry even for tears, telling herself that she had expected nothing more. After all, the only person she had really wanted there was her sister. But Lilian's telegram the day before had explained that with transport still so dear and infrequent it would be impossible for her to make the journey from London. Lilian's distress was evident even in the few highly priced words she had chosen for the message, and Hazel felt grateful that she had at least protected her from the worst of it, saying nothing about the cause of the fire and implying that it had been an accident. Secretly Hazel had harbored a wild hope that her sister would somehow find a last-minute solution and turn up at the church with her arms flung wide. But as they moved on to the minister's insipid eulogy, filled with platitudes and generalizations of a life well lived and burdens nobly borne, she accepted that was forlorn fantasy.

Soon they were standing solemnly in the churchyard, with the minister reading the Twenty-Third Psalm over the lowering of her father's coffin, and in the absence of a wake that no one had had energy or inclination to organize, she was thanking the other mourners before trudging her way back to the tiny basement room. What a pitiful last goodbye it had been, and yet fitting, somehow, given the messy nature of their final days. She felt simultaneously glad that it was over, yet jaded by the inappropriateness of it all. Certainly, it would bring her no closure, but perhaps it never could, for truthfully she had barely yet accepted her father was dead.

She sat once more at the table, thinking about Jean Parris and how inextricably entwined their destinies had become. It was almost comical that the one person who would likely understand this sudden, desperate loss was the same girl who held the key to this entire situation, the only one with the power to serve justice on Hazel's father's killers. She wondered what Jean would decide to do. She was a fearful, passive kid, but she had shown a good deal of courage in recent days, and her gift of the locket had touched Hazel deeply. Maybe she would show the world what she was really made of and do the decent thing. There had to be hope, for without that, there was nothing. She pushed the canvas bag across the table and laid her head on her hands, too tired even to move to the bed.

"Go on, Beattie, have another one. It's a special occasion." Violet waved the plate of limp sandwiches under her sister's nose, and Beattie dutifully accepted one, though her expression as she bit into it told Jean all she needed to know. Violet had hoped to provide something more festive for the occasion, even when family were the only guests, but rations and budget had dictated fish paste. Jean wondered how her mother would react to Beattie's luxurious spread of fresh crab and birthday cake for forty people at her daughter's birthday party in a few days' time.

"I still can't believe it!" Beattie's voice was higher than usual, and Jean sensed discomfort beneath the jollity. "When did you decide to do this?"

"Just last week. Once his divorce came through, we thought why not?" Violet linked her arm into Eddie's, who beamed back at her. Beattie exchanged a look with Martin intended to imply mutual delight, but Martin refused to play along and returned only a half smile tinged with contempt. Jean studied her aunt's face as Violet chirped on about Eddie's divorce and suspected Beattie was making the same calculation Jean had herself—that either Eddie's separation from Maureen had occurred long before he'd returned to Jersey, or else he was not actually divorced at all. A report of bigamy had appeared in the *Post* the previous week, and Jean now wondered how many people, separated from spouses for long war years, had decided to take that easy option rather than face the humiliation and expense of legal proceedings. Either way, it was another lie she would chalk up on Eddie's growing slate.

Jean sat holding her plate on her lap, flicking at the stiffening corner of her sandwich with her fingernail. She had said virtually nothing since the start of this horrible afternoon, avoiding eye contact not only with her mother and Eddie, but also with Beattie and Martin. No mention had been made of their last encounter or Jean's sudden resignation, though Jean was confident that was hardly likely to come up today.

"Did you not even tell the children? Looks like it came as a bit of a shock to Jeannie, getting a new dad so quick!" Beattie cast a meaningful look in her direction. Jean felt a snort of

warm air leave her nose in an apology for a laugh. As if anyone
with eyes or ears could be unaware of her feelings, a specter
in the corner of the kitchen casting dark looks at a man she
had already vowed never to call Dad. Even Daphne, always
determined to see the best in every situation, had thrown Jean
a look of doubtful concern once she'd delivered her posy of
ivy and ragwort to the new bride.

"We didn't want to make a song and dance, under the circumstances," Violet replied pointedly, avoiding Jean's gaze.
"Just a quiet, private ceremony. I'm sure there'll be a few
raised eyebrows, but if the last few years have taught us anything, it's that you've got to grab your happiness when you
can." Violet's face crumpled a little with emotion. "I know
it's not that long since we got the news of Phil…"

"Eight weeks and five days," Jean interjected without a
smile, her sudden voice sending a prickle around the room.

"But I think perhaps that's what brought Eddie and me
so close," Violet pressed on. "And truth be told, I think I'd
accepted long ago that Philip wasn't coming home. So, in a
way, I've felt like a widow for a long time."

"Oh, Aunty Vi!" Daphne jumped in to fill the silence.
"That's so sad. I think it's wonderful that you've found happiness again." But her expression did not match her words.

Jean looked at her mother from beneath her lashes, wishing she could take the plate of sandwiches and hurl it against
the wall. She wanted to scream at the hypocrisy, rip the mask
from her mother's face and tell them all the real reason for
this act of madness. For she had worked it all out as she tossed
and turned in her bed last night. This was not love, not even
a grasp for genuine happiness. For her uncle it was an easy replacement for the life he felt had been stolen from him, and
on her mother's part, pure revenge. Vengeance for a selfish,

unfaithful husband she still wished to punish, and the purging of shame for a marital love that had died long ago. Her gloomy silences in the early days of Liberation, Jean now understood, were down to the dread realization that she did not really want Philip back, the tears she shed the night of Clement's visit not tears of grief but of guilt.

The worst thing for Jean was that a large part of her understood her mother's feelings. It must have been exhausting to keep up such theater year after year, feigning adoration to hide her humiliation. Jean might even have wished her mother well, had she run off to the register office with any other man on the planet. But Violet, who had once proudly announced that she had never even been to the parish of St Mary's, never mind out of the island, had set her sights on the easiest option, a more reliable version of her husband, with whom she could rebuild a near-identical life. The die had been cast long ago, before the hymns for her father's memorial had faded into silence. For the last eighteen hours, Jean had felt trapped, suspended in propriety while Eddie's petrol-soaked boots lay waiting in the shed, crouched like criminals. Eager to check that the door had not been disturbed from last night, she offered to take the empty beer bottles out to the yard to be placed in the returns crate. Daphne tripped out after her.

"Everything all right, Jeannie?"

Jean tried to smile. Daphne's concern was real and obvious, but Jean was becoming increasingly aware that her cousin's protected world provided an immunity to darker emotions. She was simply incapable of understanding them.

"Fine."

"You mustn't mind too much, you know. If your mother is happy, Uncle Phil will be looking down and giving his blessing, I'm sure of it."

Jean concentrated on not looking at the shed door. "You think so?"

"And it's not disloyal for you to love your new stepfather. Like mummy always says, love isn't like strawberry jam, there's always enough to go round." She smiled at what she clearly considered to be a profound and helpful remark. Jean couldn't resist any longer. A quick glance at the shed revealed that the door was just where she had left it last night, with just a half-inch gap. "I'm sure that within a few weeks you'll get used to it. And Auntie Vi certainly does look radiant."

"Daphne, have you ever had to choose between doing the right thing and hurting someone you love?" The question took her by as much surprise as it did Daphne. Her cousin's doll-like features filled with confusion.

"I don't think so—why?"

Jean heard a shriek of laughter from the kitchen. Even if she wanted to confide, this was not the place. "Just a book I'm reading."

Daphne's pert little nose wrinkled in thought. "Well, surely if you love someone, not hurting them is always the right thing?"

It sounded so easy phrased like that, and Jean felt a wave of envy for a world where there were good people and just a few bad, and that like oil and water the two would never mix. Daphne's words were still hanging in the air when the back door opened and Violet stuck her head out.

"Come on, you two. Pubs are open, we're going to carry the party on at the Peirson."

Jean could see through the window that Eddie was now chivying the guests out of the house. Evidently his home stock of beer had depleted to an unacceptable level, even though a number of sandwiches still lay uneaten. Jean watched in dismay as her mother eagerly prepared to follow her new husband to a place that, three months earlier, she would have dismissed as a pit of drunks and rabble-rousers, and certainly no place for a respectable woman. Beattie was throwing Martin a pleading look for an excuse, but smelling the possibility of more beer, her husband pretended not to notice, already draping a jacket around his wife's shoulders.

"Will they let me in?" Daphne asked. "I'm not twenty-one till my birthday."

"'Course. We'll vouch for you."

"What about Jean?"

Spotting her opportunity, Jean stood up and forced as cheerful an expression as she could muster.

"You go ahead. I'll stay and get this place cleared up."

She had anticipated resistance, but it seemed that everyone had had sufficient booze not to bother with arguments. Within a moment, the sisters had reapplied their lipsticks, then with a flurry of jackets and handbags, the five of them clattered out of the house and away down the road. Jean watched them from the parlor window, then slid the bolt on the front door for good measure before heading back to the yard.

The door, swollen by rain over the months, dragged a little on the concrete, and she had to give it a decent yank to open it fully. Glancing over her shoulder to check that no one in the surrounding houses was watching, she bent down and felt around inside the shed. Her fingers immediately closed around the grubby hessian sack. Gingerly she pulled the top of it back to reveal the boots. She had not seen them in daylight before and took one out to have a proper look. Regular men's boots, grubby and worn. Could they be Eddie's size? It was hard to tell. But holding this one closer to her nose, she confirmed that the smell of petrol on them was still strong.

Placing the evidence back in the bag, she picked the sack up and held it like a puppy. It was no more than fifteen minutes to the town hall. Another ten to speak to an officer, explain why she was there and why Eddie should be brought in for questioning. In half an hour it would be done, and she would only have to sit back and watch the dominoes fall.

Jean stared at the bag. She instructed herself to close the shed door and get on with it. But still she stood, paralyzed in the afternoon sunshine, staring at the dandelions growing in the corner of the yard and the nettles poking from the gaps in the brickwork. She thought of her mother with her arms wrapped around Eddie in the public house, sipping a sweet sherry at her wedding breakfast, smiling in a way she had not smiled in months. She pictured the shock on Violet's face as she answered the door to a policeman who insisted Eddie accompany him to the station, then saw her in a courtroom, her hands gripping the back of the seat in front of her just as she had when Jean's father stood in the dock. She imagined a future, where she was happily ensconced with Horst in some far-off land, while her mother sat alone at her kitchen table, publicly shamed for a too-quick marriage to a man now linked to a murder, writing out a diatribe of resentment in her delicate looping hand.

Surely if you love someone, not hurting them is always the right thing?

Jean felt a numbness in her toes and realized she must have been standing there for some time without the tiniest movement. A large dark cloud settled over the sun and showed no hurry to move on; the bright yard and its jagged shadows turned to a dull gray, and a sharpness in the breeze told Jean that autumn was already on its way. She glanced down at her bare arms and saw that she was covered in goose bumps.

★ ★ ★

The café looked much as it had always done, except that
the interior was now as dim as a cave. Shafts of light found
their way around the plywood boards and reflected off the
tops of chairs and racked glasses like dazzling stars, for Mr.
Cauvain was as determined as ever to keep things clean and
looking as normal as possible. But there was no ignoring
the fact that the place still had no windows, and as Jean sat
nursing her tea in the furthest corner, she couldn't help but
wonder whether this was due to a shortage of glass plate or
a reluctance by local firms to come to the aid of unpopular
businesses. Either way, the twilight atmosphere on such a
sunny afternoon, combined with Cauvain's excessive cheer-
fulness to compensate, gave the whole place a dismal, abandoned quality, and she found herself wishing she had chosen
another venue.

When Hazel entered, creeping through the door in tentative steps, Jean gave a little gasp. In the context of a hospital
bed, her pale complexion and weight loss had not seemed that
shocking, but out here in the world, she looked like a cadaver.
Jean gave Hazel a nervous smile as she approached, gently
pushing a small bunch of wildflowers across the table toward
her. She had picked them on Westmount this morning, and
their scent rose up through the stale air like a pink mist.

"What are these for?"

"To say get well soon. Or perhaps for your father's grave.
I'm sorry I couldn't attend the funeral, I had…" She grappled
for the right words; it was too early in the conversation for
such revelations. "There was a family event."

Hazel shrugged. "Your locket covered the costs, I'm grateful for that."

"Please let me buy you some tea?"

"Perhaps we should talk first." Jean took the spoon and stirred her tea pointlessly, too embarrassed now to take another sip. "Thank you for the note. How did you know where to find me?"

"They gave me your address at the hospital. How is your new place?"

"Awful, but it's only temporary. I'm going to stay with my sister in London for a while."

"London?" To Jean the very name conjured up awe and wonder. "Have you been before?"

"Once, before the war. It's a huge place. Dirty and crowded, but very exciting. Museums, theaters. Everything will be opening up again now."

"Will you come back?" It sounded more desperate out loud than it had in her head.

"I don't know. Depends."

The intensity of Hazel's gaze was hard for Jean to maintain, and she found herself staring at the tabletop. "I wanted to thank you, for your advice. I'm starting a job at Summerland next week—full-time, proper pay. And I've decided I am going to marry Horst."

Hazel nodded. "Congratulations. But it's not your thanks I need."

Jean pressed her fingers to her lips, knowing that the moment could no longer be postponed.

"I found some boots in our shed that smell of petrol. They appeared the day after the fire. So if my uncle wasn't there when the petrol bomb was actually thrown, he's probably protecting the person who did it." She saw hope spread across Hazel's features and knew she had to crush this optimism before it became unbearable. "But two days ago, my mother and Eddie got married."

The silence that followed was thick with anticipation and calculation. Jean could almost hear the pieces fall into place in Hazel's head, a ghastly jigsaw of assembling logic.

"So…?"

"If I report my uncle now, with all the consequences you spoke about—it would break my mother's heart." She dared to glance up and met a gaze of steeliness and disillusionment.

"Jean, you're the only one who can help me get justice."

Jean squirmed. "Could you not just tell the police what I've told you?"

"They won't listen to me. It needs to come from someone else. Please?"

This was worse than Jean had imagined it. The guilt threatened to choke her. Her lips parted, but it took several attempts to form any words, and when they came, they were the empty ramblings of self-justification. "I doubt they'd listen to me, either. Eddie would just make up some story, and they'd probably believe him."

"But the statements your uncle's made in the past, things you've overheard… You could at least try!"

A flash of optimism struck, and she played her final card. "You know, someone might have seen something, they might come forward. The arsonists could be arrested without my help."

But Hazel just continued to stare at her. A fly buzzed around the café door, eager to escape, unable to find an opening. Jean realized she was gripping her teacup like a weapon.

Eventually Hazel gave the softest little sigh. "If you don't tell the police what you know, the people who killed my father will probably never be punished. You of all people should know how that feels. Christ, Jean. Don't you think I've lost enough?"

Jean swallowed hard, then looked directly at her, knowing it would be the end. "I'm truly sorry. But I just can't do that to my mother, not after all she's already suffered. The shame it would bring on her. I couldn't do it. I don't expect you to forgive me now. But I hope that you can, one day?"

Hazel sat very still for a moment as if considering this. Then she simply shook her head, got up from her seat and walked out of the café. Jean remained in her chair for a long time, perfectly still in the half-light, watching her tea grow cold and Mr. Cauvain throw her troubled, wistful looks from his station at the counter. The fly, having failed to make its escape with Hazel, continued to buzz pitifully around the door, its sound gradually growing fainter with its fading effort. Eventually it slid to the bottom of the door and lay buzzing pathetically on the doormat, tiny, broken and futile, and at that moment Jean felt as if her soul was entwined with it for eternity.

It was the hottest day of the summer, as if the season had decided to go out with a bang. The streets of St Helier were sweltering, and shoppers mopped sweat-covered brows and pulled at their clothes to loosen them. Old people, in the habit of wearing warm clothes every day for the last five years regardless of the weather and now taken unawares, stopped to get their breath at every available bench. Even the children seemed listless, settling for games of marbles around doorsteps instead of cricket and tag. It was a day when any sensible islander would avoid town altogether and get themselves down to the creamy sand beaches, where the lapping sea would cool their feet and ankles. But as Jean hurried down Halkett Place clutching her bag tightly in her hand, she was glad she had made the effort. Inside was the first new dress she had owned since 1939. Sewn from a light wool of beautiful yellow with white polka-dot print and a white collar, it had taken a huge chunk of her coupons, her entire last wages from Les Renoncules and every coin from her childhood piggy bank, an extravagant waste if she stopped to consider her needs for the winter. But tonight was the biggest of her short life, and she was determined to look her best. Tonight she would see Horst and agree to be his wife.

She pictured herself on the quayside, watching his distant figure approaching on that rubber boat. She thought of his crinkly smile and the warmth of his body as she finally gave voice to the words that had failed her last time. And not just saying them, but declaring them with real commitment, so that he would know she meant every word, understand that no matter how long they had to wait, the certainty of their future would sustain them both. The thought of it brought a rush of excitement, immediately submerged in a surge of remorse and ignominy.

"No!" she muttered aloud to herself as she turned the corner into Bath Street, causing a passing housewife to glance at her with concern. Not today! She would not allow these feelings to cast a shadow—the decision had been made and she would not, could not, change her mind. It was not as if she had had any choice. And, she reminded herself, it was not as if her suspicions about her uncle constituted any kind of evidence. It was not as if she was personally responsible for what had happened to the Le Tourneurs' flat that terrible night. Not as if, not as if…

She had repeated this incantation to herself every hour since leaving the café three days ago, but it had failed every time. The memory of Hazel's face was her first thought on waking and her last each night, the hurt in her eyes causing a cold drag of shame through Jean's gut. For the truth was, she would never know whether she was protecting Violet or herself. At 3:00 a.m. she was a courageous defender of her mother's happiness, by four a pitiful coward who hadn't the courage to face life's consequences. But worse was the sense of loss. Hazel had been her only friend, with her supportive chats and calm perspectives. She owed the woman so much, and the unpaid debt sat inside her like a stone. Even the new dress in her bag, though she'd told herself it was for Horst, was a feeble attempt at consolation.

She gritted her teeth and picked up her pace, despite the heat. She had enough time to join her mother and Eddie for an evening meal, then get changed for her pretend date with Tom Maloret, slipping down to the harbor in plenty of time for sunset. As she neared the house, she rehearsed her alibi in her head, anticipating every possible reply. In fact, her mother's novel interest in her new husband, with all its incumbent cooking and cleaning and flirting, would now work to Jean's advantage, even though it turned her stomach to witness it. Her uncle's move from the box room into her mother's bedroom, occupying the same half of mattress where his brother had once lain, and the giggles she had heard emanating from behind the door, made it difficult to be in the house. But once more, she told herself all this was temporary. She would start work next week and her wages would start accruing right away. She just had to keep her eyes fixed on the prize.

The atmosphere hit her as soon as she opened the front door, a tangible acrimony that crackled through the house, even before she reached the kitchen. Her mother's wailing and her uncle's muffled shouts of anger raised every hair on her body. Immediately Jean's mind leaped to a police visit.

Had she been right, had they made the link to Eddie with-out her involvement? Perhaps one of the members of his lit-tle troupe had become loose-lipped through guilt and given Eddie's name to save his own skin. But the looks of rage and disgust on both their faces as she entered the kitchen, directed firmly at Jean, killed that notion instantly. It was her mother who struck the first blow.

"How could you, Jean? The shame of it! Tell me it's not true?"

Jean's stomach began to collapse into her body. "Is what true?"

"You, with a bloody Kraut?"

It was a hammer blow. Jean backed away toward the kitchen door, but it was already closed behind her.

"What are you talking about?"

"This!" Her uncle's face was the familiar purple of his alcohol-fueled rages. She could tell from his breath he had already been drinking. He pointed to a sheet of paper on the table covered in neat cursive handwriting, a sheet that looked as if it had been torn from a spiral notebook. Jean moved only fractionally closer, fearful of the proximity; the handwriting was unknown to her, and she could not read it clearly without picking it up. But even from where she stood, a few words and phrases jumped out. *German boyfriend...harbor...think you should be told*. At once, Jean knew. A tidal wave of emotions swelled in her—fury, horror, but above all, terror. Eddie was alarmingly close to her now. "Arrived second post, unsigned."

Jean opened her mouth, her mind whirring. There was no time for hurt feelings about Hazel turning on her so savagely. She needed to talk her way out of this, invent a lie, create an escape route. Perhaps if she told them who had written it? One mention of Hazel's name and they would dismiss this letter as another trick. But she had already hesitated too long, and while she could see no reflection of her own face, she knew that her stricken expression already confirmed everything. Eddie's lips pouted in anger, his chin jutting. "That note I found in your room weeks back—that was from him, wasn't it? I was right all along! Got your little pal to lie for you!" Without warning he grabbed her shopping bag from her hand and pulled out the new dress. It unraveled from its paper wrapping, a smoking gun in polka-dot fabric. "And what's this? Suppose this is for his benefit? You little slut!"

It was over. Denial was useless now. Jean turned to her mother.

"It's not like that! Nothing happened between us. He's a good man who wanted nothing to do with the war. He wants—" She stopped, thinking better of mentioning the marriage proposal at this moment. "He just wanted peace, same as us. We...we love each other."

For the second time in days, her mother snorted at the word. "And how long has this little love match been going on?"

Jean shuffled numbers in her head. Almost two years was not, she knew, an acceptable answer. "A few months. He's a prisoner of war now. He knows he has to be punished for what his country did. He's not a bad person, Mum, I swear." She willed the words into her mother's soul, begging her to understand. But the mother who might, at one time, have accepted this out of love for her daughter had withered weeks ago. Violet slumped down at the table.

"My own daughter, a jerrybag. We'll never live it down. Never."

"No one's going to know." Eddie's voice was increasingly steady now, but no less frightening for that. "Whoever wrote this has said nothing till now, or I'd have heard about it." Privately, Jean sneered at her uncle's concept of himself as the font of all island knowledge. "And if they were after money, they'd have said so. So, chances are they're just trying to do the right thing by this family." Again, Jean scoffed internally. If he only knew who he was commending. "This information never goes outside this house, understood? We take it to our graves." He turned to Violet. "Just because we know what this little hussy is, there's no reason anyone else has to."

"I am no such thing!" Jean heard her own voice, clear and stronger than she thought possible. "And how dare you judge me, after all you've done? Creeping into my room at night, stealing my underthings. You think I didn't realize what you wanted? And I know you were behind that fire at the Le Tourneurs' flat. You're responsible for a man's death!"

Her mother's horrified gasp was topped only by her uncle's detonation. His face grew so purple now she considered he might be having a heart attack. It would be her only hope. He grabbed her arm before she had the chance to duck away from him and yanked it behind her back where any struggle would only cause further agony. Jean threw a whimpering look at her mother for mercy, but Violet's face was still buried in her hands, and Jean sensed that whatever path Eddie now chose, her mother would support it.

"That is it. We'll decide later how to deal with you." He was forcing her toward the kitchen door and into the hallway. Her previous courage vanished as quickly as it had risen and now a panic was enveloping her.

"Let go of me. You're not my father, you can't do this."

"I'm your bloody stepfather, and I can do what I like!" Eddie's voice was bubbling as he pushed her down the hall and up the staircase. "One foot outside your room and you'll find out what I'm capable of." She stumbled on the steps as he propelled her upward, every twist of her body trying to protect the angle of her arm, the bashing of her shins on the treads nothing to the agony of her shoulder, which she feared might rip from its socket at any moment. As he threw her into her bedroom with a force that dumped her half on and half off her bed, leaving her winded and weeping with pain, she deliberately avoided looking up as she heard the slam of the door and her uncle's wheezy gasps outside it, grateful only that he was no longer in the room. She glanced up to catch a reassuring glimpse of the bolt on the door, thinking that at least she would be able to keep him out. But what she saw there caused a spasm of panic that momentarily blocked the pain. Where the bolt had been there was now only a chiseled-out hole in the wooden frame. And the unmistakable sound of the metal bolt sliding into its casing on the outside of the door was followed only by her uncle's heavy footsteps clomping down the stairs, then the stifled sound of his continuing rage from the kitchen while her mother sobbed.

As soon as she felt strong enough, Jean dragged herself up and onto the bed. The pain was subsiding a little, telling her that nothing was dislocated. The heat of the day, trapped in the upstairs rooms of the house, was unbearable, and she yearned for a drink of water. But slowly it dawned on her that thirst and pain were the least of her problems tonight. She hauled herself onto her feet and staggered to the window. Somewhere beyond those jutting, sloping roofs was the sea. She thought of Horst paddling across the harbor on that tiny dinghy, where he would find no one waiting on the quayside. She wondered how long he would stay, scanning the darkening land horizon for her running figure with an ever-rising sense of despair, before eventually climbing back into the boat and returning to the ship for the last time. Then he would ruminate on their final conversation, recalling her doubts, and assume that she had dismissed marriage to a German as more trouble than it was worth. He would slump miserably into his hammock and the slow journey through disappointment and resentment would begin, finally telling himself that she had never loved him and perhaps he was better off without her. And later tonight he would chug out of the harbor and out into the Channel, alone and abandoned, to disappear into an unforgiving penal system.

Jean slowly dropped to the floor and propped herself against the wall beneath the window, her mother's and uncle's voices still reverberating through the floorboards. Then she rested her head against the wall to cry. At some point she must have fallen asleep, for when she woke in the same crumpled position, the moon was high in the sky and starlight lit her bruised arm. Her shoulder ached, her eyes were swollen and her body cried out for water. But what was unbearable was the realization that she was now a prisoner, too, that her opportunity to escape all this had passed and that everything she had dreamed about had collapsed in a pile of dust.

11

Shafts of moonlight found their way through the high window and fell in bright geometric shapes on her moth-eaten blankets. Hazel turned over for the fiftieth time and accepted that she was not going to get any sleep. Her burned hand and swollen ankle were still sending shooting pains around her body, and she was experiencing a vague all-over tremor. Smears of sweat formed in every crevice of her body and her heart was going at over a hundred beats a minute. She tried to tell herself it was because she no longer had any tablets left from the hospital, having swallowed the last one too early yesterday, or that it was delayed shock from the trauma of the past two weeks. But deep down she knew the cause. It was shame.

She turned again, shutting her eyes to close out the world, a dozen hot pokers prodding at her soul. Why? Why had she, Dick Le Tourneur's daughter, commended all her life for her moral center, allowed herself to be swept up in a moment of pure insanity? A tsunami of poison, and a betrayal not just of that hapless kid, but of her own parents, who raised her to be good. And what on earth had she expected it to achieve? Would Jean's misery in any way counter her own suffering?

A memory of that night forced its way in. She saw herself, a deranged mess she scarcely recognized, sitting at that grubby little table, overwhelmed with despair in the grim charcoal hours before daybreak. The bitter words had been scrawled out in less than five minutes, and she had bolted to the postbox as if sprinting from her own conscience. That night the drugs had knocked her out for several hours, but the next morning no sooner had she opened one eye than reality rolled over her like a tram. Grabbing her shoes, she had run back to the postbox, prepared to beg the postman to return the letter, to bribe him if necessary. But she had been met only with the sight of a distant figure on a bicycle and the faint sound of whistling as he cycled away. She had intended to lurk in St Mark's Road and try to intercept the letter at its final point but had to stop for breath so many times on her trudge across town she had again missed her chance. She tried to comfort herself with optimistic scenarios—perhaps Jean had found the letter first and destroyed it, or maybe the new Mr. and Mrs. Parris had taken pity and responded with sympathy and understanding. But in her heart Hazel knew exactly how it would have played out.

Of course, the girl would now despise her. She would remember nothing about Hazel but this, and take it as the definition of her character. She might even decide that her uncle was right all along, and that Hazel was nothing but a backstabber who betrayed people for petty vengeance—the informant they had always seen. Hazel looked across the room, where she could see the outline of her notebook and the tatty canvas bag. Poking from the top of it was her ticket for this evening's mail boat, purchased with the remains of the locket money—

an additional twist of the knife. But at least she would be out of here tonight. She wanted nothing more now than to run far, far away, to put miles of churning white water between herself and this island. Although she already knew that no journey would ever distance her from this.

Giving up on thoughts of sleep, she eased herself gingerly out of bed and moved toward the window, staring up at the black rectangle with its filthy lace curtains. At such moments she felt her father vividly, and today his disapproving voice rang in her ears, chiding her and demanding apologies, until a precise thought pushed itself forward. An apology was exactly what was needed, even if it could not undo the damage, and no matter how horrendous an encounter it might be. Fumbling to find her clothes, almost relishing the pain as an appropriate punishment, she got herself dressed and slipped out into the street.

It was not yet six, and the streets were deserted except for a lone road sweeper pushing an unwilling broom along the gutter. The moon was fading, a pale ghost of its nocturnal glory, and in the distance the earth was tipping toward the sun, revealing a line of bright gold along the horizon. Hazel walked as quickly as she could, glancing about her as if she expected assault around every corner. Finally, she turned into St Mark's Road and limped her way toward the Parrises' home. The house sat silent and closed-up in the center of the terrace. She stood nervously looking up at it, wondering if the upper window on the left might be Jean's room. Weeks ago, leaving the café, Jean had mentioned in passing that the evening sun could overheat her bedroom in the summer; it was not much to go on, but it was all Hazel had. She decided to risk it. If it brought the mother or uncle to the door, if they knew her to be the author of the letter and attacked her on their doorstep, let them do their worst. Scooping some gravel from a neighbor's garden, Hazel threw a few tiny stones at the pane. She waited for half a minute, then threw some more. She was starting to think it was a waste of time when the curtains pulled back and she saw Jean standing at the window, pale and red eyed, staring down at her with distrust and alarm. Hazel made eye contact and placed her palms together in a begging gesture. For what felt like a long time Jean just stood there, doing nothing. Then she reached forward and pulled the sash open about a foot, bending down to speak through it.

"What do you want?" Her face was rigid and her voice damped down to keep volume to a minimum, but her distress leaked through. "Go away. Haven't you done enough?"

"Jean, I'm so sorry." Hazel echoed her half shout, half whisper. She felt a rock in her throat but swallowed hard—self-pity would not help either of them now. "It was a moment of madness. If I could change what I did, I would."

The girl's expression didn't alter. "We have nothing more to say to each other." She went to shut the window, but Hazel rushed toward her next sentence, desperate to keep her there.

"Please just tell me—did you get to see Horst before he left?"

She saw Jean glance anxiously behind her at the mention of his name. Then she shook her head. "They locked me up here. I think they're going to keep me here for days."

Hazel scoured her mind for something useful to say. "I'm sorry. But you know you can still reach him?"

Jean scoffed. "I'll never see him again."

"No!" Hazel stepped forward till she was almost on their pathway, so eager was she to impart this information. "The British Home Office will know where he's been sent. You can trace him. It might take months, but it can be done. Please, Jean, don't give up on this because of me."

The girl's expression showed nothing but skepticism. "He'll think the worst. He'll forget about me."

"He won't. Find him, write to him, explain. If he loves you, he'll understand." She heard the intensity in her voice and felt that she might be getting through. But then she saw Jean's shoulders slump.

"I have to go." Again, her hands moved to the sash.

"Just one thing. You asked me if I could ever forgive you, when it was never necessary. But can you do the same for me? I'm not… This is not who I am." For a second they simply stared at each other, suspended in time and space like some absurd parody of the Romeo and Juliet balcony scene. Then, in a gesture mirroring Hazel's departure from the café, Jean shut the window and disappeared into the room without another glance.

Hazel stood for a moment, staring up as if her eyes alone could bring the girl back to the window. Then she turned and stumbled slowly back through the streets, now stirring with early workers, edging her way toward her new building and dingy basement room. She played out the conversation over and over, wondering if she could have said anything different or more effective, but knew it would have altered nothing. She thought of the prayer her father had once read to her from a magazine: *grant me the serenity to accept the things I cannot change, courage to change the things I can, and the wisdom to know the difference.* All she could do now was move forward. In twelve hours, she would be on a ship sailing to England and, by tomorrow evening, she would be with Lilian again. She would leave behind not just the last few weeks, but five years of Occupation, a stack of memories, her entire childhood. Twenty-seven years of work and family, highs and lows, all parceled up into a past she would never revisit. She recalled the day she and her father had moved into the flats above Parris's ironmongery, and the hope they had shared that it might be a new start. If they had moved to another address, if she had never clapped eyes on Philip Parris, if she had not watched him and his grubby associates going to and fro in that backyard…how different her life might have turned out. But it was pointless to think such things. On reaching the flat, she pulled back the curtains to let in the day, stripped the linen from the bed and stuffed her handful of possessions into her canvas bag. There was nothing left for her in this place.

Jean put down her pen, held the letter up and gave it a little nod of approval. It had taken her most of the day, but she was happy with the result. This time there had been no doubts, no second thoughts about what to say. The resolve that had hardened since Hazel's dawn visit had sharpened her mind, and phrases had simply poured out. All she had to do now was to find a way to get this letter into a postbox and en route to her brother as quickly as possible. She slipped it into the envelope, wrote his address and slipped it under her mattress. An opportunity was bound to present itself soon.

Sitting back in her chair, she tried to picture Harry's face. She knew that the photo on her bedside table, snapped on a cheerful family visit before the Occupation, would be hopelessly out-of-date. Since then, he had been through army service and fathered two children; he would be slimmer, tougher, but probably more serious, and maybe more understanding. That thought had sustained her as she churned out page after page, describing the new domestic arrangements at home but keeping back any information that could damage her case.

Conversations about Horst, Hazel and the whole sorry saga of recent months could be put on hold until they were sitting face-to-face over a cup of tea. Neither did she mention the violence, Eddie's disturbing behavior toward her or anything that might encourage her brother to contact Violet directly, thus letting the cat out of the bag. All that mattered now was to get herself out of this house and into the safety of her brother's home. Once there…well, that was more complex, and short on detail. But she knew it involved making herself indispensable to Harry's family, finding a job and finally introducing Horst into the conversation. Surely an ex-soldier who had witnessed the misery of the ground troops on both sides would understand? Perhaps, with his army contacts, he might even know how to trace a POW? But all that was far in the future. For now, Jean kept her requests simple and straightforward—some money for the fare, wired directly to her childhood Post Office account, and an agreement that Jean could visit for an unspecified period. One step at a time.

It was now a full thirty-six hours since Eddie had shut her in here. Other than brief forays downstairs to use the lavatory and to get a glass of water and a crust of bread to take back to her room, she had seen nothing but these four walls, and while the first few hours had been sheer despair, she could now feel an emerging determination, as tangible as the bruises on her arm. As so often before, Hazel had been right: the road ahead was now longer and more complex, but not impossible. While she could no longer take up her job at Summerland—the family would never allow it now—she had been hired easily enough. That meant her plan to work, save and eventually marry was just as viable in a new location. She looked up Chelmsford in her atlas and wondered what it was like. The idea of such an adventure terrified her.

But then she remembered the J.D.M. speakers, who did not let a few rotten tomatoes and the antipathy of the local paper deter them from their goal. And, when she thought about it, caution could be just as dangerous—her refusal to report her uncle had taught her that. It was no longer a question of finding the courage. She was simply out of other options.

She thought again about Hazel. She partly regretted not accepting her apology, but the old sense of *Schadenfreude* was strong. It had never occurred to her that Hazel could be so vindictive, and the shock trailed ugly suspicions in its wake. If Hazel was capable of treachery like this, had Jean misjudged the woman from the start? She replayed Hazel's account of her father's lover, the mysterious woman in the green coat. Was any of that even true? Now she would probably never get answers to the questions that pursued her every night and may have to live forever with scarred memories of her father and emotions she did not yet fully understand. But perhaps, in the end, none of it mattered. The truth about herself and Horst would have had to come out eventually, and it seemed unlikely she would ever set eyes on Hazel Le Tourneur again. It was all about the future now.

The footsteps outside her room and the sliding back of the bolt on her door alerted her to a visitor. Checking that Harry's letter was properly hidden, she arranged herself on her chair to look as collected as possible. Whatever punishment Eddie and her mother had cooked up downstairs, she was determined to face it with grace and use it to her advantage. But she was relieved when the door swung open and she saw only her mother standing there.

"Time to have a little chat." Jean nodded and gestured to the bed, the only other place to sit. Violet plonked herself down on the mattress, her hands folded neatly in her lap.

Whatever she was about to say, Jean suspected she had discussed it with Eddie many times. "Your stepfather and I—" Jean winced at the phrase but tried not to let it show "—have discussed things at length. What you've done, and the things you said—well, words fail me, Jean. I thought I knew my daughter, I really did."

I thought I knew my parents, too, Jean reflected, but said nothing.

"Still, as Eddie's pointed out, the most important thing is that no one ever gets to hear about this—not even the rest of the family. So, what we're going to do is carry on as if nothing's happened."

Of course, Jean thought. When had her mother ever done anything else?

"It won't be forgotten, mind, and there are conditions. You are never to repeat any of those dreadful things you said about Eddie. There'll be no more talk of jobs, you'll be back in this house by nine every night and we'll always want to know where you're going. But it would do no harm to be seen around with that nice Tom Maloret."

Jean stared down at her hands. So that was the plan—marry her off to the pleasant, dull civil servant. That poor hapless man, used by the entire family as some kind of permanent fig leaf to cover the Parrises' shame, a trajectory Jean herself had set.

"Tomorrow morning," Violet continued, "you'll go to the market to buy some vegetables, and on the way back you'll call into the States offices and ask to speak to him. You'll apologize for the disgraceful way you behaved when he came for tea and ask him to accompany you to your cousin's twenty-first on Saturday. Is that clear?"

Jean thought of the letter tucked away under her mattress

and remembered how close the post office was to the market. It would take several days for the letter to arrive, and, with luck, the same for her brother to respond. Once the money was in her account, all she had to do was book her ticket and slip out of the house with a bundle of basic items hidden in a bag. By the time the leaves were turning golden in the Royal Square she would be on her way, searching for Horst and starting her new life. She looked at her mother and nodded.

"Perfectly clear, Mum. I'll go first thing."

The water today was a flat, blue-green pond, with tiny wavelets that foamed and sputtered as they curled, then seeped up the sand. The gulls coasted on the high thermals, saving their energy for hunting, while out in the bay Elizabeth Castle sprawled, confident in its centuries of history, a picturesque reminder of the transience of human beings. Soon the tide would turn and begin its long journey out, revealing the crumpled mess of rock and seaweed beneath. Tonight it would rush back in to lie glistening, black and mysterious under the light of the moon, before reappearing the following day as a choppy dance of frills and crashes. Nothing in this world was permanent, Jean reflected; even in the darkest, hungriest days of the Occupation, the islanders had believed that one day the war would end and they would be free, and so it proved to be. Her shoes dangling from one hand, she relished the soft muddiness between her toes and held her face upward to feel the breeze and taste the salty air. It felt good to be outside.

She thought of her childhood trips here, paddling in the freezing water of the marine pool. Her mother could recall bathing huts along the water's edge, in the days when the merest sight of a female ankle was considered unseemly, and Jean herself could remember riding a donkey along this very strip. Her father had often bought them ice cream from the kiosk above, despite moaning about the cost. How joyfully that six-year-old girl had taken the cold sweet cone from his hand, believing her father to be the kindest man in the world and her parents to be the happiest people she knew. It all seemed so very long ago.

She had deliberately taken a circuitous route through town, avoiding scrutiny by telling her mother that she needed a new sanitary napkin from the chemist (this, she knew, would halt any further discussion with Eddie). Her first stop was the post office to buy a stamp and push Harry's letter into the post-box, her fingers already trembling in anticipation. Then this brief, welcome respite along the beach before completing her roster of duties, calling in on Tom Maloret and finally stopping off at the market before home. As she clambered up the steep stone steps from the shore, brushing the sand from her feet, she wondered what kind of reception she would get. Tom had not contacted her since that disastrous afternoon in their front parlor, though whether that was down to her behavior or her family's she wasn't sure. Still, as Jean cared not a jot whether he accompanied her to Daphne's party, she felt no nerves about asking. And while she felt guilty about this ongoing manipulation, she could at least promise he would be well-fed.

Within fifteen minutes, she was at the official-looking door that led into the States offices, the same one they had entered all those weeks ago for that very first interview. Having persuaded the ancient spinster at the front desk to admit her, she made her request for two minutes of Tom Maloret's time in her best school-assembly voice. The woman gestured to a chair, and Jean arranged herself neatly on it. A few minutes later Tom burst into the waiting area, wearing his familiar work suit and his hair slicked into place.

"Hello, Tom. Sorry to bother you at work." She gave him her most welcoming smile.

"Jean! I certainly wasn't expecting to see you today." It was a troubling response. Gone was his usual benign attentiveness, replaced by a twitching anxiety that suggested her presence was none too welcome. Perhaps after her abrupt disappearance from tea, Tom had assumed things to be over between them, or maybe their "romance" had been a secret in the States office. But she sensed that there was more to it. Could rumors about the Le Tourneur fire have reached the ear of officialdom after all? Her best course of action, she decided, was to plough straight in.

"I'm sorry I've not been in touch, but there's been so much going on. Perhaps you heard, my mother and Uncle Eddie got married?"

"Yes, I saw the announcement in the classifieds. Please give them my congratulations." His voice was tight, and she noticed his eyes kept flicking away from her as if a sustained gaze was difficult.

"Anyway, I'm here to invite you to my cousin's birthday party on Saturday."

Tom hesitated. Her anxiety began to rise sharply. What had happened to that keen, pliable clerk who was always trying to help? She waited, feeling a light film of sweat form under her long-sleeved blouse, chosen to hide the bruises on her arm. Eventually he replied:

"I'm sorry, Jean, I'm just not entirely… I was actually going to call on you."

"Oh, what a coincidence." She heard her own stupidity.

"In fact, now would be a good time for you to come up-stairs to one of the offices, where we can talk privately."

Jean felt the heat of her body dissipate into a chill. Apart from the woman behind the desk, some feet away, there was no one to intrude on their conversation. Why would he need to see her privately?

"Well, of course, Tom, but is that really necessary?" She faked a laugh. "You look awfully serious?"

He finally met her eyes. "I'm afraid it is rather serious. Would you care to follow me?"

By the time they reached the rear of the building, Jean's heart was pounding, and not only from the staircase they had ascended at alarming speed. Tom showed her into a side office stuffed with filing cabinets and a small desk in front of the window, then disappeared for several minutes, leaving her listening to the sound of passing cars outside and the authoritative footsteps of civil servants scurrying about in the offices above. The room was no larger than a generous cupboard, uniformly gray and not the kind of room where you brought anyone in order to deliver good news. Jean sat awkwardly on the edge of one of the chairs, hardly daring to think where this might go. A few minutes later Tom re-appeared carrying a red file, closed the door for privacy and took the other seat behind the desk.

"Tom, what is this about?"

His expression was as neutral as he could make it, a skill she assumed he'd picked up from working around officials all day, but there was a gloom in his eyes. His slim pale fingers opened the top file and pulled out what appeared to be a large plain white envelope.

"This was delivered to our office yesterday." He cleared his throat a little. "I have to warn you, it's rather distressing."

He pulled out a black-and-white photograph and placed it on the desk. "I must ask you to look at it."

Jean's eyes dropped to the picture. At first, she couldn't make it out—it looked like a black lump on a squiggly gray background. But as her eyes adjusted she realized it was a human body lying on the ground. On a beach. A male body, clearly dead. And it was wearing a German uniform. Then...

"Oh, my God." Her hand jumped unthinkingly to her mouth. A shriek of shock and despair still managed to escape.

"You recognize this person?" Jean continued to stare at the photograph. The face was bloated, distorted, but there was no doubting it. In some odd part of her brain, she convinced herself that if she kept her eyes fixed on the image, another explanation would present itself, and another meaning would materialize; in addition, if she kept her eyes forever averted, she would never have to look at Tom's face. For a second, she considered trying to pass it off as the shock of seeing any dead body, to say she had no idea who this person was. But then he added: "He has been identified as *Obersoldat* Klein. You do know him, don't you?"

She could barely manage to speak at all, never mind construct some convincing lie. Her voice sounded faint and far-away. "Yes."

"A small photograph of you was found in his wallet. Some letters, too, although they were disintegrated and illegible."

She nodded. What else could she do? Finally, the only real question she wanted to ask fought its way out. "How?"

"His body was washed up on Portelet Beach yesterday. While on the British vessel en route to Weymouth, it seems he somehow managed to escape onto the deck unseen. He may have slipped, but more likely he jumped overboard. It's not uncommon among German soldiers—families are dead, nothing to return to but shame and imprisonment. By the time he was missed, it was too late."

Drowned, Jean thought. The boy who was terrified of water. How desperate to leave this world he must have been. She pictured him flailing in the open sea, the land nothing but a blur, the ship steaming away toward the horizon. The arms that had held her instinctively smacking down on the waves, the mouth that had pressed hers gasping for its last breaths. The tears swelled in her eyes unbidden, but she made no sound. She longed to scream, wail, cry out his name, but nothing came out. Tom took the photograph and replaced it in its envelope, while Jean kept her eyes firmly on the desk, wondering why he wasn't shouting at her in fury, demanding that she get out of the room and never speak to him again. Then his hand crept halfway across the desk and lay there, an obvious olive branch.

"I realize you probably need time to take this in. But I would just like to say..." His voice was full, and she could tell he was struggling. "Please don't consider yourself in any way responsible for this." He stopped, and she heard him swallow. Looking at him was still out of the question. He cleared his throat again. Jean stared at his hand, lying still, untouched. "Would you like me to sit here with you for a few minutes? Or I can leave you alone, if you wish?"

She shook her head, not really knowing what she wanted. A drip fell on her lap, either from her cheek or her forehead, which was soaked with sweat. It was very possible that she might vomit at any moment. She took a few tentative breaths before speaking. "What will happen now?"

"The body will probably be buried in the Strangers' Cemetery with the other German military."

"And who knows? I mean, about me? Who will you tell?"

Tom sat back in his chair. "The only people who know are a few British officers on the ship and a handful of people here. No one will find out, I'll make sure of that."

"But it will get out. I'll be called a jerrybag. I'll be punished."

Tom shook his head. "You're not a…one of them. You formed an ill-advised friendship, that's all. It's not your fault this young man harbored delusions."

Jean finally dragged her gaze to his; his eyes were clear and calm. "What do you mean?"

"I know you, Jean, and I know you could never behave like that."

Her mind swam. The lines between truth, lies, wishful thinking and pure fantasy were a blurred mess, and she could make no sense of them. "I don't understand?"

"It's quite obvious what happened, at least to me. This young man befriended you, probably helped you with food for your family. And being a kind person, you showed him consideration, which he misinterpreted to be something else. That's understandable. But not your fault." The desperation in his face was obvious, willing her to accept his story. Perhaps Tom was already picturing a future with her, and needed to set this version of events in stone before other, more subversive thoughts crept in. She wanted to shout at him that he was wrong, tell him that Horst was the man she wanted to spend the rest of her life with. But she could not muster the courage or cruelty. The word was out of her mouth before she could stop it, limping passively along the path he was clearing for her.

"Yes…"

"So, I'll file this photograph away, and we'll forget all about it. I think that's best, don't you? For everyone."

"Yes." She was denying him. Her dead sweetheart, the man she had intended to marry. But she didn't really know what she was saying. She could hardly think straight. Her future was falling away like a sandcastle in the tide, leaving her with nothing but this place, her mother and Eddie. And she would never see Horst again.

"We should focus on the present, not the past. Think about the good things. You mentioned something about a birthday party?"

It felt as if all the light was leaving the room. As if high doors were clanging shut around her and there was nothing she could do to stop it. "Yes…"

"Thank you. I'd love to come. We can have a pleasant day together, and we won't mention this at all." She was pinned by him, a butterfly on a board. He reached a little further across the desk, and this time she let him take her hand, not knowing what else to do. "I think you know how I feel about you, Jean. We've got so much to look forward to."

She remembered nothing of leaving the building, but found herself sometime later at the harbor, the place of her and Horst's last meeting. Small white clouds blew across the sky, and the breeze gently shook the first leaves from the trees. But Jean saw nothing, felt nothing, just sat with her memories until she could bear it no longer. She did not go to the market for vegetables, nor visit the chemist to furnish her alibi; she spoke to no one and walked through passersby as if neither of them existed. Horst was dead and she had betrayed him. Their beautiful hope-filled future was gone forever, swollen and seaweed-strewn on Portelet Beach. There was no lower place for her to sink. And nowhere else to go but home.

12

"Another one? Go on, you look as if you could do with it."

Hazel accepted another cup of stewed brown tea, taking in the room around her. It was a decent-sized kitchen, and very different to the rooms she had inhabited recently, with its pink floral curtains and cozy family feel. Lilian had never been overly concerned with tidiness, which had got her into trouble when they were children, and Hazel had often won praise for tidying up after her. But here, the wooden toy train in the middle of the floor and the coat hanging loosely on the back of the chair instead of on its hook actually made the place feel homely. For the first time in months, she felt secure.

Somewhere outside, the unfamiliar rattle of a train running at speed along the track caused a slight vibration through the entire house, and Hazel craned her neck to peer out, hoping to catch a glimpse of it. How thrilling to have such a network of travel just outside your door, with connections that could take you anywhere across the entire expanse of the country! The 10:05 she had boarded at Weymouth, still bilious after twelve hours on a choppy sea, had run through miles of luscious rolling hills before tottering through the

London suburbs. Entranced, she had abandoned her newspaper and gazed outward as the winding track allowed her to see directly into the backs of terraces and peer at families hovering behind private windows. England's own, different war was evident everywhere, in the piles of rubble on every corner and the gray exhaustion written on the faces of everyone. But the newness of this world filled her with optimism. She took a long gulp of tea and removed her shoes with her noninjured hand.

"Thanks. I really appreciate this."

Lilian continued to fold clean nappies at the table. A bucket of dirty ones was boiling on the stove, filling the kitchen with steam.

"I still can't believe he's gone. Only last month we were talking of going over for Christmas. And I feel terrible about not making the funeral."

"Don't feel bad. It was a small affair. I was in no condition for anything else. Dad would understand."

"Do you think he was looking down on all of you?"

Hazel smiled. "Not sure he believed in the hereafter himself—all that Quaker stuff came from Mum."

"And you?"

Hazel returned her gaze to the window, losing herself in the unfamiliar view of a tiny garden. A greenhouse had miraculously survived the Blitz and tomato plants were bearing fruit at the far end. As a kid, she had been taught at school that all nature's bounty was God-given, but her father's politics and her own questioning nature had restrained her faith. And now, after all that had happened…how could she believe in an all-powerful benevolent being? One who allowed Hitler and doodlebugs and concentration camps? What kind of omnipotent god would send such destruction as a test of faith? The strong sense of her father's presence that visited her frequently was just as likely to be a trick of the mind. She turned back to her sister.

"I really don't know, these days."

"Do they know any more about what started the fire?"

Hazel watched Lilian piling the white toweling squares on top of each other, then looked down at her tea, choosing her words carefully. In the long hours of her journey, she had reflected whether or not to tell Lilian the whole story, thinking perhaps to relate it in person would be more acceptable. But now that she was here, surrounded by cozy domesticity and the smell of babies and new life, she saw no point. It would bring nothing but anger and upset, demands for action that would amount to nothing. And if it was a heavy burden to carry unshared, perhaps that was a suitable punishment for the way she had treated Jean Parris.

"No. Probably a candle, or Dad's pipe. Ironic really, considering how impossible candles and tobacco were to get during the war."

Lilian shook her head. "I can't believe you had to live under Occupation for all that time. It was bad enough here, but at least the Germans weren't living among us!" She sighed sorrowfully. "Just seems so cruel that Dad survived all that, only for this to happen now."

"Try to think of it as a release from his pain. That's what I do. He went downhill through the war. Well, we all did." Her sister reached over and touched her hand. Even a gesture of this innocence forced Hazel to bite her tongue to stem the tears. Lilian was all she had left in the world now, and it was impossible to express how grateful she was to find herself here.

"So, what do you intend to do?" Lilian gathered the nappies up and placed them on a shelf at the end of the kitchen. "Will you try and find another teaching post?"

Hazel pulled a face. "I don't know. Feel like I need a completely fresh start."

"Won't be so easy now the forces are back," Lilian pointed out. "Though I was in the local library the other day, and I heard them talking about taking on a new assistant."

Hazel considered this. "Maybe I should pop in and find out more."

"You should. I mean, you're welcome to stay as long as you need, but we can't afford to feed another mouth for long, if you're not earning."

Hazel nodded. "Of course."

"And, I'm sorry to say it, Haze, but finding a husband's not going to be as easy as it once was. So many taken in the war. And you're not...you know..."

"Getting any younger?"

Lilian shrugged her reply. Hazel smiled to herself as her sister raised her whining daughter from her cot and plonked her on one arm, expertly continuing various chores with her baby balanced perfectly. Despite their father's firm principles of female equality, Lilian still subscribed to the notion that a woman could not be complete outside of a conventional marriage. It was futile for Hazel to point out that she still had no interest in marriage if it meant giving up everything else, nor was she sure that motherhood was a vocation she craved. Hazel turned her head and caught her reflection in the glass of the kitchen door. The bloom of youth had long ago died, her precious auburn hair hung lifelessly, and her once-porcelain skin was tinged with gray. Who would have her anyway?

"Is there anything I can do?" She pushed herself upward.

"You can peel some spuds for tea," Lilian replied, jogging

the little one as she heated milk on the stove. "Sit at the table if you like—that ankle still looks a bit puffy. I'll give you a hand when I've fed her." She hesitated a moment, then turned, a look of real concern on her face. "Do you think Jersey will ever be the same?"

"Hard to say. It will be hard to dismantle a lot of the new infrastructure. The bunkers might end up staying forever."

"And what about you? Are you going to be all right?"

Hazel looked at her sister in her snug Clapham kitchen, remembering the prewar island of Lilian's imagination, the place she remembered without anti-tank walls and gun emplacements and turret towers. She thought of her father's head cradled in her hands on the street, and Jean Parris slamming the window in anger. And then, without answering, she took a large handful of potatoes from the vegetable rack and began to peel. Somewhere out in the rainy afternoon, another train thundered along the tracks carrying a thousand different lives.

Les Renoncules had not looked so lovely since before the war. From the luscious ivy folding over the exterior, to the gleaming rooms within, decorated with small posies of wild clover picked from the farm's meadows, and the polished dining table awash with plates of food, it was an impressionist fantasy of a previous life. Guests mingled cheerfully through the rooms, cigarettes were lit and gratefully inhaled, and Daphne moved amongst it all with ease and pleasure, her lustrous curls tossing over her shoulders, those perfect sapphire eyes flashing joy at everyone she greeted. The dress Beattie had made for her did indeed look beautiful, and Jean watched her sail through the rooms like some glorious tall ship, glad that joy still existed in the world.

There seemed, in the bustle of the rooms, a determination among the guests to enjoy themselves, to laugh and chatter as if no one had been affected by the last five years. Jean wondered if she was the only one who noticed the women's pilled cardigans and the clumsily patched collars, the telltale marks of glue on ancient shoes. And the number of older, bony frames huddled around the house's fireplaces that spoke of malnourished bodies not yet adjusted, even though the day was pleasantly warm and the sun still burned hot on the courtyard stones. But as she pushed through the crowd, it was also quite evident that this group largely comprised the more fortunate. The children may have been stuffed into hand-me-downs too small for them, but none looked as if they had gone shoeless in that last, bitter winter. The powdered noses of the women may have dripped cold and rosy in months gone by, but the quality of their skin told Jean that there had always been a scrap of cheese or a portion of rabbit to skim off the worst effects of deprivation, and she guessed that their lips had never been short of a lipstick for special occasions.

She watched Martin, resplendent today in a tweed jacket and pink cheeked from the drink, sucking on his pipe and chuckling at a joke with several other farmers who looked almost identical, and reflected what he actually knew of the people he had abused that day in the square. You would never look at Martin, with his thickset features and hairy arms, and assume him to be a rich man, but at the same time one would know he had never truly been without. Once, in 1941, when Daphne had needed a minor surgery after a fall, he had traded half a pig with a local doctor to access some precious anesthetic. Health care would always, somehow, be within his resources.

There were, indeed, forty guests. Almost everyone invited had come—who would turn down free food and drink?—

including Tom, whom Beattie had happily agreed to accommodate at the last minute, apparently thrilled that timid little Jean had finally nabbed herself a beau. Jean threw him a half smile as she swerved her way through the crowd, knowing that Eddie was once again boring him to death on the evacuees' compensation issue. On arrival, Beattie had taken Jean aside and explained that as there were so many people here, would she mind passing round some drinks and perhaps washing up a few plates? Before Jean could object, Violet had accepted on her behalf and Jean had felt too empty-hearted to argue. But she quickly realized the advantage. On a day when polite conversation felt like a mountain she could not possibly climb, it was helpful to have a reason to weave through people at speed, not engaging too long with anyone, and free to move on when the long looks at her gaunt face and glazed eyes threatened to become a direct question. By the simple virtue of holding a jug of cider in one hand and a plate of sandwiches in the other, she became semivisible, a ghost who flitted through the farmhouse demanding no more than the briefest of thank-yous or a casual condolence about her father. And today that suited her just fine.

Since her interview with Tom, nothing seemed to matter much. Emotions, even despair, had drained away. Color appeared to have vanished from her spectrum, everything she glanced at now seeming grayer and dimmer. The quietest noises set her nerves jangling; even music assaulted her ears. Her resolve, too, had bled out, replaced by a state of inertia; without the long-term goal of marriage, her plans to leave the island now seemed futile and, if she were honest with herself, overwhelming. Horst's tragic, pointless death had closed the door to everything good, and all she desired now was to hide from the world, secure in her rabbit hole of oblivion.

She wanted nothing, expected nothing. A vacuum was the only comfortable place to be.

She had decided before arriving home from the States offices not to tell Eddie or her mother what Tom had reported to her. Better to deprive them of the satisfaction and avoid the derision. They had peered at her, sensing her darkened mood and stony disengagement, but had allowed her to disappear into the privacy of her room without questions, although she had heard them muttering and speculating together in the kitchen. Neither had Daphne nor Beattie made any comment when she slouched in today with Tom, looking nothing like a girl with a new sweetheart, although Jean had seen them exchange concerned looks. Inquisitiveness, she realized, was not encouraged within this family. Inquiries were something to be battened down and buried for fear of causing fuss or, worse, finding out something you never wished to know. Perhaps, she reflected, as she offered crab sandwiches to some elderly women, this was how her mother had managed so successfully to live out her deception of the perfect marriage for two decades, drifting through a world where everyone chose to look at the sun on the water, never the rocks beneath.

But maybe it wasn't just her family. After all, the Germans had deified a madman and called this island Summerland because that was what they wished it to be, even when they were corrected. Even after they turned the place into a perpetual winter. Jean tried to imagine a different world, where people sought out truth and freely communicated emotions. She wondered how it would feel to live in it. But then she remembered Hazel, the one person from whom she had demanded honesty, and with whom she had shared secrets. Look how that had ended up.

The rituals of the day came and went as the sun made its slow passage around the room. The cake, a magnificent affair that must have cost Martin a pretty penny in black-market sugar, was wheeled out and the guests summoned around to sing "Happy Birthday" to Daphne, which then slipped quickly into a tipsy rendition of "Twenty-One Today." After the cutting and passing around, the compliments on its moistness and the delight at eating proper treats again, the plates and little forks were cleared away to the kitchen and the older guests began to make excuses to leave. Eddie sat with Martin and his pals smoking in the snug, with Tom hanging reluctantly on the outside of the circle, desperately trying to attract Jean's attention while she pretended not to see the doe-eyed looks and keen smiles he kept throwing her way. Watching him shuffling from foot to foot, answering all questions politely, she imagined herself married to him and wondered if that was now an inevitability. Certainly, her family would conspire toward it, desperate to throw earth over her terrible stain, and at this moment she knew that she had little resistance left to fight them.

As the St Mary's cousins began to gather their belongings for the journey home, Daphne sidled up to her and whispered in her ear.

"Would you like to see my birthday present from Mummy and Daddy?" It was, of course, a rhetorical question, and a moment later Jean found herself dragged up the farmhouse staircase by Daphne's excited grip, hurtling toward her bedroom. Jean tried hard to plaster on an expression of enthusiasm; she really couldn't give a fig what trinket or heirloom Daphne had received for her birthday but could see that an ardent audience was required. "It was such a surprise," Daphne burbled on as she opened her wardrobe door, "because they gave me no clue what it was. And I know it's secondhand, but it really doesn't matter because it's just so beautiful. And sometimes, something that's belonged to someone else is more special, isn't it?" She hauled down a large, rectangular cardboard box from the shelf at the top and placed it on the bed, lifting off the lid and removing layers of tissue paper. "Mummy told me that Daddy bought it for her in Paris when they were on their honeymoon, and it was always her favorite. But she never gets the chance to wear it anymore, so they decided I should have it. Just take a look—isn't it lovely?"

As Daphne took it and draped it around her own shoulders, twirling and turning with pleasure and satisfaction, Jean felt her mouth dry up and her heart begin to race. It was indeed utterly beautiful. And very much not the kind of garment you would have seen in the local shops, even before the war. A beautiful twenties-style coat in dark forest green, with a velvet collar.

She had picked her moment carefully. It was getting on for six. Only the dregs of guests were left milling in the garden. Martin had long since fallen asleep in an armchair, smelling of cider and whiskey. Daphne had taken a couple of younger cousins to see the horses in the neighboring field, while her brothers played an impromptu game of cricket out on the meadow. Tom had volunteered to drive Violet and Eddie back to town in his father's car after Violet declared herself exhausted by the excitement of the day, though Jean firmly suspected it was more to do with the three glasses of cider she had seen her mother put away, a habit she seemed to be embracing in her new marriage. Tom was clearly dismayed by Jean's insistence on staying behind and desperately tried to persuade her to go with them. But her logic of helping to clear up and getting the last bus was so impeccably plausible that not even Eddie could object. She even made a point of waving them off on the step, telling them she'd be home in a couple of hours.

The kitchen, she decided, would be the best place for what was to come. Its position meant that anyone from the court-yard could be seen approaching, and the footsteps of anyone coming from the house could be heard in the hallway—an ideal place to have an uninterrupted conversation. Jean hovered around the butler sink, her eyes fixed on the flagstone floor she had mopped so many times in recent weeks, and waited. She could hear the clacking of plates being stacked in the dining room, so she knew it would not be long. Sure enough, within a minute Beattie appeared holding a pile of dirty crockery, a tired smile on her face. Her hair had fallen a little out of place and her red painted lips had faded since their lunchtime application, but as Jean looked at her in the golden light of the late afternoon, she recognized a genuine beauty she had never really seen before. Bright eyes with un-usually long lashes, full lips and a pleasing smooth complex-ion. It was obvious, really, that compared to her sister, she was the one that most men would choose. But to Jean she had always been Aunt Beattie—Violet's sister, Martin's wife and Daphne's mother. She had never really seen her in the con-text of a sexually attractive woman.

"I think that went pretty well, don't you?" Beattie beamed. "Those crab sandwiches went down a treat. And thank good-ness for that cider, that's kept everyone happy. Did you have a drop of that yourself, Jeannie? Delicious, it is." She placed the pile of plates on the draining board. Jean looked at them with passive curiosity.

"Are those for me?"

Beattie looked a little nonplussed. "Well, if you wouldn't mind. There's still loads out there." She must have sensed something in Jean's tone because she added, "There's no hard feelings, is there, about that money business? Because we've forgotten about it already. In fact I've already got another girl from the village starting next week."

Yes, Jean thought. Of course Beattie had got another girl from the village. Same as her husband had got more French workers to labor on the farm and had found illegal sugar for a birthday cake. Martin and Beattie had always had enough money to acquire what they wanted, and the only time money had failed them was during the Occupation. The shock of it must have been immense, and no doubt stirred the need in Beattie to compensate herself. Especially as the war coincided with Daphne's true blossoming into a gorgeous young woman, who absorbed every drop of Martin's attention. And how infuriating it must have been for Beattie, the prettier and richer of the sisters, suddenly to find herself stuck with what appeared to be the less interested husband. The irony of that almost made Jean smile.

Jean leaned back against the sink, expecting that her legs would be shaking. To her surprise she realized they were strong and firm, and that she was feeling quite calm.

"How long did it go on, Aunt Beattie?"

"Sorry, love, what you say? People arrived about one, didn't they?"

"No, not the party. Your affair with my dad." She watched the bomb bounce a few times across the surface of Beattie's consciousness before it exploded. She saw her cheeks flush red, the panic in her eyes. Jean wondered if this must have been how she had looked to her mother and Eddie when they confronted her with Hazel's revelation.

"I *beg* your pardon?"

Naturally, Jean thought. The denial. The first obvious response. This stage was likely to drag on, so she would need to get her cards on the table as quickly as possible, before someone came in. "I know all about it, you see. Your visits to Dad's shop every Thursday, in your special coat from Paris. Suppose it was part of your disguise, like the headscarf? Suppose most people wouldn't expect a farmer's wife to be dressed like that."

Beattie fumbled behind her for a chair, and finding the edge of one, dragged it into her body before falling onto it. The initial flush had faded, and now the blood seemed to be draining the other way, rendering her pale as her delicate pearl earrings.

"Why are you saying these terrible things?"

"I suppose you thought you wouldn't be seen, going out the back way. Trouble is, there's one window that overlooks that backyard. Funnily enough, the person who saw you thought you were German. At the time, I thought that if that were true, it really couldn't get any worse. But it turns out it can."

"Who are you talking about? Who told you this?" Beattie's eyes were wild, her mind scavenging for sleights of hand and possible loopholes.

"A neighbor, who then went on to speak to the authorities." She saw Beattie about to ask another question, but Jean had promised herself from the start that her aunt would not take control of this conversation. "Where did you tell Uncle Martin you were going every week?" Before Beattie could reply Jean let out a bitter little laugh. "Oh, of course! You said you were visiting Mum! Bringing us food from the farm! I wondered why you kept telling everyone how much you helped us out through the war, when really you only ever came over a couple of times. It all makes sense now." She could see that Beattie was crumbling under the onslaught. The facts were coming too thick and fast; she had no time to think, to wriggle, to create. The gleam of sweat was on her forehead and top lip, and her eyes darted toward the window and back toward the kitchen door, perhaps calculating how long she had before Martin woke up or Daphne or one of the boys clattered in. She sat for a few more seconds, suspended between her options, between past and future. Then Jean saw her face crumple and knew that the last wall had fallen.

"Oh, my God. Jean, I'm so sorry." Her face fell into her open hands.

Jean nodded. She was astonished at her own serenity. "You need to tell me everything now."

The voice emerged through Beattie's fingers. "I don't even know why it started. I went over to the shop one night for the wireless news. There were a few of us there. Then everyone else left, and it was just us. He had this black-market calvados from France…" Her momentum dropped and she trailed off, already crying. "Maybe I just wanted to get my own back at Martin. Prove that someone still wanted me."

Jean nodded. It was more self-awareness than she had expected.

"Then you carried on seeing him every week? Until… when was it, Christmas eighteen months ago?" Beattie's head nodded. "When he told you it was over?"

The hands dropped for a moment, and she looked up, tears on her cheeks, her lips trembling. "No. I told *him* it was over. It had gone on far too long, I was terrified it would all come out. But he said if I ended it, he'd tell Martin. Then Vi would have found out…"

Jean felt her eyes grow wide. "He threatened *you*?"

"We had a massive row. I was so upset with him. That he was prepared to ruin my family, and his own."

Jean scoffed. "Bit late for that."

"I know. But that's how I saw it."

"How come you swore at him in German?" Beattie looked confused. "The word *schwein* was overheard."

Beattie shook her head a little, not seeing the relevance. "We had that German au pair years ago. Helga? She taught me some German swear words. More polite than swearing in English."

Jean tried to absorb the incongruity that Beattie had been concerned with verbal etiquette during an affair with her own brother-in-law. But the biggest question was yet to be asked.

"So that's why you were angry. And it was you, wasn't it, who wrote to the Germans, telling them about the wireless?"

The explosion of tears was so intense Jean wondered if it might bring someone into the kitchen. Each sob contained a wailing noise. It sounded faintly familiar, and Jean realized it was the same one her mother had made the day her father was arrested. Beattie's voice battled through the chaos of it to be heard, stuttering and falling over itself.

"I never knew they'd deport him! I thought his Jerry contacts would protect him, that he'd just get a month or two in the local jail, give him time to come to his senses. Jean, you have to believe me, if I'd known what would happen…if I'd known Violet would lose her husband…" The tears overcame her, and her entire body shook silently for a moment. Jean had to lean forward to make out the words: "You have to believe me, you have to believe me."

The volume of her crying fit only emphasized the quiet in the rest of the house. Jean glanced nervously toward both doors. It seemed impossible that no one else had heard Beattie's wails, and while no one was yet on their way, Jean realized she only had a short time to end this. Swallowing hard to overcome her instincts, she edged toward Beattie and gently pulled her hands from her face.

"I believe you. I believe that you never intended my father to die." To her horror, Beattie reached her arms around Jean's waist and hugged her body close.

"Oh, thank you, thank you, Jeannie. The guilt, you've no idea… I'll never forgive myself." Very slowly the sobbing eased, and she pulled back until she was once again sitting straight on the chair. Then she looked up at Jean, a whimpering puppy. "Will you tell them? Your mother, Martin?" Her eyes filled again. "Daphne?"

Jean looked down at her aunt, for so long a paragon of calm and comfort and stability, now utterly broken. "No, I won't tell them. But I need something in return."

The water in the bay today was the deepest blue she could remember, with crisp white curls of foam on its surface. The wind, though not yet cold for October, blew loud in her ears, threatening to whisk away her little felt hat, so as she climbed the steps onto the ship's deck, she took it off and stuffed it in her pocket. Better a bare head than her precious hat flying out across the ocean, for she would have to take care of all her possessions from now on. She glanced around, searching for a place to settle, and chose a varnished slatted bench near the stern of the vessel. Later she would need to find herself a seat in the covered areas on the lower decks and make herself comfortable with her copy of *The Little Prince*, which she had been saving for the journey. But having never seen the island from out in the bay, she was determined not to waste the opportunity. How different would Elizabeth Castle look from the other side? How would the town appear from such a distance, and would she be able to see her house? Jean smiled to herself. For days she had fretted about this journey, imagining every possible catastrophe, but now that the moment was here, she felt nothing but excitement. And as for embarking on this trip alone, the solitude only sharpened the experience. It was nice that there was no one around to chatter on or distract her, and that she was free to let her mind wander. She lowered herself onto the bench and took the salt air deep into her lungs. With it came smells of fish and sand and seaweed. She was going to miss that.

This morning her mother had hugged her tightly, the way she used to when Jean was a child, and told her to write as soon as she arrived. Eddie had shuffled in the background, nodding at her as if she were one of his tavern associates, awkwardly offering a five-pound note that he pretended to find in his wallet at the last moment. Jean knew he'd expected her to refuse it, but she took it without question and put it in her purse, figuring it was the least he owed her. Neither he nor her mother had volunteered to go down to the quayside to see her off, but the hurt was more than outweighed with relief. She had had her fill of difficult conversations and had sidestepped questions in recent days. She was content to let things lie. And if the mess of loose ends, half-truths and wicked deceptions she was leaving behind still woke her in the night, she had the comfort of knowing that she had done the best she could in an impossible situation.

It was a week after Daphne's party that Jean returned to Les Renoncules, after a great deal of thinking and several days' intensive research in the library. Choosing a day when Martin was busy with the orchard harvest, she had slipped around the side of the house and knocked on the kitchen window to avoid alerting Daphne or the boys. Then she and Beattie had edged quietly into the courtyard to have their conversation on the seat by the toolshed, far away from prying eyes. There she had laid out her new plans to her aunt and told her what she wanted her to do.

"No, Jean, it's out the question!" Beattie had protested as they sat, arms crossed against the breeze. "We've already offered to help out with bills until Eddie gets his finances straight. How am I supposed to convince Martin to cough up that kind of money?"

Jean patiently went through it again, point by point. That, given all the shocks and upset of recent months, and her mother's new married status, it was the perfect time for her to leave the island. She spelled out her plan to stay with her brother for a while, adding that Harry had already accepted her request to visit and wired money for her fare. Once settled, she would apply to one of the new teacher training colleges funded by the British government—she even told her aunt about the new enthusiasm in England for women primary teachers and the shortages in the labor market. Then she repeated her crucial point: that Beattie and Martin could easily afford, over a couple of years, to support their niece financially in something she really wanted to do. After all, she was only asking enough to cover tuition fees, dependent on any grants available, and a basic income until she could become fully independent.

"See it as a way of compensating me for the loss of my father," Jean finished, looking directly at her and watching her aunt shrink into herself. "If you tell Martin it's to help our family, I think he'll agree. And if he argues, get Daphne to persuade him—you know he can't refuse her. In return I will say nothing about what you did, to anyone."

"How do I know I can trust you?" Beattie muttered.

"You just have to," Jean replied simply.

"What if the authorities charge someone else as Phil's informant?"

"The main suspect was Hazel and she's already moved away. And anyway, it looks like there aren't going to be any arrests. People here will just have to live with the uncertainty and the injustice."

Beattie sat for a while, considering all this. After a few minutes she looked at her quizzically.

"Teaching little ones? I never knew you were interested in that?"

Jean shrugged. "Neither did I till recently. But I've given it a lot of thought. I want to be able to live my own life."

"How does your mum feel about it?"

Jean thought of her mother and Eddie together at the kitchen table, playing rummy and giggling together, and gave a wan smile. "Honestly, I think they'll like the idea of me going away for a while. And they'll be very touched by your incredibly generous offer." Again, she looked at her aunt with obvious meaning, and this time she knew that she had won. There was nothing Beattie wouldn't do to preserve her security and position. And if it wasn't the righting of a wrong, it was the closest Jean was going to get.

Later that day she had sat on a bench in the Royal Square, waiting for Tom Maloret to emerge from his office, and when he appeared, suggested a stroll through the little churchyard where they had picnicked all those weeks ago. As they moved around the paths, shaded green under the branches of the trees, he listened in respectful silence to her announcement and her apology for springing the news on him so suddenly. He hardly complained at all when she gently rejected his re-

quest to write regularly and stay in touch, perhaps finally realizing that in their handful of assignations she had never once
shown any real enthusiasm or returned his interest.

"I hope you're not doing this because of what happened
to the German boy?" he asked her as they stood beneath a
spreading chestnut tree. And Jean had replied, with honesty,
that Horst's death had played only a part in her decision. "Will
you come back?" he asked as they reached the gate, and Jean
had considered for a moment before answering:

"I don't know. Perhaps one day."

A rumbling vibration told her that the engines had fired
up and her hand gripped tightly around the handle of her
brown leather suitcase. Inside was squashed her entire life
plus a selection of new underwear, for she wanted no remind-
ers of the misery and degradation of the last months. There
was so much to regret: her blackened memories of her father,
Eddie's unpunished crimes. Her broken friendship with the
woman who had set her on this road. And the loss of Horst
was something she doubted she would ever truly get over.
But it was impossible not to feel a surge of hope. As the ship
began to veer away, she looked down at the quayside and out
over the harbor. As she took in the vast stone walls and the
harbor surround, memories crowded in. Her father's prison
boat with the Germans lined up, their rifles cocked and ready.
Eddie pounding down the gangplank of the first passenger
ship, still expecting to find his old house as he'd left it. Her
stolen night with Horst just across in the French Harbour, in
what had turned out to be their last meeting. So many life-
altering events, in such few weeks; if the next ten years of
her life passed by in tranquil uneventfulness, she might yet
feel exhausted by it.

The mail boat slowly chugged its way out through the harbor entrance and soon they were out in the bay of St Aubin. Jean turned to look back. Jersey did, indeed, look entirely different from this perspective. The castle was as strong and impressive as ever, but its shape and form were entirely contradictory. The town no longer appeared as a bustling complex of streets but as a tiny village, its buildings crushed together like tiny gems on a chain. She could not see her house or anywhere close to it, but she could spot the trees on Westmount and the dock of St Aubin's harbor at the far end of the bay. It was the island she had always known, but smaller and more vulnerable, unrecognizable from the long dark days of Occupation and even from recent weeks. They sailed out around the point and past St Ouen's Bay, and as she spotted the cliffs at Grosnez, where only months ago she had walked and watched the last Germans clearing the bunkers, one thing struck her above all else. Despite the gray anti-tank walls and the hulking gun towers, those permanent hideous disfigurements of a world gone mad, it was still a green and golden shimmering jewel in the swelling blue waters of the Channel. And it was beautiful.

AFTER

Jersey 1972

The Gaggia machine behind the counter made a loud gur-
gling as it spluttered its frothy, richly scented brew into one
of the café's oversize coffee cups. Jean smiled her gratitude
as the young man brought it to her table, spilling not a drop
into the saucer, and set it before her. The pale foam sat perfectly on its surface, inviting her.

"One cappuccino. Enjoy."

"Thank you, I will." Adding a small sleeve of brown sugar
from the pot on the table, she lifted the cup to her lips and
savored the flavor; it was full and generous, so much better
than the instant stuff at home. She resolved to look into getting a proper percolator next week; it would be lovely to have
coffee like this every morning, and to serve it to friends when
they came over. Perhaps she would have a look at the selection in De Gruchy's before she went home. But that would
rather depend on how today panned out.

She sat back to watch the shoppers walk by and the stream
of traffic up Halkett Place, allowing her eyes to drift to the

huge abstract painting on the wall opposite. In recent years she had struggled to match her husband's enthusiasm for Rothko, but she loved the bright colors and bold design of the prints here, and the collection that lined the café's plain white wall seemed to add to the feeling of peace and space, almost like a gallery. In the background, some pop star was singing about a Rocket Man, and she found herself swaying imperceptibly with its rhythm. There were only three people at the other tables, for it seemed tourists had not yet found this place tucked away from the main shopping street, but it had certainly become her favorite haunt in the last year. She decided that they would come here next Saturday for Stephen's birthday and try one of the new "pizzas" advertised on the menu.

She sipped at her coffee again and felt a flutter of excitement. It was ten minutes past three. She tried not to look up every time someone ventured close to the glass door but found curiosity hard to resist. She was just about to get her emergency paperback out of her handbag when the door opened and she heard her name.

"Jean! So sorry I'm late."

Jean was on her feet immediately, pushing back her chair to give herself space. As always, a floodgate flipped open in her head, memories instantly rushing in; the sculpted cheeks and the confidence in those eyes never seemed to change. Jean wrapped her arms around that familiar body, now older and perhaps a little weightier, but still with the same proud height and steady gait. She kissed one cheek, feeling the soft skin beneath her lips.

"It's good to see you, Hazel."

"You, too, my dear."

"Cappuccino?"

"Lovely, thank you." Jean indicated another order to the

waiter, then sat back in her chair to take a proper look. Hazel's hair, now a steely silver, was long for her age, still worn past her shoulders and straighter than it had once been. She wore a full-length dress of Indian fabric in the Woodstock style with a trailing scarf and silver rings on every finger, giving the impression of a floating, gleaming apparition as she settled into her seat. Jean glanced down at her own canary yellow jumpsuit that until five minutes ago she'd considered a bit racy for daytime. Hazel beamed at her and looked around. "Nice place."

"New Italian chain." They exchanged small ironic smiles. "And how is the Belle Vue? Comfortable?"

"Perfectly lovely, thank you."

"I meant what I said, we'd have been happy to put you up. You were so kind last time we were over, giving up your room for us."

"Well, I couldn't see you in that awful bed-and-breakfast again, and anyway it was a pleasure. But I'm afraid I'm an impossible houseguest these days. I'm up and down all night reading, padding about. Never been a good sleeper, not since..." A shadow passed across Hazel's features and disappeared just as quickly. "Well, decades." She graciously accepted her coffee from the waiter and took too big a gulp immediately, wiping her mouth with the back of her hand. "But I can't believe the changes here! So much new building. I hardly recognized St Helier as I flew over."

Jean nodded. "Lots of new hotels—you can't move in King Street for holidaymakers. They keep telling us it's progress." She smiled. "I've been telling you for years you need to come back and see for yourself."

"Now here I am, and how right you were. But frankly the whole country seems to be on a consumption trip. You should see Carnaby Street on a Saturday now. Every freak in London turns up, proving their anti-Vietnam credentials by buying the latest James Brown record." She laughed and it sounded like a waterfall. Jean realized how few times she had ever heard that sound.

"It's good to see you again. Last time, you and Jeff were midseparation. But by the look of you, you more than survived."

Hazel gave a giant shrug and held the pose for a moment. "What can I say? Divorce seems to suit me. I mean, it was ghastly dividing everything up, and the solicitors now have most of our money. But Betty Friedan was absolutely right—domesticity and women's careers don't mix, at least not for me." She took another giant swallow of coffee, even though it was clearly still too hot. "Although you continue to pull it off with some aplomb, it seems?" She sat back, cup in hand, her eyebrows raised in mischievous expectation.

Jean smiled, embarrassed by the compliment. "Don't know about that."

"Your letter last Christmas said you were going back to teaching?"

Jean nodded while pulling an apprehensive face. "That was always the plan, as the boys got older. But Stephen's radio for schools project has snowballed this year, so it looks like I'll be assisting him with that instead. I'll have no idea what I'm doing, of course."

The laugh came again, then she leaned forward and patted Jean on the hand. "Any woman who taught ragamuffins in Bethnal Green for four years straight can manage anything she puts her mind to, trust me. It sounds terribly exciting, you must tell me everything." She drained her coffee and slapped her hands on her knees. "It's lovely out there. Shall we take a walk?"

Five minutes later they were pressing through the dawdling, aging couples in town. Tourists swarmed on and off the pavements, the women in their fancy straw hats and the men with pink peeling noses pointing vaguely at duty-free brandy in shop windows and counting out their cash. Jean and Hazel found a path through and scuttled into the Royal Square, both glancing at each other with unspoken memories.

"Whatever became of the J.D.M.?" Hazel asked as they passed the George II statue.

"Swept away by the tide of high finance, I think."

Hazel scrunched her lips toward her nose. "Yes, I follow the progress in the *Financial Times*. What do they call them, High Net Worth Individuals?"

"We just call them millionaires. New luxury villas going up all over the place. Alan Whicker's just bought a house here."

"Let's hope he brings in more money than carnations, or it may not turn out to be a good swap." They slipped down past the church toward the Weighbridge, where Hazel suggested a walk up South Hill. "For old times' sake? I used to walk here a lot." She gave Jean a guarded look. "Well, you remember." Jean nodded silently.

Slowly they climbed the rising incline of Pier Road beneath Fort Regent, watching the vista open up on their right. Beyond the sloping roofs of the commercial warehouses, the harbors were crowded now, packed with pleasure boats, fishing vessels and dozens of private yachts in their expensive moorings, while cranes created a jagged silhouette against the pale blue sky. At first they chatted genially about work and families, Hazel holding forth about funding for her new community library, which she complained was taking up all her time, Jean recounting the struggles of getting the boys through O levels and her plans for the literacy worksheets that would accompany Stephen's series. As they neared the spot over the French Harbour, where it had all begun, they both fell quiet, only the sound of their breathing audible between them. Without saying a word, they stopped to lean on the rugged granite wall and look down at the flat green water. Eventually Jean broke the silence.

"I walked past your old flat the other day and thought about your father. I'm so sorry, Hazel. I still..."

Hazel held up a palm. "No. What I said in that very first letter, remember? Raking over the past solves nothing. Anyway, I'm sorry for my part, too. Were it not for me you might have had an entirely different life."

Jean stared out across the distant bay. "Who knows if it would have been a happier one? I was a child when I knew Horst. And if we'd married, I would never have had a career, never met Stephen. I probably wouldn't have come back here."

"You never really explained why you decided to move back? You obviously thrived in London. I thought you might stay."

"It was when my mother died. Eddie was already in the care home, after his stroke. I thought I'd just come back for a few weeks to take care of Mum's affairs, but then the job at St John's came up. And Stephen thought it was a good place to raise children." She turned to look at Hazel. "But it was more than that. I wanted to face the ghosts. To return here with some pride. I didn't want those awful days after Liberation to be the end."

Hazel slung a loose arm around her shoulder. "There was so much damage. The injustice and the rage. And for so many here it's still not over, still hurts every day. That's why I was so glad when you came looking for me."

"Me, too."

She looked at Jean. "Did your family ever... I mean, did the facts ever come out?"

Jean shook her head. "I made a promise to Beattie. And anyway, what good would it have served, after all that time? My son bought a poster the other day—The Truth Will Set You Free. He was horrified when I told him the quote was from the Bible. But I think some truths can just as easily crush you. You know, Beattie died last summer, and I don't think she had one happy day after the war."

Hazel's eyes narrowed a little. "And your uncle Eddie? When did he die?"

"Oh, he's still alive. Still in the nursing home, seventeen years now."

Hazel grimaced. "Do you visit?"

"Only at Christmas. He doesn't know me anymore." She felt Hazel's arm tighten around her shoulder, felt the solidarity. "Come on, let's walk on round to Havre des Pas. You can get a bus from there."

Around the sea lido, hardy swimmers were larking in the chilly, early summer sea. As the two women stopped to watch them, the laughter and sound of splashing water carried across the breeze and made them both smile. Jean nodded to the guesthouse a little further along the front.

"That's Silvertide, isn't it? I wonder how many of those swimmers know that they're only two hundred yards from the old German secret police headquarters?"

"Those walls must have some dreadful stories to tell. But the tourists create an antidote, somehow," Hazel mused. "I'm so happy they came back."

"What are your plans for the rest of the day?"

"I thought I'd visit my father's grave. It's actually not far from here."

"I know. I lay flowers there every year on the anniversary."

Hazel's head tipped sideways, her eyes glistening. "I never knew that."

"Would you like some company? I know a little florist we could pop into near the cemetery?"

"Lead the way." They set off together down the road, Jean's platform sandals click-clacking next to Hazel's quiet, hippie flats. The sun was just starting its descent but radiated a heat that made promises of a summer to come, and the cool Atlantic wind on their backs blew their hair in a dozen directions, making them both laugh. While they walked in a comfortable silence that told of conversations no longer required, Jean realized that her mind was filled only with thoughts of sweet peas and white gardenias for the perfect posy to place at the graveside. And what she felt was not just a sense of peace, but an overwhelming gratitude. Gratitude for Hazel's company, for the mellowing of distant memory. And for the gentle warmth of a late May afternoon that smelled of kelp and brine.

★ ★ ★ ★ ★

ACKNOWLEDGMENTS

Thank you to my old friend Bruce Labey and other pals involved in Jersey's 13th Parish Independent Film Festival for the pub conversation, which partly inspired this book.

For the research I would like to thank Dr. Gilly Carr, Associate Professor in Archaeology at the University of Cambridge, UK—probably today's leading authority on Channel Islands Occupation history—for generous access to her book *Victims of Nazi Persecution in the Channel Islands: A Legitimate Heritage?* (Bloomsbury), for the informative Frank Falla Archive she instigated, created and continues to curate, and for her assistance in fact-checking the background material for this book.

Also invaluable were Paul Sanders's seminal works *The British Channel Islands Under German Occupation 1940–45* and *The Ultimate Sacrifice* (both Jersey Heritage Trust), Charles Cruickshank's *The German Occupation of the Channel Islands* (The History Press) and the blogspot of Jersey Deputy Sam Mézec, which provided useful insight into the Jersey Democratic Movement and their 1945 manifesto. And I could have done none of this without the Jerripedia section of theislandwiki.org, which provided so many details of the period.

Thanks also to writer George Aboud for her early editorial assistance, to Rick Lecoat for my website design, Sean McTernan for the legals and my now-retired agent, John Beaton, who spotted the structural problems with my first draft but persuaded me to keep going.

Enormous gratitude to my agent, Lisa Highton of Jenny Brown Associates; my UK editor, Alison Rae; and US editor, Susan Swinwood; rights supremo Fiona Brownlee and all those at Birlinn and HarperCollins for their faith and support.

And lastly, thanks as always to Gary, for all the encouragement, suggestions and cups of tea, and for telling me to shut up whenever I whined that I couldn't do this, which was most days.

AUTHOR'S NOTE

I was born in Jersey, Channel Islands, the only British territory to be occupied by the Nazis during World War II. The Occupation lasted for five years but cast a long shadow, which still exists today.

In 2019, a conversation with old island pals about our parents' wartime childhoods set me thinking. For while much has been written about the island's suffering in the years of 1940 to 1945, far less has been written about the aftermath, the sorrows and resentments amidst the joy of Liberation, the eruption of long-repressed fury and the post-traumatic stress.

Then, in the COVID lockdown of 2020, I found myself again contemplating my own family history. My grandfather's siblings sheltered an escaped Russian and were betrayed by local people to the German authorities in 1944; my great-aunt Louisa Gould paid with her life at Ravensbrück (the basis for my 2017 film, *Another Mother's Son*). The two elderly sisters whom my family accused of the betrayal were never prosecuted, and no conclusive evidence was ever presented against them. But my family continued to hold these women responsible, and the sisters were ostracized for the rest of their lives. I still do not know whether or not they were guilty.

In a world increasingly divided by opposing certainties, and with so many reluctant to challenge deeply held convictions, this story emerged. The characters and events are fictional, but the story's setting and background are real.

BEYOND SUMMERLAND

JENNY LECOAT

Reader's Guide

GRAYDON
HOUSE

1. Jersey in 1945 was an island traumatized by the Occupation, its population wretched and divided. What parallels would you draw with other contemporary societies?

2. What complexities do you see in Jean's relationship with her mother, Violet?

3. What do you make of Jean's feelings toward Hazel?

4. The story deals with themes of certainty versus doubt, and loyalty versus duplicity. Do you think we view these issues any differently today?

5. How do you feel about Jean's changing perception of her late father?

6. Compare Jean's developing friendship with Hazel and her relationship with her cousin Daphne.

7. There are a number of betrayals in the story. Which

of these seem justified to you, and do any seem
unforgivable?

8. How much has changed for the role of women in society
    since the 1940s?

9. By the end of the book, do you believe that Jean's
    character made the right decisions in relation to her
    family?

10. How do you feel about the friendship portrayed in
    the final pages, and what does it tell us about female
    friendships?